Roots & Branches Series

My Beard

Memoir Stories

Sharon Doubiago

Spuyten Duvyil
New York City

SOME OF MY BEARD APPEARED PREVIOUSLY IN THE FOLLOWING:

"25 maybe 28," Zyzzva "the last word: west coast writers and artists,' vol. XX11, Number 3, Winter, 2006.

"Kimmy in Camp Moistness of the Soft Woods," The AVA, Boonville, CA, 2013

"Psyche and the Vidyahara," earlier version, *My Father's Love, Volume 11*, Wild Ocean Press, 2011. www.wildoceanpress.com

"Our War," earlier version, Ink Fish, Newport Oregon, 1996

"My Beard," earlier version, Portland Oregon Magazine. vol 4. # 2

ISBN 978-1-944682-91-0

cover photo by Bob Peterson

Library of Congress Cataloging-in-Publication Data

Names: Doubiago, Sharon, author.
Title: My beard : memoir stories / Sharon Doubiago.
Description: New York City : Spuyten Duyvil, [2018]
Identifiers: LCCN 2017038608 | ISBN 9781944682910
Subjects: LCSH: Doubiago, Sharon. | Poets, American--20th century--Biography.
 | Short stories, American. | Biography as a literary form.
Classification: LCC PS3554.O814 Z46 2018 | DDC 811/.54 [B] --dc23
LC record available at https://lccn.loc.gov/2017038608

for Love
    for Robert Yoder

The World's Worst Mom

He steps out of the trees with his backpack and violin as Moonlight and I come up Highway 20 to the 5-mile marker where he's camped. He throws his stuff in the back, opens the driver's door, slides me over, slides in.

We turn back for Highway One, head north to Westport, past the Blues, Danny's favorite surfing place, then northeast into deep forest. He pulls over every few miles, his face flushed with emotion, marijuana. I take a couple of puffs. Heads together, waves of energy passing through us, Moonlight whimpering behind us. Whenever Ĉelo touches me a million lights turn on a million images of Max through our nine years. *How much I love you, Max.*

"What are you thinking?" he demands, as we start up again.

"Oh, everything," I say to the redwoods, the cold, clear, blue sky high above them.

At the next pull-off, he jumps out, throws himself down the ravine. I assume he's peeing, let Moonlight out to do so too. God, I'm always talking to Max in my head. It's hard to grasp that I do this, like second nature, like talking to God when I was a girl.

Then they're back up, throwing themselves around the car, Ĉelo banging on it. "You're still in love with Max!" he screams. Then sobs, "you find the trees and sky, your dog more interesting than me."

So, climbing twisted Highway One through the giant redwoods, the world obediently disappears. He stares at me wild-eyed as he wheels the curves, he loves me so much he can't miss. How refreshing he is after my men, my cool ones, my unemotional ones. Next stop, I'll make sure to get the wheel.

"I love you!" he gasps. "I just had no idea who you were

before three weeks ago. I was just attracted to your beauty. But, now, you are my One!"

I recognize the Mormon polygyny I've told him of. Wife Number One stands on the highest rung of the ladder on the left side of God. She holds the door open for the Procession of Wives which follows—Wife Number Two, Wife Number Three…Wife Number Twenty-Seven ad infinitum. The right side is for the husband of all the wives.

"There isn't a man on earth who could think you up," he gesticulates to the giants. "The way you think. There isn't a man who would believe it."

I take this as a compliment. I enjoy his thinking, his visionary Yalie, Mendocino-stoned rock and roll fiddler, the brilliant child prodigy of the cello, his seeing in me the potential of a great writer. I love the dancer his electric violin has opened me to in the past few weeks, my soul to fly. I love his physicality, all of it—three days without a bath. I may not be in love with him, but I enjoy him—body, mind, heart and soul.

We come out of the dark into the sun. 101.

"My heart goes with you, right into yours, right into your kids, to all your family, the Edens—how perfect that your birth name is of the Garden—and, so, there's Max. So I love him too. Because if I didn't I wouldn't love you.

"Basketball," he starts in about Danny "is an art form. That's why they have penalties—because when you fuck up you've stopped the flow of the dance."

I see your hands, Max, showing Danny how to make a basket.

He sucks deep on the joint. "I see Max's hands all the time. Telepathically. On you." As usual he knows my thoughts. He exhales equally long. *I see your hands, Max, all the time, too.* "His fingers are longer than mine, classically beautiful, the palms are flatter, and they are darker."

I see you walking out of your office at Christmas to us, our first encounter since you left, so thin, your hands too large, I never noticed the burden of them, too large, too lit, too hot. When you put them on Shawn's shoulders in greeting I thought I'd die for the pain in your hands, their loss of her, her loss of you. How much they hurt. Even Danny.

"The soul of the Cancer," Ĉelo drives on, north, ever north, "is in the skin, unlike the rest of us with the soul deep inside the body, protected as armor. This is why Max is so afraid, Cancers are sensate types, experiencing the world in the most immediate sense, through sensations, why they, crabs, build elaborate shells over their skins for protection."

I'm a master, as you finally knew, at disguising my feelings in order to please you, but Ĉelo is open to me, he knows what I'm thinking, it's eerie. I've begun to experiment, letting a thought into my mind, then watch him get it. He doesn't even think this amazing. "Of course," he says. "I love you, you think I don't know what's going on?"

I puff on his joint.

"You made it so good for Max, and their real father, they couldn't leave though they wanted to. They hated you for this blackmail. They weren't entirely conscious of this, it just felt like you weren't responding to them, but to the rules of the game: until death do us part. But what's that code have to do with them, with their living flesh in the now? Despite everything you did your men felt unloved. Unseen. Unknown. And trapped. You seemed like a retard to them. At the same time, like their mothers, superior to them. So they kept trying to break the code, break through to you, communicate, that's why they were such assholes. How could they trust someone who'd eat so much of their shit? They couldn't, so finally they left."

"There isn't a man on earth like you," I sigh. Laugh. Reach for Moonlight in the back. "The way you think."

After four or five hours we emerge to the mirror beauty of the Humboldt Basin, its deep blue passivity, the ominous quiet so different from the roaring ocean, the majestic redwoods. Everything is reflected in the Bay waters.

"Winning is as bad as losing," he says as we near Eureka. "When you beat them you have to eat their hearts."

Rachel Love is walking Eureka's Main Street, the line of old weathered buildings, the former whorehouses that are now Eureka's department stores. She's walking the sidewalk towards us as we move up the street in search of the high school, her head held high, her hands deep in the pockets of her beige slacks. Shawn's middle school P.E. teacher walks like she had to get away from someone, or from everyone. Everyone knows she's having an affair with Russ, Danny's football coach and now his "father figure" since Max left. (And before that, his father.) Though as far as I know their affair is a secret. I feel fear for all of them, his wife and kids. "Hard," Ĉelo says, nodding at her, re-entering civilization."

We make our way to the north end of town.

"Cars destroy the integrity of these old towns," he says pulling into Sambo's at the 3-way intersection.

I'm grateful for coffee. But as I turn to leave with our steaming styrofoams I spot Danny's Driver's Ed teacher in the far corner, Mr. Blackwell, twirling the left end of his black waxed handlebar, giving me the Evil Eye.

As usual, I shrug it off, smile, sort of nod—how strange to see these mythical Mendocinians here in another town so far north. Suddenly I see Danny, the years of his growing, feel the deep heartsickness I've harbored for so long, the fear that he'll never get up off the gym floor, the deep ache for him for his deep ache for his father. I'm grateful for these men that he's found, that he loves, has great need of, but they are so straight! And as Ĉelo puts it, their disgust of me is palpable. How Danny will you ever sort it all out, your love of me, of them, the values by which I've raised you, with theirs, the values of American sports? As I hurry out of Sambo's I catch the headlines in the stand: **Mendocino Whale War: Soviet Ship Still Blockaded!** I recognize friends in the little boats surrounding the Russian whalers in Alameda.

It's dark by the time we find the gym, a high old redwood saltbox.

"Another doubie, Doubi" he says, lighting up.

I try not to breathe.

Through the fogging windshield I spot Danny's ex-girlfriend, Jan, wandering forlornly around the lit-up, jumping gym, through the parked cars, the milling festive crowds, the lines at the doors, and back around the gym again, from which the cheering for my son is bouncing the thing off its foundation, walking as if she's invisible, in a trance, but, headlines too, in mourning for the star inside. I've never asked him what happened six months ago because he doesn't want me to ask. But everyone knows of her heartbreak. "Jan wants to get married. Can I?" he asked. I experienced a slight panic but even then I wasn't going to say no. I've never said no to him or his sister, they know my philosophy, that this empowers their own decision-making. I believe that in this I protect them from rebelling just for the sake of rebellion—that I protect him from the confusion of blaming me for his feelings and actions with her. And that I protect myself as their mother from confusing love with abusive parental power and authority. Your responsibility, your decision—that I respect them that much. I did note that he didn't say "we" want to get married, but even so I thought deeply and seriously about the possibility of his marrying her and realized, as preposterous as others would see it—others would see this as negligence on my part—that it would be as good an education for a sixteen year old as any else. If his father, George and I had been allowed to be together as teenagers we would have done much better than we did. Danny broke with her right after I gave my permission.

Now, my eyes glued to the back of the proud, betrayed girl wandering the cars of the parking lot, the sickening thought comes for the first time: Coach Mastin got him to drop her.

We pour out of Roses, Moonlight settling into the sleeping bags in the back. I head straight for her, unusual aggression for me—all I wanted at her age was for the adults to leave me alone. She turns abruptly, wild seventeen-year-old Medusa black snake hair flying, hand raised, "No!" Turns, heads down the redwood slat fence into the fog, while I suffer Coach Mastin's exact words, I just bet, about her, to my son. Crazy.

We enter the small door to the lit-up people filling the stands both sides to the ceiling. The sounds of this other world hit with shocking force. "MENDO, MENDO, MENDO! MENDOCINO!" The echoey slaps, slams and squeaks of rubbered feet, the whistling refs, the yelling coaches, the bounce and clangy dribble of the ball down the court, *the whisk! bang swisshhh* through the basket, the cheers and stomps and songs and boos of the crowd. We move deep into this room, Ĉelo following me, across the floor, to Mendocino's side.

Mr. Stinnett, Albion's postmaster way up in the stands, signals excitedly across the crowd for me to sit with him and his wife. This is a surprise, two seasons, he's never acknowledged my presence at a game before. Only in his post office and only then about Danny. "Danny's the kind of player who does well when he gets mad." I was stunned the first time he said this. I thought only I knew this trait about him, normally so conscientious and sensitive to others he becomes paralyzed to his own powers. I thought only I knew his dark side, that he does have one, that he does get mad, can be very nasty, to me— how his fans would love to see that!—and when he does, he's devastating—focused and directed. We're just like my mother and sister in this. "Donna needs someone to take it out on,"

Mama would say. "She's so wonderful to everyone else. I'm just glad it can be me." Hey, what's a mother for? "If only you could get pissed at whatever's keeping you from reading," I've said to him since the first grade.

We inch our way down the coat-piled bleacher, over and through the knees and feet, eyes riveted on us until I return the gaze, inch in on the far side of Postmaster Stinnett. "Thanks!" But he's looking askance at the longhaired, bearded Cêlo behind me climbing over his lap, his dirty, ragged, flag-patched Levi jacket hanging down in shreds. Climbing over me I get a whiff of not only his last dubie but his campfire of the last three nights.

And then there you are. *Oh Danny Boy....* How thrilled I am to see you, though how startling somehow, as with Rachel Love and Mr. Blackwell, to see you here. You come down the court so beautiful with the other beautiful Mendocino players I'm glad to see too. The ball leaves your hands, flies through the air, slides whistle-clean through the basket, *hwuum!* and the crowd goes nuts. Wow! When you're hot, you're hot. How good a basketball player you are. Your large blond muscular body comes back down the court through the others with breathtaking grace, the timing of a ballet dancer. I can't take my eyes off you. Little laughs of joy for your dazzling beauty gurgle up. Pride is a feeling I don't easily allow myself but suddenly I'm overwhelmed seeing that DANNY! DANNY! spiraling ever higher in the leap for the ball intended for the other team, spiraled out of me, feel almost shame that I've not allowed pride in you before.

"Yes!" Cêlo chimes my thoughts, "you should be proud of him." Then staring cosmically at me, "he is the product of your whole life, the glorious culmination. You have done well, One."

I want to say I feel proud not because you're the star, but because you've overcome so much, but words won't come out. *Ba-boom, ba-BOOM!* I'm lost in the pounding feet on the wooden tier, my heart beating with everyone's.

Mr. Stinnett shouts to me over the din. "That floor has springs under it!"

I laugh, delighted. I've always heard about the old dance floors of the West.

"That's why they're jumping so high!"

The other team is St. Bernard, a big Bay Area Catholic school. Catholic schools are good, you said, because the priests scout for players, Catholic or non-Catholic, it makes no difference, just winning does.

"How could my Protestant parents have sent me to Catholic schools?" Ĉelo suddenly slumps. "For the better education they said. Ha! For an education in sado-masochism!"

I snuggle into him sympathetically, seeing a large puppy licking his face. "Who was St. Bernard?"

"No wonder I'm an alien," he moans.

We watch the game for awhile.

Then he says, "And they hate you too, One, that's clear." He's looking at the Mendocino fans fanning out all sides below us. "They can't help it, One. They just don't understand. They don't *know* Danny, that he's a boy of enormous sensitivity, that their straight life would destroy him. Like it did me." He sighs deeply. "Drugs, the only thing that's saved me."

You're up and down the court in a long wild dance for the ball with the other young gods, as Ĉelo calls them. *You should see him now, Max, he's at magic level. The improvement since last year is astounding! When the ball doesn't roll in, there's no sign of his old self-blaming, his hurt. He springs back, puts it in the second try. Do we have the Nazi, Coach Jim Mastin, to thank for this?*

But then, shockingly, a little wave at ebb tide, and then another, my habitual understanding starts sliding out to sea. Suddenly *I can't stand that you aren't here, Max, witnessing, as these strangers are, the result of your parenting, witnessing our boy's hard-won glory.* Then I'm back to that same terrible question, *how could you leave us?* Then the loss of what we built crashes like the tidal wave from Alaska that hit this coast when he was still a baby, washing Crescent City down to Humboldt Bay. *I cannot, I will not bear your betrayal of our son.*

The crowd hushes, holding its breath. You step to the line, blow through your mouth, take a deep one, bounce the ball twice, rise up and in the most precise, delicate flip of the wrist, shoot. In a perfect arc the ball sails through the basket without touching. The crowd stomps, whistles, applauds. The ref gives you the ball again, again blows the whistle. As you begin the little ritual, toe-tapping the painted line, I feel the tear of losing you rip a little more inside me. One more year. Postmaster Stinnett is on his feet now, *oh Danny Boy...,* cheering ecstatically with everyone else their deep acclaim of you. *It's you must go....* Now Jim Mastin's hands, the most ruthless this side of the Alleghenies and the French-Indian War, are on your shoulders, instructing you. Claiming you. *And I must stay....*

It's half-time. We're way ahead. I begin to see that you really do belong to them. Not to me, this woman who can't hold her man, your fathers, this unworthy daughter, this hippie, this poet, this feminist, this welfare mother! Suddenly, their terrible, sanctified disapproval drowns me. Me! The One who made you! Who feeds and shelters you! Who brings you to them! Who loves you the most! Whom you love the most! The one who loves you when you lose. The one now under the water, drowning again, heart hurting so bad it will explode for the loss of its great love, first love, most taboo love. Give me an *M!* Give me an *O!* Give me an *M! Ba-boom!* Go to hell, Mom! My heart breaks for the enormity of the realization. They hate me because I'm your mother.

Suddenly, just as they're coming back on the floor, from out of nowhere there's an exquisite long stem red rose quivering in the air in front of me.

"For the real star of this game," Ĉelo's eyes are luminous

with light and tears. "Me to you and all your parts, including the part that loves Max."

"Where...whenever did you get this?"

"This rose is my vow to you," he says very tenderly, staring into my eyes. "To never betray you. To love you forever. Oh, One, I've never known a woman so beautiful. So intelligent. So mysterious. A woman with such a large heart."

The crowd is stomping "PUT IT IN! PUT IT IN!" The cheerleaders are tumbling upside down, Ĉelo is pleading let me in! The golden god that is you, my son, is leading the players back down the court, and I'm having a heart attack.

"I *love* you. I *love* you. I *love* you."

I'm a woman who has waited to hear those words all her life I'm a woman starved for a man who can say those words, for the evidence of a man who can love. For the evidence that you, a male, will be able to love. Goethe says a man can love only in relation to his feeling loved by his mother. But what if she loves him and he doesn't feel it? I keep saying there are men who can love. There have to be. Sometimes I shout at you. "You better be a man who can love. Or the world's going to die!"

"My Rose, my One," Ĉelo has somehow twisted his body around to almost face me on the narrow bleacher. "Will you marry me?"

His arm, which has been around my neck suddenly pulls me to his mouth. He kisses me, long and hard. I pull away—no telling what this lunatic will do if I object too strenuously, lose the game for us with one of his fits, he's that crazy—lovingly help him settle back around in his seat, prop the thorny rose which has fallen into Postmaster Stinnett's lap back into the air, trying to avoid the 1960s beehive hairdo bobbing at my knees—Coach Russ' sister!—trying to see who has the ball. "Sorry." Laughing a little. "Careful!" I laugh some more. Where is Rachel Love sitting? Where's Jan?

"You are as closed to me as Max is to you!"

This hits me like God saying it. It's true! I'm no more in touch with him than your father and Max were with me. Holy Goddess. (I'm trying to learn to invoke her name, despite how weird it sounds.) I'm hit by the mirror reflection. I thrive on the emotions they deny. They thrive on the ones I deny. This is why I'm drawn to Ĉelo, feel gratitude for him…to pierce my walls to find me. If I can't open to him I'm as guilty as my men who couldn't open to me. Holy Goddess, what greater sin? The power of his words, his yearning for me is like the centrifugal suck of the wave that threw me to the bottom of the sea when I was eleven. It's impossible to get up.

My right foot gets caught in Postmaster Stinnett's left white-socked, shining black rimmed ankle. "Excuse me," I sigh, yanking it free.

I am kissed as I have never been kissed.

Crowded in like sardines with the loggers, fishermen, coaches, scouts, classmates, ex-girlfriends, betrayed wives, employed, respected adulterous husbands, their secret loves at the California Small Schools Basketball Playoffs, as the mill belches out its deadly toxins over Humboldt Basin and the whales are being butchered in still another war with Russia, Ĉelo V'ec, Russian for *good person*, and the star's mother, as the third quarter ends and the fourth begins, are making out. You miss the shot. From the huddle at the bench down in the east corner, you, a truly gifted basketball player, though just a Junior, are looking up directly at us. "Your mom's making out in the stands with some weird hippie. Tier 16, Section D." Scott Honeycutt, from the bench. Coach Mastin too.

You miss the basket again. Foul again Number 5. Keep turning again, the briefest glance, taking all eyes with you, Coach Mastin's, crouched in his grey suit on the boundary line, up to the stands where the hippie rock-and-roll fiddler and your mother are necking.

In the cold, dark, pouring rain parking lot behind Sambo's, I see in the first huge drop as it wobbles on the rim of my right eye, you on the gym floor looking up to me, your mother, being tongued by a freak in the stands.

In the next drop on the left side, I see your father and me coming down the aisle, I'm tugging on him so hard, he's falling over, what's wrong, Love? I'm your wife now, just as you dreamed all your life, the lie of our big smiles for the guests and the photographer, the beginning of the biggest Seven Year Lie ever lived.

In the next drop I see Max, the man I let raise you, our son from age five, in the rainy window of the car that's taking him away from us forever, silently, cruelly mouthing the words I've begged from him for nine years, *I love you.*

And then I commit the crime second only to making-out in the stands at your son's state playoff basketball game.

"Ohhhh...Max...." I groan to Ĉelo who has me wrapped in his arms. "Oh, no-ooo!!!" I scream but in this terrible moment I cannot remember this guy's name.

"I'm sorry! Sorry! Sorry!" I try to ward it off. "It's the first anniversary of our separation!"

And the hysteria. The sobbing comes from so deep you hear me in the showers, understand and forgive me, though Postmaster Stinnett will never speak to me again, never will I stop crying from this night, I who have worked every waking moment of my maternal life to do it right, how could I have blown it so monumentally, lost such complete control, humiliated you like that? Oh, whatever is happening to me? Did Ĉelo slip me some of his drug therapy? Maybe dancing all month to his band, all my life I've wanted to dance, his rock-and-roll fiddle unwinding me from all the lies I've always had to live, his saying he loves me, how strangely frightened I've been, because of those longed-for words, I love you, because the walls are tumbling down, because all I've denied all these years is standing there behind the walls glaring at me like the crowd.

St. Bernardo 76! Mendocino 65!

I bawl so hard, I sink so low I'm drowning and resurrecting again and again in the oily puddles beneath Roses' whitewalls. No punishment will ever be great enough for my sin this night against you.

You too will never get over this night.

But Ĉelo V'ec is holding me, tight, soothing me, actually encouraging me. "Cry it out, One, don't hold back!"

Never have I known such a man!

"You make me think of my mother," he says into my hair, squeezing me tighter. "Blonde and beautiful. Someday I'll tell you about her."

"Tell me now!" I shriek.

"When I first saw you waitressing that night at the Foghorn, I remembered the big buttons on the pale pink cotton blouse I undid to nurse her."

I pull myself together.

Drink the hot coffee he gets me.

Then I realize the problem.

My period's started.

As I enter Sambo's, the blood soaking my crotch, I glimpse Mr. Blackwell sitting beyond the plastic palm tree the boy is being chased around by the lit-up tiger so fast they're melting into pancake butter, sending me now a million Evil Eyes. *How could you, Mrs. D…?*

I don't know, Mr. Blackwell.

Into the toilet I bleed as if I have adenocarcinoma of the endometrium, tiger stripes of melted butter, blood, urine and tears, my head between my legs cramping, my head against the tin door and wall, my Tampax case empty, the dispenser empty, the sanitary disposal box overflowing at my feet, our collective waxing Virgin moon hysteria bleeding out so we can't stop, oh Danny Boy the pipes are calling the pain of the years and years of holding it together against their stupid, cruel judgments, their small minds, their insidious gossip, Mama telling me as a girl, pay no attention to them, only you know the truth. Yes, but Mama, they're gathered around the toilet rim to finally flush me, a procession of women on the right side of God, Rachel Love and Jan, and Coach's wife and Postmistress Stinnett marching around and around the whorehouse with their universal, collective horror: *a mom like you.* My lifelong resistance to my community's protest of me breaks completely down, how they've tried to rescue you from the deprivations and degradations I've caused you. How could I? I'm worse than shit in the bowl, I die, cry, sob, bleed for my inability to play the game, though see in the same shit that I've always played his fathers' games, made it too good for them to leave, how they've hated me for this blackmail, how they can't trust me. Nor can you. If I'd freaked like any normal free spirit, if I'd ever demanded my equal to a man, I would have found a man like Ĉelo long ago. I cry now for the guilt of double crossing his fathers. I'm the Russian whalers in the Alameda Estuary. I'm the Girl in the Sea named Joy you witnessed drown last summer, pulling the boy driving by so innocently in his Volkswagen off the bluff to her.

My new love charges right into the women's bathroom, snaps the lock right off the tin cubicle.

"Oh, One! What's wrong?"

I sob into his white meaty chest. He lets me. His sympathy for me, his understanding, his compassion is unlike anything I've ever known, have always prayed for. Have not been able to understand its absence in my life. I sob purging cries into his heart until in unison with the Hoopa vomiting in the far stall they are gulps, hiccups, then laughs.

The three of us laughing in unison so fragile in our stalls.

Then, over the sinks, looking into the mirror, recognizing each other. Smiling shyly, so sweetly.

We sleep in Roses, her shiny white body glistening crystals under the I-5 overpass in the mudflats with white herons rising all around us, make cosmic love behind the frosty windows, the rose arched in the front window, Albion Moonlight turning around and around on the front seat holding back his howls at the full moon moving over us all night as we turn again and again into each's body, through my blood and tears and his words.

"It's good, One, that you made love in the stands of your son's basketball game, anything else would have been betrayal of him, all you've taught him, perpetuation of their hypocrisy, the same old killing game. Our kissing in the stands was our wedding ceremony, now we are married, you are my Rose of Sharon, the Lily of my Valley, this thing we do with our bodies, this Roses our altar, our sacred home that will not be fouled, for you are the Bride who can read and I am your Groom."

What your mother did to you. What you are going through. What your coach is telling you.

My pain, my regret, my guilt will never leave me.

Nor will it you.

I was sunbathing on the platform out over the ocean when he arrived, and so felt not just secure and beautiful but a bit insistent on my nudity. Like that, he was on top of me.

Vaginal. Low and deep and pretty and effortless like the ocean coming in beneath us.

Then he turned me onto him, so that I was on top. Clitoral. He came fast, too.

In ten minutes we were kissing again.

"You sure got your rebirth together, Scorpio." I laughed in his fleshy ear, fingering his pink cock ballooning on his sunlit thigh. "Next time I want to do it on our sides."

We did it on our sides. Then I was on top again, then going down and sucking his cock. Then he wedged his thumb between my mouth and it. Soon his gyrating thumb was another penis. Soon it had more power. I dropped his penis for his thumb. Ĉelo, Ĉelo, this is so incredible. Moving rhythmically, pressure and oceans and movements so sexual, I was gone. Though never forgetting where we were. The narrow platform over the Pacific Ocean, the two hundred foot fall.

We must have climbed the steps to the house because next thing I knew we were on my bed in the big windows. On my back. He played with my vulva. I came. And about seven or eight more times. He started counting, he told me later, after the seventh. "Twenty-five, maybe twenty-eight, I sort of lost count." Crying and sobbing and shaking. Once past the barrier or pattern or program of the usual once or twice of the past few years it was limitless. I could go forever. The experience of second wind. My son had told us that in school they learned "second wind" and "muse" are the same word in ancient Greek, the same concept, it means ghost. It means this other spirit takes over your body and gives you unlimited energy from heaven. Actually, I'd recently learned this myself, from him, as a dancer, dancing to his electric violin in his rock and roll band.

We talked, all the while his hand delicately pressing on my mounds, up the place where the thighs come together. I became afraid. Afraid that he would remove his hand. I was extraordinarily sensitive to any pressure. His finger on my inner thigh began the spasmodic contractions, the walls of the vagina throbbing, a wave coming. His tongue passed around my neck carrying with it more pressure than I could bear, so I came again. He said "Sharon." The sharp pain in my heart closed, then opened to all the world. Call my name, the poet says, in the act of love. The ocean out the window gleamed with day starlight, that's how bright it was, you could see the stars through the blue sky.

The more I came the more afraid I became of him. I opened and opened, or rather, he opened and opened me. This was not something you could ever masturbate. He was in control, as if he was playing his fiddle. To allow this required complete submission that took utter will power to maintain. Each time I took him in deeper, I came in greater sorrow, greater fear (but also the opposite, undone from these, to joy), the fear that he was not true and faithful as he so passionately, vehemently claimed. I was helpless, totally trusting, this was how I was showing him, knowing him, getting closer and closer to the truth of his betrayal. Of life itself. Trust was the key to this knowledge. Stop trusting and I'd stop coming, stop knowing. The rhythm, the mentality, the mutuality, the dependence on opening to the rhythm. Each orgasm opened me to another opening. Opening. I was the onion peeling open.

He watched from some terrible distance, the student musician, curious and fascinated at what he'd opened, though he whispered, trust me, I love you, I love you, do not be afraid. He always pleaded with me to believe him. "You always know everything, you always know what's going on." Later I would learn I'd been right, he was sexing another woman. He was practicing.

I grew afraid that he was growing disgusted, that I was a turn-off with my helpless animal sounds. I was getting tired of the sounds myself, of my own groans, the sounds I'd become, groveling and dependent and crazed. Like the sound I heard from the labor room when I was in the hospital birthing my son. The sound of an animal trapped in the air ducts, that's what I thought then, a rabbit, a coyote. "What's that sound?" I gasped to the nurse who spit back, "you're next, girl." The sound grew stronger. The sound of a woman moaning too deep, too guttural, crying too low for anyone outside herself to understand, and so it was now, I felt his revulsion, I was afraid of him, I was helpless under the weight of his breath, though compelled and intrigued, these orgasms wouldn't stop, they came now as regularly as the waves beneath the window, pounding, throbbing, hissing, jostling, crashing at the land to tear it away, to dissolve it into liquid, into air, into spirit, ghosts.

Or like the abortion: oh dreadful groan spasms, strange and weird, too painful. I felt every scrape, a stranger's hands inside the deepest part of me, scraping and scraping, and hearing a strange sound, realizing only later it was my own moaning, though I was too paralyzed to move or to object, or do anything else. A powerless entity, consciousness/unconsciousness, whatever, but no comprehension, just pain buffeted in black universes.

The Mendocino Fault Line cracked open a little, coming straight up from South America the whole way up, coming, coming, north, past Peru and Ecuador, caressing Central America, teasing Mexico, so sad and terribly coming right through Ramona and LA, right to here, Navarro Bluff, this place we fuck. And then out. Out into the Pacific Ocean, to the Glob, a massive cellular glob out there, a living entity that is nothing but millions of acres of pure single cells floating off this coastline.

As I came again I thought: a short novel. Have a chapter for each orgasm. Chapter One, first sentence: That evening the kids went to the prom. Nonlinear. I couldn't remember the exact succession of orgasms, which images came when, though that would be interesting to investigate. There was the first—in daylight, in bright afternoon sun, out over the Pacific Ocean, the San Andreas Fault which is Point Arena, where the telephone cable comes in from Japan, protruding way out on the southern horizon.

Afterwards, as we smoked a joint as the sun fell toward the horizon, he described it. "I had my hands around all your pelvis. Hands in front, holding on. Hands in back, pushing and squeezing, pulling and coaxing, till your orgasm felt like your insides were coming, were turning out. I never felt anything like it."

Then night came and the fishing boats and the constellations and a crescent moon just into Leo. I was naked, a funnel-shaped hollow gradually circling, contracting circles, the lowest and smallest of which was the earth.

"Your bird sounds."

"Birds? That was the clitoris."

"Clitoris? Well, I don't have one." He sucked on the joint.

"Birds!" I rejoiced. "Remember when you said sex is the soul's yearning to be a body?"

He turned toward the window. He was singing. "He puts his bow right there, and rubs it back and forth. Until she sings her little celestial song."

"You said 'Georgia' is the most difficult tune to play." I snuggled down into the question mark of his back. "Why is that? It's just about my favorite all-time tune but it seems so simple, well, especially for you to play."

"Because the difficulty is not technical. The notes are simple, anyone could learn the notes. The difficulty is the mood, the emotion, the simple, exquisite beauty. You can't fake that mood. You can't fake it, you can't *perform* it. To play 'Georgia' you have to go there emotionally every time."

He turned back to me. "Like making love to you."

"I saw a quote from Patti Smith the other day," I said, waylaying him a bit, my tongue on his right nipple. "She said women who've been through labor are potentially the greatest vocalists. You know, having screamed and moaned, stretched their vocal cords through that."

The phone rang. It was Feather. As she read me an article in the *San Francisco Chronicle* about the Cosmic Clothesline the Mendocino artist Max Salkin has strung, from the Heeser Drive headland to Goat Island, he played again with my pudendum, poking around. Soon he had his thumb all the way into my anus and his middle finger in my vagina and his index one on the clitoris, moving around and probing and pushing, holding the whole thing lovingly with his head and left hand just like he plays his violin. It felt so meaningful, it seemed really possible that we could go through anything and everything, other lovers, betrayals, death. He is capable of pure love, I thought. To be held, my pelvis, in his magnificent violinist hands, to be handled so deeply.

Feather called again, this time she read a book review from the *Chron*. "Our myth of the female's relative sexuality is a biological absurdity. The more orgasms a woman has, the stronger they become; the more orgasms she has, the more she can have. For all intents and purposes, the human female is sexually insatiable in the presence of the highest degrees of sexual satiation."

"Gee, Feather, you wouldn't believe what's happening to me right this minute as you read." But she was so excited she couldn't stop reading, something about the unheralded vestibular bulbs of which the clitoris is only the tip of an intricately complex and magnificent organ which rings the vaginal shaft and engorges with blood during arousal triggering the muscle contractions of orgasm.

"Voila," I sighed. "That sounds exactly right. Exactly what it feels like."

"And your girlfriends, too," he sighed when I hung up. "They always know what's going on."

Me and my girlfriends were in a café over the harbor at sundown. Maryna said that conceivably she could have sex for money. Be a prostitute. But she could never be a nude dancer.

Feather concurred. And so did the working harbor, the incoming fishing boats glittering behind her.

I was struck by this. I could never fuck for money—I'd rather be killed—but conceivably I could be a nude dancer.

Feather said that in a room full of men, men are the enemy. With one man I have a fighting chance.

For whatever reason I couldn't be nude with either of them, though they were easily enough with me. Feather was so beautiful it was hard to imagine that she felt any insecurity regarding her body. About being exposed to the gaze of a roomful of men.

Maryna, every bit as beautiful as Feather, though both so different from each other, told of being a teenager, hitchhiking down Sunset with her best friend and the guy giving them five bucks to lift up their shirts.

We're all so different, I'd die before I'd lift my shirt for money, sex for me is always about love. I hate money, I could almost take up arms against money, but for the first time I heard how easy, fun and freeing, even sexual, it is for some women. And I saw the nude dancer on the job, for money.

But I remember the first time I just wanted to show my body, my self, to Ramon. Eighth grade. Just to let him see. Just for the relief of someone seeing me. Other than Daddy.

There was sex in that. But something else far more profound. Beautiful or ugly, I was God's creation. I had been so unseen. Especially by Daddy.

Oh, Suzi, I wrote to my great girlfriend from high school, *Ĉelo is beautiful. Amazing boy, man, human. His capacity for loving so total. I gave up long ago finding such a man. Believing in one. How OPEN he is to me. How he knows me, learns me, opens me. How he doesn't misread me. How he knows on some psychic level just WHO and WHAT I am.*

The more I came the more I became him. His cock became mine, I drove it into him, and out and back, feeling the incredible yin and yang of it, how we are true opposites and the orgasm is the Sufi Chain of Transmission, God descending and we ascending, the run, the speed, the equal successive parts of each angel coming, our cries all up and down the Chain of Being, the Cosmic Clothesline.

"Of course I love you," he'll say the night he leaves me. "I make you come, don't I?"

Later when we are completely broken and I am completely heart-broken we'll meet in front of Mendosa's Market.

"Oh," I'll say, daring to reach out and touch his chest now so touched by another. "When I'm near you, even now, I just go inside you, go with you. As I think you move into me, go with me."

"Yes," he'll say. "With all others there's a vacuum behind them, there's a stillness you hear."

Morning. Gulls. They came into the window suddenly, a huge white flock turned on wing, filling the whole space, then falling with the wind straight down the bluff. There was one black one.

I remembered my husband when we were teenagers. He wasn't a good lover by any stretch, but in his negligence I was free to explore myself, beneath his large passive body. Within the boundaries I could do what I pleased. Sex with him was light and joyous (when I could overcome the heartbreak) because he did not love me, but I loved him. He did not care, he was gone, he was so far away, but for me sex was the place we married.

Then with Maximilian Rainbow. His dark and heavy lust so full of sin. The only sinner I've ever really known. No, there's Hunter. Hunter's sadism. (Not even my father was a sinner; he was just weak, sort of helpless.) Max's violent fantasies. His turn-on, his ejaculations by porn, by sin. His anger. It took six years from the time we started down that road till I finally succumbed to his fantasies, fucked that artist up Topanga Canyon as he wanted me to, now that Jesus Freak in Whale Gulch. Well, to do it, I had to fall in love with him first.

"*The first time Ĉelo and I made love he wasn't so hot,*" I wrote to Suzi. "*I accepted—completely—that's the way it'll be. Sex is never primary. But by the third time together he had become my most fantastic lover, playing my unloved body like a classical violin. That was typical of him and much of why I loved him, how he learned, how he changed, grew, loved. His penis was small by the standards but I've learned that the smaller the penis the more active I become, my vagina encircling it, the entire circumference and length it explores, grabs, pulls into its banging walls. And it turned out that even his poor performance that first time was part of his beauty. His ex-wife had not been into sex and he respected that, learned to let it go.*"

The sun rose over Cameron Ridge. I sat up in the bed, he asleep beside me. The sea washed around us, washed ashore into the Navarro, over the rocks in great white leaps. I watched this in the same mirror I watched from my crib when I was a baby. I was reading Virginia Woolf's *Orlando*. Feather said I had to read it. I was trying to think what a novel is. How you write one. When he woke I told him how important the first sentence must be.

"*He—for there could be no doubt of his sex….*"

Kimmy in Camp Moistness of the Soft Woods

Adrian Newton lived in Philo, fifteen miles up the Navarro. He was 76, recovering from his third heart attack. He wanted to tell a writer the history of prostitution on the Mendocino Coast. He approached Nancy Littleriver when she was playing the part of a madam in a local theater production. He offered to coach her. The stereotype is all wrong, he insisted. No one understands. They've got a completely wrong view of those women. And no one will take this information from me. Recently there'd been government-funded Bicentennial efforts to get the oral histories down from the old timers. No one would take Adrian's oral history. He said it's important, it's the early history of Northern California. It's as important as the history of logging and fishing.

I know a writer, Nancy responded, who would be interested in your story.

On the way to Philo, the long, windy, high ocean bluff south from Mendocino, we passed, at Dark Gulch, my ex, Ĉelo, and his new love. For the rise up out of there and next curve I was nearly blind. The pain of losing him, the pain of his exceedingly callous abandonment, of seeing him for the first time with her, a glimpse of her behind the wheel, of seeing in that flash his complete involvement in another life, his amps in the back of her station wagon. To see her, what she looks like. When I came back to the road in front of us, Nancy was saying Ruth is still unbending about you. She can't believe anyone as beautiful as you could really experience pain, doesn't have, in fact, everything she wants.

"Right," I managed. A guy in the Seagull had said something like that last Sunday. I'd just published some first poems in a local paper. "Girl," he said. "You'll never be a great poet, because, obviously, you haven't suffered enough."

I took a deep breath, still trying to get free of the devastating image but at the same time coveting it, the joy of having glimpsed him, in knowing exactly where he was at that moment. I shared this with Nancy. We both laughed, hard.

At the four point five marker up the Navarro she had me pull off into the giant redwoods. She led me down the path, the solstice sun flitting through the old virgins, to the river, to the famous swimming hole where the last time I was here I watched a couple making love. She was showing me the late sixties hippie encampment here, pointing out where everyone lived, who and how, the magical stories. She lived here in a tent with her four children for almost a year.

"It was a glorious time."

She was weeping.

"I'd been Minnesota's Catholic Mother of the Year, 1966, married to a professional football player, and so miserable. So humiliated, so annihilated. Coming here, discovering nature, marijuana, like souls, you know, fellow travelers, it saved me, so many of us, from suicide."

She pointed to a particularly old, if screwy-looking redwood. "Alfonso, and John Griffith on vacation from the post office, were camped here. It was cold. We called it Camp Moistness of the Soft Woods."

"The poet Sam Hamill was here, too," I shared. "His epic poem, *Triada*, begins in this encampment."

"When the rains came the second winter we finally got it together to get a big house in Little River. That's when I got my name, so people'd know how to find it.

"Adrian lives down the road. When people started coming from the city he would spend his time driving up and down, picking up hippies, helping them out."

"Did he have girlfriends?"

"Oh, for sure. You'll see, Addie's very sexual. He believed the sexual revolution was going to save mankind. He'd been waiting for it all his life."

It may have been my first hit on the time, my generation's time, as "history." Will there be government grants for our counterculture history or will it be as it is with Adrian Newton, no one will write it down?

Nancy went for a walk in the woods. The cabin was tiny, redwood, two rooms. He was an average size man, slim, with a thick mop of white hair. He sat by the fire feeding it redwood chips. He placed me with my pen and tablet on a small ottoman in front of him.

"I don't cut wood. No need. I just go outside and pick up the bark. It keeps me perfectly warm. Place is small, these burn a long time. I just bend over, throw a handful in, keep it going all night."

He stared at me a moment.

"People approached sex different in those days. It's not understood now."

He looked again at me, his eyes soft, sensuous. I became conscious of how we looked, facing each other. The interviewer, the interviewee. Nothing in our manner betrayed our seriousness and objectivity regarding this particular subject. Most oddly, on the wall behind his head was the famous photo of Robert Kennedy splayed on the kitchen floor of the Ambassador Hotel, a young Vietnamese man in a cook's smock kneeling to him, looking with great anguish into the camera.

"In those days there were few women outside prostitution who had any understanding of sex. They were just ignorant." He bent to his box, threw in more chips. "They still are. They don't know how to please a man. They don't understand. They don't know how to treat a man as a man. I'm not talking about as an equal. But as a man."

I felt myself beginning to fall into my oldest hole but I didn't let him see this. I knew what he meant. I certainly was a woman who understood.

He was born in 1904 in one of the houses in Eureka. "The line," he called it. "The entire Main Street there of Eureka, they were all houses. Every one of them. In the Twenties there must have been a hundred houses on the coast. My mother was very young, very pretty. She was still young, very pretty when I was grown.

"No one understands prostitution, the prostitutes. They got a completely wrong view of those women. In those days there was one woman for every thirty men. They were *loved*. Many of them loved their work, felt they were living the best life. Chose to live that way.

"No, of course I didn't know my father. Who cares? Though all my life I've wondered about him. Which one. All men are your father, my mother told me. I never cared much for men anyway. Until the hippies came. I much prefer the company of women.

"Yes, sure, there were other children. The children had chores. One of my first jobs was delivering linen to the different houses. My mother got into the linen business as one of her sidelines. Eventually she became a madam.

"The rest of the family, my brother and sister, they live over in the valley, they don't speak of this past, they deny it, make up all sorts of lies. My sister bought a family album at a garage sale, has it on display in her living room in Vallejo. Sometimes I think they've denied it so long they've forgotten where they came from. But I've always been proud of my childhood. It was great. So much better than most kids'. I couldn't have stood milking cows, hoeing and going to church. I loved the women, all kinds, like a harem, you know. Their perfumes. I loved certain ones, and they loved me. I'd babysit, I'd wash their little basins, you know, empty their chamber pots, make their beds. They would tell me their stories, cry on my shoulder, tell me of the men. Where they were from, how they got there. I was in love with them. I loved their smells. They called me Love

Boy. That was my name. Sweet Adrian. Sometimes, Tender. You know, it means—I tended them. I loved the smell of a room after a customer. I'd get food and drink for them. Some girls were so popular I had to bring them sandwiches, they didn't have time for a break.

"The sad ones were the ones in the window cribs. A tiny space. There were girls who never left those cribs. The cheapest, the most likely to be diseased. The girls who got too old and deformed, out of shape. Well, you couldn't really stay in shape lying in a crib day and night. But some men were really turned on by this. The girl who's sole function in life is to lie there and be fucked. When the 1918 flu hit they lay there dying. Didn't stop a lot of guys. Food was brought to them, the curtains usually drawn when a customer went in."

"Streetwalkers? No, they were a whole other thing, the lowest. Filthy, no respect."

"Tell me what the different women were like," I said. "You know, specifics."

He jumped at this. "They were *all* unusual! There were women who had peculiar things about them. Physical, yes. Well, some had unusual personalities, or faces. Or minds. In those days there was much greater human variety, not like now, there's so much cosmetics and plastic surgery, and everyone is supposed to be the same. Variety was the key, the moneymaker. Something unusual. One woman had a club foot, she was the mother of my best friend in Eureka. She made a lot of money, bought a ranch near Willits. There was one woman in our house, she was famous everywhere. Her private part was seven inches thick, and it was reversed."

"Reversed?"

"It protruded way out in front. When you touched it, it was spongy."

He had some old photographs, a pile on the floor beside his chair. In one, four women are coming out by carriage to a logging camp, hundreds of men waiting.

"The look in everyone's eyes is wild," I laughed, looking at the photos. "The men's eyes, the women's eyes."

"Yes," he said. "I don't know who made who wild, but yes the energy was wild."

"I remember when I was five we lived out on the road from Comptche, you know where that mobile home is now, that's where the schoolhouse was in those days. There was a woman they'd bring out in a covered wagon. They said she'd had six hundred men. Such women would stay in the camp a month or so, then be taken on to the next camp.

"There used to be a hermaphrodite, is that how you call it? Androgene? She was installed in a special buggy and taken in the caravans from logging camp to logging camp. Her sole function to be fucked. You'd crawl in there with her. After awhile she'd been in there for so long she couldn't walk. Her clitoris was very large, like a small penis. There were men who were very turned on by her, that she never left that space. She was known about, everywhere. Sometimes great efforts were made to get to her."

"Who were they?" I ask. "I mean as time went on, this wasn't the Gold Rush, this was 1904, the Twenties. Was it a tradition, was it acceptable? Did girls grow up saying I'm going to be a prostitute?"

"No. There was some stigma. Girls from Mendocino went to Eureka. My mother was from Mendocino. Girls from Eureka went to Albion. Usually it was a young girl that was in love with a man who convinced her to become a prostitute for him, for them, and for love she would do it. Whore house, we just called them whore houses. In Mendocino there were none. The churches, the families, you just passed Mendocino. You'd go to Albion or Caspar, Fort Bragg. Those places were wide open. Mendocino was dry. You know, alcohol goes hand in hand.

"I can still see the cribs on the line, the cribs that lined Eureka's Main Street."

And I'm seeing the ocean voyage between Mendocino and Eureka, the road—was there a road?—from Eureka to Albion?

"Yes, of course, you went back over and over to the same woman. You became very good friends. I had many friends. During the act though she never talked. It was always the same. They washed you. Yes, a disinfectant in the water. And then they did this little motion, which was how they checked for venereal disease. They would hold the penis and underneath with a quick motion move it way back and that way they could tell. The cleaning/checking method. The same procedure, always. It got to be a real turn on. You looked forward to it. You kind of wanted it."

"What did they wear?"

"They just dressed like you. Well, no, they always wore a dress. A simple dress. The rooms were simple and comfortable."

"What about sexual practices? Was sex the same?"

"There was *no* oral sex. I *never* heard of it. And no Blacks, Chinese, or Indians in those places. But the girls when they got too old, diseased, whatever, ended up in the places for Blacks, Chinese, Indians.

"They had an exercise they did that kept them in shape. I don't know how to explain it. It developed the muscle down there. Some were especially good at this. They were well known. Actually, the thought was that some women had an extra muscle."

I asked about the nature of the relationships, between the men and women, for the men with both their whores and their wives.

"That's when love comes in and it gets funny," he laughed. "What I could never understand is how one guy would have two or three girls in the same house and each one thought she was his only one. Common sense should have told them that it wasn't so."

"Did the wives know?"

"My wife, I'm certain, had not the faintest idea. She was a rare one, she had sexual knowledge, but not about that."

Something in his voice was different then. I didn't ask him if her knowledge came from him.

"Could women's ignorance have been a front? You know, the way a woman is supposed to be. Feminine?"

"No," he assured me.

He said "There are women still here, well-known Mendocino County names, whose original money came from prostitution.

"They'd sell out, buy land, develop big ranches, respectable businesses. Marry well. It's just like the marijuana farmers now."

"What about the burning of Mendocino's Chinatown in 1911? The whole headland, several rows of streets, on Main Street in front of the Hotel area." I'd discovered this fact somewhere, had delivered it to the Historical Society, though they didn't seem much interested in that history either.

"Well, I was only seven, but yes, everyone knew who all was responsible. It's still a well-kept secret. Some of those people are still here. It was planned. Another fifty years it'll come out. Same thing happened earlier with the Indians. My grandparents were Indian killers. In Chico, that area. Well, my grandfather. My grandmother would hide the Indians. I always did like women best."

We drove him to Boonville to grocery shop. I stayed in the station wagon, writing. A list of my next questions. The name of the Eureka house you were conceived, born and raised in. Tell me of first sex, how old you were. The well-known Mendocino County names. What did you do for a living as a grown man? More about your mother, her girlhood growing up in Mendocino, her name?

"I loved my mother," he said. "A beautiful, proud woman from Mendocino."

He came out of the market a few minutes before Nancy. Why is oral sex a contemporary phenomenon? He leaned against the wall, his foot up behind him, lit a cigarette, and watched 128, the main drag north and south through town. 1904, two years before my grandparents married. Twelve before my father, their last child, was born. He was wearing faded baggy dungarees, a leather jacket, and a logger's cap with something in Boontling, the outrageous secret, local tongue develop to throw off trespassers of Boonville, written across the front. *KIMMY*. I imagined it meant *FUCK*. Or maybe *PIMP*. Maybe that's what he did for a living. Max always wanted to pimp me. Now I know kimmy means man. I'm not talking about as an equal. A man's needs used to be understood. My broken heart and the hook: I want to please a man. I want him to know I understand. This goes back to Daddy, even before he raped me. Even as a toddler when he messed with me, that was the main feeling I always had, as did my sister in the bed next to us, my whole being rushed forward past myself, wrecked and bleeding, sawed in two, it's okay Daddy, I forgive you, I love you, and God does too. You are not going to hell. You're a man, made in His image, you couldn't help yourself.

Adrian's heart was bad but he wasn't old, leaning up against the Boonville store. I saw, as Nancy Littleriver said I would, his deep sexual essence. A boy who was raised in a house of prostitution. He was centered in his groin, he came from sex. Of course we all do, but he was grounded there. Like my father, like Max, his whole identity there. Too bad our soldiers raped the Indian women, I'd just read in an anthropologist's 1952 dissertation on West Coast history, but that was a good thing they were there, or, men being men, at the mercy of the sex drive, they would have been forced to turn on each other in homosexual sex. And love is fleshly even unto spirit, St. Augustine said. And spiritual unto the flesh. I could see softness around Adrian's eyes, a sensuousness; his whole being glowed when he talked. I love the body, the loss of physical pleasure must be the real horror of age, I pray never to lose that. So what is wrong? Why am I falling so deep down my old, sad, scary, ringing hole?

We dropped him off at his Philo cabin with his bag of groceries. Philo means love, I sighed, saying good bye. I'll be back soon as I can. Then on down to the coast, past Iron Bridge, the four point five marker, Dylan pleading Lay Lady Lay.

I was here with Max and the kids, they were swimming, I was sunbathing on my belly. A nude couple up the sandy slope. At first, they were reading, sunbathing on their backs. But after awhile they were on their bellies, in a sort of huddle, their faces to each other. Then in the warm golden sun, beneath the towering redwoods, they were on their sides, and her leg went up over his hip. One glimpse of his hard penis going between her legs, her behind gyrating slowly around the backpack that obstructed part of my view. Trying not to look, but wanting to, that strange mix of feelings, wanting, not wanting this to be happening. They were being still, quiet, this position was the least obvious. They fucked. And I watched. I finally got Max's attention. A gift to him. The voyeur so great in him.

Darkness falls last on the Pacific, you can drive in its direction a long time, to the light. But then darkness does fall. The dark mimicry of the owl at Dark Gulch, a gull, and the gall that I have been left again.

Lay across my big brass bed.

I'm not sure when Adrian died, it seems it was soon after that. I intended to return, take down more of his story, but I kept putting it off. Writing always takes me to the truth of myself, whether I want the truth or not. Even an interview, just writing down another's story. Like the Historical Society, I wasn't ready yet.

Fornography

I got back from Oregon and California on Thursday in time for the two week writers conference.

For the three days before it started, I cleaned the cabin and moved in my stuff that'd been stored for eighteen months in a friend's barn in Mendocino. We finally agreed that the back room should be mine, even though I am the one who needs a view to write and he has to be blind to everything outside himself. He made me a book case. It was thrilling unpacking my books, shelving them; I'd forgotten about some of them. My dog, Albion Moonlight, kept casing the place, happy to be back too.

We had exchanged very emotional letters. In all of his he begged me to come back, apologizing profusely for having asked me to leave. On the same day we had both written asking if the other wanted to have a baby. When I turned off Highway 101 at Discovery Bay I pulled over and searched through the back of the station wagon for my diaphragm. To have it near. Later, I cursed myself for not putting it in then, but I was so broke, I was budgeting the cream. Spermicide is one of my biggest expenses.

We made love in the dirt driveway, next to Roses' left front tire, still hot. He said he'd thought of doing it there the whole time I was gone. The sun shone wildly through the high cedars, casting dark lacy spiders over our bodies. The images of a woman in a shower, the water rivering down from her dark pubic hair, from the magazines I'd taken from Ĉelo's the night I'd gotten home from South America and he told me he was living with another woman flickered around us too. I'd begged Ĉelo for the letter I'd written him from San Andreas Island asking him if he wanted to get married, its existence in his keep now feeling like a betrayal of the sacred. Reluctantly he'd given it back to me, but during that awful first night I regretted it and so returned it to his loft over the Caspar Inn. He was sleeping in Elk, at her house. Beside his bed was a stack of porno magazines. I left my letter on his pillow, took the magazines. I will study these, I will understand him. Eventually I threw them out but now as Patrick and I made love I saw again that dark one, the shower water down her pubic hair, her inner thigh.

I didn't have my diaphragm in. My body still didn't feel fully recovered from the abortion eighteen months before. I've gotten pregnant every time I haven't used a diaphragm between the eighth and twenty-second day.

But it seemed a test of our love. Mine, anyway. To interrupt to put the thing in would bring up the whole issue of our letters, marriage and a baby, and the problems of our love. Besides, I'd had whole days on this journey dreaming of being pregnant again, of having another child. Devreaux and Tom's pregnancy moved deep inside me. It was from their cabin on the end of Middle Ridge, over the mouth of Salmon Creek and the ocean, that I wrote, Patrick, do you want to get married? Do you want to have a baby?

I wasn't very relaxed and it wasn't exactly sensuous, but it was fun. In the dirt, under the cedars towering over us, over the gleaming silver water of the Strait, back home in this beautiful place.

How hard it is to reach him, to open enough, to make this love real.

It was almost an hour before I freaked. Silently, not telling him, not to spoil our much needed moment. On the floor of the back room that was to be my room, on my back again, I squeezed and squirted gobs of spermicide up inside.

About three hours later, when we began to make love in the loft, he discovered dirt all over my rear-end and in my vulva. We got to laughing, teasing each other. Sticking out my butt and tongue to him as nasty as I could. That's when I counted the days and saw that more time had passed than I'd figured— twenty-four since my last period. That's cutting it close, but still I was sure I was safe. Eighth to the twenty-second day just to be safe but actually I've always conceived between the eighteenth and twenty-second day, my ovulation later than most. After this last pregnancy I'd upped the diaphragm time to the twenty-fourth day, but until then I'd gone without protection every twenty-fourth day of my sex life. So we made love again without protection, and this time I came. Powerfully, gloriously, a long deep-heart and pelvis-throbbing vaginal orgasm. Then, very gently, he turned me over, put it in from behind. "Do you mind?" he asked, apologetically "It seems the only way I can come with you."

I loved it.

Afterwards, lying there in that sweetest of exhaustions, the trees wavering in the skylights of the rent-free, caretaker, cedar cabin we'd lived in on and off for a couple years, the sea below in the lower windows, the sounds of lapping at the bluff, Moonlight's paws clicking around on the cedar floor, I shared with him my month of travel. Then, suddenly, I remembered: my period started on that morning I started down from Ashland, through the thick fog, crossing the California border, turning east on 89 to seek out Ishi's places, to mark my return to California.

That wasn't three weeks ago.

That was two weeks ago.

I pulled my Celestial Guide from my red backpack beside the mattress.

It was true. I'd counted wrong.

Now I was filled with dread and fear. As he was when I shared it with him. We lay beside each other very still. Then I filled the diaphragm full of the cream, inserted it, on the hope again that the semen had not yet entered the cervix.

"I saw a show on Donahue at my parents'. You know, you always learn new things about this. There's a substance, like hard plastic—that's how he described it—that seals off the cervix at all times except those forty-eight hours of ovulation."

"Well, at least we were open to it," he said.

By late Sunday it was clear it wasn't working out. But he denied it when I asked. I was sorting through the box of photographs, my old places, lovers, father and mother and brother and sister and my kids, when I happened to look up at him. *"Every man I've ever loved/has looked at me/with murder in his eyes."* Finding that line for one of my poems was a breakthrough. I vowed I would never stay with a man again after seeing it.

That night we both agreed that we should live in separate places.

In the morning after love he descended the loft ladder, made me coffee on the tiny propane stove. I lay there working hard against my emotions. Ascending, his naked body golden and furry in a shaft of sunlight, the sea and gulls flashing behind him, the most golden body I'd ever seen, the only one whiter than mine, he explained that he had had a month with the cabin to himself, had written well, had evolved—he bent then to kiss the top of my head—a schedule of discipline. Of writing all morning and afternoon, then going to town to get the mail (my letters, mostly), and then to Happy Hour at the Town Tavern, and drinking late. Getting up the next morning and starting over. "I've always written my best poems with a hangover."

It took me until three Monday to move my stuff back into Roses, everything except the books. I was so tired of moving, packing, unpacking, packing again. The grime of the cabin, the twenty-six floor-to-ceiling windows I'd washed, plugged the cells of my body, filled the crevices beneath my nails. I had three weeks to finish my book. The publisher was waiting for it. I'd have to finish it in Roses. We had an argument about my wasting time going to the conference. He implied I was selling out. I worked to cultivate excitement in being independent again, to not give in to the brutal spasms of hurt clinching my heart, washing all through me, threatening to drown me. He had begged me to come back. He had promised me this wouldn't happen again.

At 8 p.m. on Monday he sat down next to me at the opening reading in the Fort's theater—Leslie Marmon Silko's. "It was hard," he whispered. "I've been drinking all afternoon."

He reeked, more of perspiration than beer.

"I worried about you. Please come home tonight."

Right then a friend from California climbed over both of us for the seat on the other side of me. "I can stay with you guys, can't I?"

Caitlin was penniless, intended to crash the whole symposium.

"They're cracking down this year, Caitlin." I'd crashed the conference myself the year before, though I hadn't attended the workshops, just the lectures and readings, and I'd given a reading in exchange. As a result, my book was going to be published by a Minneapolis press, Caitlin having made the connection, being partly responsible. The local press had had my manuscript for almost two years until I'd realized that Sam was messing with me: soon as I slept with him he'd publish it.

"I'll go right up and tell Jane I was in Canada, there's the mail strike and so I couldn't apply for a scholarship."

We took Caitlin back to the cabin with us, made love twice in the next safe days, silently in the loft above her, the quarter moon waxing in the skylight. The need to be silent while coming has always been erotic for me.

The morning broke in thick fog, drizzles. I got us both out of there early. To leave him alone for his writing discipline.

I parked at the beach at Point Wilson, took my ten cent shower in the campground restrooms—the cabin had no running water—let Moonlight out for the day, sat in the passenger seat, the typewriter in my lap. I started in again on Wyoming. Even with the overcast a few female bodies sprawled naked on the sand.

I stared across the Strait to Whidbey Island. In 1910 they strung a net from here to there to catch Philippine ships trying to invade. This is the military origin of this place, now run by Parks, Recreation, and Arts. I stared at the cement bunkers.

I could write a book about trying to write Wyoming. "The killer poem," I've called it, the one that will make or break my book-length poem. It takes place at midnight on the crest of the Big Horn Mountains. I try to tell my story as a poet, how it was the Vietnam War and the U.S.'s genocidal policy against its Natives, *"the fuck of history,"* and getting a Master's Degree in English, being taught male academia's law and order of poetry which seemed to me of the same fascist spirit as the law and order of the army, that caused me to take *"a vow never to be a poet/ because art I was taught/is too delicate to sing of genocide./But what else could I sing/while whole peoples were being murdered/in my name?"* "There can be no poetry after Auschwitz," the well-known line went (though I didn't learn of it until long after my own crisis). *"The poem as museum piece/where words are molded like human skin to shade the light//like special collections of gold filled teeth."* Wyoming is about breaking my six year vow not to be a poet.

So it is also that greatest of academic taboos: a political poem. Wyoming begins with the testimony of a soldier who participated in the Sand Creek Massacre of 1864. *"I heard one man say he had cut out a woman's private parts/and had them for exhibition on a stick./I heard of numerous instances in which men/had cut out the private parts of females/and stretched them over saddle horns/and wore them on their hats/while riding in the ranks.*" This is followed by the testimony of Chief Oury of the Utes: "*The oath of a woman is almost worthless/among the Indians.*"

I worked for years on these two testimonies, to keep them true to the originals and at the same time, to set them as poetry, as lyric, as art. Many times this work struck me as immoral, as in the quote about Auschwitz. I'd been taught, indirectly, that the words of a woman are almost worthless. When the phone call came from the Minneapolis press saying they wanted to publish my book my first reaction was Wyoming. Wyoming's not right yet. I'd spent the months since working on a new version, one in which I, the female narrator, was more distant, more objective, not so "strident" (the main charge against political poetry), and, more lyrical, that is, somehow, preposterously and more beautiful. Mainly I got rid of the woman urinating at the top of the Big Horns.

On Tuesday afternoon Patrick came to Bob Hass's craft lecture. He'd photocopied my pass, *FIRST CLASS GUEST*, glued a gold star on it to get into the lectures and readings. This had caused great glee among our friends, the local poets, most of whom were fiercely resentful of the conference and were boycotting it.

The only thing I remember of Hass's lecture, other than the gossip that once again he was hitting on every young woman in the audience, was his mention of Denise Levertov's "bad writing during the Vietnam Era." Denise, seated in the front of the middle section of the theater, didn't move. Thankfully, he went on, she has returned to her early, lyrical voice so that he once again cares about her writing. I could hardly believe it. He who had done more than anyone to discredit the great Robert Duncan was now siding with Duncan in his vicious war against Levertov for writing the poem "Advent 1966," about the widely published photograph of the napalmed nine year old Vietnam girl running naked down the road. Duncan attacked her anti-war poems as too violent, accused her of contributing to the violence by writing them. Then he read his own poem in which the image of the nine year old girl on fire is *"a mirror of the drama of the self's necessary struggle and undoing in pursuit of the imagination's Art, its end."*

"This is not a baby on fire but a babe of fire,
flesh burning with its own flame, not toward death
but alive with flame, suffering its self
the heat of the heart the rose was hearth of."

It became a raging burn from which the Duncan-Levertov long and important friendship never recovered. Last year there had been a similar confrontation between Robert Bly and Levertov. In his craft lecture—again with Levertov in the audience—Bly insisted that the violence of her language created violence. That conference was now said to have been so disturbing and wild that three female participants ended up in the nut house. It felt like the Fathers against the daughters—that she would dare threaten their authority! Jane, the conference head, had decreed that from now on the conference would be intellectual and conservative. I wanted to scream and never stop.

"I was wandering around the cabin depressed," Patrick started in as soon as Hass was finished. "No sleep in so long. And I was looking at your books. I pulled *Amerus* off the shelf, opened it to an extraordinary poem, was sucked right into the middle of it. It was *beautiful.* I looked back to see who had written it." He grabbed my arm then, as we walked up the aisle. "It was you! It was Wyoming!"

Someone passing us in the aisle was muttering Neruda, *"and you will ask: why does his poetry not speak of sleep and leaves and the great volcanoes of his native land? Come and see the blood in the streets! Come and see. The blood in the streets!"* Outside we managed to get clear of the crowd. *"Come and see the blood. Running in the streets!"*

"Oh, God, Patrick, I've never been able to read that version since it came out. It embarrasses me. It's the original, I've written many versions since." I saw the large cardboard box in the back of Roses marked Wyoming. I put my arm through his, jumped a little for the wonderful synchronicity. The very day I started to work on the poem again, he opened to it in a magazine. As I said, I could write a book about writing Wyoming.

"Don't change it. Every word is perfect, is right. It's beautiful."

"Well, I have changed it. Many times." Then I asked him, in fear and dread, "Would you read and critique my latest version?"

"Sure," he said.

We met a few minutes before the evening's reading. I gave him two versions, the one in the manuscript that the press had and the one I'd completed two weeks ago in Oregon. (The one I was now working on was nowhere near finished.) He stayed outside the theatre on the grass with Moonlight while William Stafford read inside. He was shaking his head in disgust when I came out. "It's prosy, Ramon's not right." Of the two he preferred the manuscript version. I couldn't fathom how this could be. The newer version is much more lyrical, I was sure. But in fact my editor had said the same thing.

"Your language is too passive, '*when you reach me/traversing the great plains of your brotherhood….*'" Shaking his head in disgust.

And again he begged me to come home with him. "I'm in bad shape, you just have to come."

"I'm moved out, Patrick."

"I've started hallucinating. I'm afraid I'm going crazy."

He walked over to Caitlin and told her to come. I could feel the progress I had made in my withdrawal from him, in not succumbing to the chaos of heartbreak. He's freaking out, but I've been kicked out. He's got our beautiful rent-free cabin all to himself, I have three weeks to finish my book in a car. And now I'm worried I'm pregnant again.

Again, our two vehicles, Roses, my white station wagon, Caitlin's green Volkswagen, followed his silver Saab the six miles out Hastings Road to the cabin, cedar-glowing in the dark woods on the bluff over the Strait. *"You come damned/by your Creed,"* I said aloud on that little journey the rest of the stanza he'd been so disgusted by, *"to withhold love/from your sister."*

And again, in the early dawn, Caitlin and I drove back, me with *Amerus* in tow. She was attending Margaret Atwood's daily workshops. I drove down to my beach and after my shower, started in on Wyoming. Moonlight played all morning with a barking seal in the surf. The day was overcast.

I read all four versions, the three that Patrick had read the day before and my newest version. And saw it. Truly, I'd had a failure of nerve. None of the versions were right, but the original and the earlier drafts were superior. With each reworking I'd lost a little more of the original meaning and outcry. Then I was afraid. Did I want approval too much? Had I sold out as he kept implying? Recently I had been reading academic poets, trying to see, to learn some of the tactics I'd always scorned. I saw myself again on Navarro Bluff in Mendocino sitting in the front window over the ocean first writing Wyoming and Ĉelo has fucked another woman at his gig the night before at Caspar Inn, has spent the night with her. The hurt, when I found out, was devastating. He comes in, I look up, "Oh, honey, I think I finally got it! I think I finally got Wyoming!" I'll never escape the image, the smell of the cool March sea air on him, a bag of groceries in his arms. He'd charged it at the Albion Market, to bring me and the kids food. Later, when I learn the context, he screamed, "I didn't bring those groceries out of guilt!"

That he had not returned after his gig was not that unusual. Ĉelo had pursued me for a long time, constantly saying "I really love you, One, as Max obviously did not." Falling in love with him was a long process; it was falling out of love with Max and overcoming my distrust. I wouldn't let him move in but he was spending more and more nights with us. The day before we'd fought; he'd had a fit of jealousy over Sam's visit from Washington.

"How was the gig?" I asked then. "I'm sorry I didn't come. I just couldn't." He'd called me an exhibitionist, a groupie, and a whore for poetry.

We made love on my son's bed in the back of the cabin because mine in the front window was covered with Wyoming. I pulled him back there, into the dark knotty pine. Football posters, basketball trophies. When he put his hand on my hip, he gasped, "Oh…" In that moment, I knew. But quickly I shined it on, I had to work, I couldn't handle such hurt now. Me, the great denier. The sex was the joy of my success with Wyoming. Then I drove him down the coast to Elk for practice with his new band, bought a Moosehead in the continuing spirit of celebration, the first alcohol I ever bought myself, and drove Roses back the long way over Greenwood Ridge, ecstatic about my poem, saying it aloud as I descended to the Pacific, *"until I knew/I would die if I didn't write."*

A week later, with the kids in the back room watching a TV that Danny's girlfriend loaned him so he could watch an important sports event, we were lying on my bed in the front window over the ocean.

"Have you fucked someone else in the past week?"

I didn't know I was wondering this. I surprised myself with the question. I wasn't prepared for the shock when he said yes. Then the uppermost thought was not to freak out with the kids in the house.

"I played hot that night, my last night with the Electric Harmonic Blues Band. I got out there on a solo and she was dancing right in front of me. She was so sexy, her little hips, her bare midriff, just inches from my face and violin. Every time I came down from a solo I'd be praying for you to be there. Please, One, oh please, be here. But you never came. She's one of the truckers camped out on Flynn Creek Road. After the gig they wanted to know if I wanted a ride to Albion Ridge. I got in the back of the truck with her, but when we got to Albion Ridge I didn't get out. I went on with her. She lives with her kid in a beautiful gypsy truck. Oh, One, I've been sick all week for not being able to share this wonderful thing that's happened to me. It was so sexy to wake up in the morning in a strange woman's bed."

He reached then, pulled my limp body to him. "I didn't want to hurt you."

In one sitting I wrote another version, finding a more suitable place in a preceding poem to insert some of the historical facts. When I rose from Roses I was bleeding.

A whole week early! I wasn't pregnant, I was free at least of that worry. I marked it on my Celestial Guide calendar. I had no money for Tampax. My Levi's a bloody mess. I crawled into the back, searched for my sponges. A jogger was running by in the drizzle as I inserted one way too dry. She was wearing a gray sweat shirt with *WYOMING* in red letters across her chest. I laughed out loud. However the number on her back as she ran east toward town was 74, not my son's 72 (Utah), and I knew I hadn't done it yet. But I was close. In my gleeful relief, despite the mess of my crotch, I found myself suddenly writing a whole new poem, *Ramon/Ramona.* "*Even now I do not understand/ her terrible name,*" Betty Hotbox. That's what the boys called that strange girl in high school, slightly retarded, maybe just emotionally, who they all fucked and then scorned, and in that moment I knew a rare self-censorship: I would not carry forth that horrible name into the poem. I'd protect her even this late.

For her craft lecture late that Wednesday afternoon Margaret Atwood discussed "The Muse." A questionnaire was in every seat. I've always felt confused about the Muse, mainly if I have one or not. Once in Vermont I sat in on a class by Richard Grossinger, "Ibn al Araby and the Sufi/Arabic Archetype of the Muse." I actually pondered then if Jesus could be my muse, the archetypal Christian figure I no longer believed in but whose image from childhood was a permanent part of my psyche, the Bible being my literary root. I kept silent in Richard's class even when Lindy, his poet wife, argued on behalf of women writers against "the muse problem." "The muse problem," according to Richard, was that Male Writer/Female Muse is the Sacred Archetype, the primary Form and Relationship, an insurmountable spiritual fact, a Cosmic Law, and to attempt to break it a sin, and ultimately impossible; women can't become real writers. I was dumbfounded, my Jesus hole filling with the oldest sea of wordless sorrow and knowledge. I didn't know then about the Goddess.

Atwood's questionnaire was: *1. Are you male or female? 2. Do you have a muse? 3. Is your muse a real person or a mythological construct? 4. Is it male or female?*

I answered *yes* to number 2. I struggled to answer number 3 thinking now of Crazy Horse instead of Jesus, how just before leaving Mendocino he'd visited me in one of the most powerful dreams of my life, how he had come to be the center of my book poem. For number 4 I answered *Male.*

In the middle of Jon Anderson's reading that night, a poem about the Milky Way *"when I was a boy,"* which oddly evoked an image of my son at sixteen with a famous one of Marilyn Monroe, Patrick walked out. Then lights, lines of light were crossing and circling Anderson's body. Jon Anderson was one of the first poets I'd heard read, eight years earlier in Vermont. I was shocked by his appearance. He'd been a boy then. Now he looked on the far side of middle age. I worried that the lights were affecting his heart's electrical system.

I was the first one out of the reading. Patrick was across

Battery Way playing with Moonlight. I could see his insanity, it stood out in contrast to the severe military setting. "I'm sorry," he pleaded. "I had to get out of there. I kept hearing voices. I wanted to scream at the guy. I thought his poems sucked."

I leaned into his body. We leaned against Roses.

"You're right," he said. "We shouldn't live together."

"O.K."

I left him, headed back to the crowd, fighting the hurt, to tell Caitlin. She'd have to sleep with me in Roses.

"But I can't sleep now."

We went down to the Town Tavern, her green bug following my white Roses. Like me, Caitlin has lived long periods of time in her car in order to be a poet—and in her case to found and run the Sonoma State Poetry Center. Wednesday is Jazz night. "We took a vow of poverty," I laughed as we danced. Her leotard strap broke. I removed my tiny ceramic red heart pin to use as a safety pin. I'd worn it since Devreaux gave it to me when I got back from South America and my heart was broken for Ĉelo. I had it pinned on the lapel of the man's classy suit jacket she'd also given me. I loved that little heart, but sometime in the wild dancing it fell off her leotard, disappeared in all the flying feet. We danced to the end, an exercise for exhaustion, a prayer for sleep. But when we came out, 2:30 a.m., it was barely dark.

"Summers here, Caitlin, this far north, there's only a couple of hours of total night."

I knew this from sleeping on the beach with Patrick last summer. On the night of the Solstice it never got completely dark.

There was a note on the windshield.

I'm in bad shape. I'm afraid you were hurt by me tonight and may have decided to not come home. Please come home. I really need you, tonight especially. I wanted to say that at the Fort but I was afraid to. I just can't go inside the Tavern. I need your friendship. I love you. Patrick.

The handwriting of the body I so loved was shaky, each word shakier than the last. But I was sick of being his yo-yo. I wasn't going to make a fool of myself to Caitlin.

I pulled out in front of the Volkswagen, led her to North Beach. I will not go back to him.

"So what is your relationship with Patrick?" Caitlin asked after I'd cleared the back of my heavy boxes, piling them in front around the steering wheel, keeping a space for Moonlight. When I'm alone I pile them on the passenger side, leaving space at the wheel for a quick getaway, Moonlight sleeping with me. We lay on our backs, me trying not to be nervous with the intimacy. I listened to the soft lapping of the waves on the beach, my favorite sound. I'd never spoken of my relationship with Patrick before, had never put it in words to anyone. I was interested myself in what they would be. Then I heard footsteps. I felt love for him, and concern. He said he was in bad shape. He begged me to come home.

"It's been nourishing, healing, I think, for both of us. For me, after Ĉelo, Max and Mendocino. For Patrick there's a lost love too."

When Charley and I finally got to the top of the Big Horns—we'd taken the wrong turn—I got out to pee. He didn't get out, just crawled to the back floor of the van, fell asleep. All the way from Mendocino, he wouldn't share the wheel. I'd been in great misery, my stomach churning, like an ulcer, sick the whole trip for the loss of Max, with being with this man I did not love.

Wyoming is where she starts driving for the first time.

"Patrick seems like the kind of man who gets deeply attached," Caitlin said, now in deep breathing. "You are beautiful together."

"Yes, I know."

"You look like brother and sister."

"Yes, I know."

Yes, she was still with Lee, a poet too.

"Wasn't it over last year when you were here?"

She was asleep. I listened to her light, feminine snores, and vowed again not to get upset. I haven't the time, only two and a half weeks now. Fuck him and the cabin not big enough for him to write with me there. I'm the one with the deadline. I'm the one who needs support now. I fell asleep.

I woke to headlights approaching. Caitlin screamed, "they're going to hit us!" grabbing me. We waited in each other's arms for the car to crash into my side. Moonlight rose from his sleep on the passenger side, looked out. The car came to an abrupt stop, headlights blazing through the cracks of the drawn curtains, the motor gunning.

"Just a car turning around," I said. Could it be those guys who attacked me sleeping in Roses in the woods during last year's conference. Foolishly I didn't have Moonlight with me that trip.

"Once Lee and I were sleeping on a bluff and someone came and pushed us over. There was a tree that caught us. I guess I've never gotten over it."

And I'll never get over those guys. She fell back to sleep. Then again I thought I heard footsteps. But Moonlight didn't budge.

We were up at the crack of dawn. Caitlin took off. I watched the green VW disappear over the hill to town. I'd heard that Jane intended to kick her out because she hadn't paid. "Kick out a real poet who hasn't money because her whole life is dedicated to poetry and poets," I said to Moonlight, opening a can of organic dogfood. "A writing conference for middleclass housewives and overworked school teachers on vacation who think they can pay to learn how to write poetry."

I made the bed, got the boxes back in the back, found my shampoo, a towel, a change of clothes for my morning shower, another sponge. I looked up.

Patrick was coming down across the field.

As he came nearer I looked away. I could not look at the pain in his face. My priority has to be my book.

"Are you okay," he cried, embracing me. He was wet. "Are you okay, are you okay?"

Everywhere I touched, lay my head, his heart was jumping up and down. In his sweaty neck, his shoulder, his chest, both arms.

"I love you. I love you. Why didn't you come?"

"I'm not coming back, Patrick. You'll just ask me to leave again. I'm tired of moving in and out."

"I was up all night. I found you here at 4:30. Maybe you heard me. If she hadn't been here I'd have gotten in with you. I walked back to the Fort, to town, had coffee. It's been a long time since I slept."

"I have to finish my book."

"I love you," he went on. "I don't want to lose you. I've been fucked up, I'm sorry. Come at least until you finish your book. *Please.*"

I was so weary. And afraid. To go through it again. Weirdly, my period stopped.

On the way to town the next morning he handed me a letter from Shilla in Mendocino. Because of what happened to Shilla's daughter Nikki and the fact that she can't seem to recover they're moving from Mendocino to LA. I told the story to Patrick. Nikki was in Danny's class. She was finally moving to the city, San Francisco. She'd been afraid to leave home so everyone thought this was a good step. She found a nice apartment. She was making trips back and forth to her car, the apartment on the eighth floor. In one of the trips down she left the door unlocked and a man got inside, waited for her. He held a knife to her throat saying he was going to kill her, and raped her. Then she managed to get out of the apartment, running through the halls naked, screaming help me, help me.

No one did and he came after her, dragged her back into the apartment, and raped her again. Someone did call the police. The police surrounded the apartment building. She got away again, running down the eight flights of stairs, naked. He came after her again.

When they hit the street, he right behind her, the police grabbed her, held her back, and riddled him with bullets. This is an image that haunts me now. I tried to explain it to Patrick. I thought that witnessing his death must have been almost as traumatizing as any part of it, that his murder was abuse of her too. I didn't want my father hurt, Patrick, for molesting me, that's just about my earliest memory. He was crazed, he needed protection, I did too from killing him. But everyone I've tried to share this with has called me sick, as if the desire for revenge is healthy, normal. But what about love thy enemy as thyself, Patrick, what about turning the other cheek? What about that Japanese discipline to somehow, if possible, protect the crazed person out of his mind attacking you? I just don't believe that anyone's ever healed by the eye-for-an-eye philosophy.

On Saturday afternoon William Matthews gave his craft lecture: "You Don't Have to Live a Good Life to Write Good Poems." He'd just been fired as head of the University of Washington's Creative Writing Department for sexual harassment of his students. Now he had been hired by an Eastern school for more money, more prestige.

On Saturday night Margaret Atwood gave her reading. She read from a novel in progress. She explained that she was a little hesitant to read this chapter as she had recently read it to a high school class and the whole class, teacher included, got up and walked out. "But I feel I need to further the dialogue going on here, to say something about the importance of looking at our culture, of removing the blindfolds of ignorance labeled tradition."

A main character was a woman in her late thirties, who writes a lifestyle column, like where the best places to eat in town are, etcetera, for a Toronto newspaper. The woman's editor assigns her to cover an exhibit of pornography at the downtown Toronto police station. "You must know, this is a true story," Atwood interjected, looking at us in her ironic way. "I didn't make this up. This isn't fiction. You can go to the downtown police station in Toronto and tour their three rooms of pornography."

There's the scene describing the devices and things. "Here's something," the policeman says, "that even we haven't figured out." It's a dildo on a squat, wind-up thing that runs around the room, pumping up and down. "Maybe it's for midgets," the reporter says, distracted by a mannequin with a dozen dildos penetrating her face and head.

The tour proceeds to the room where the films are shown. They see a film of a woman's vulva. That's all that's shown. It's a black woman. Just a little of her inner thighs and pubic hair. But then slowly something is emerging from her vagina. When it is fully out you see that it's a rat.

The reporter vomits on the policeman's shoes. He is polite, sympathetic. She tells her editor that she can't write the story. For the next six weeks she's unable to have sex with her husband. The chapter ends with them in bed. She asks him, hesitantly, if he would enjoy seeing a rat coming out of her vagina. He jokes, "dead or alive?" And then quickly, seeing her distress, says "no, of course not. Come on. What's the matter with you?" She tells him and the chapter closes with his question:

"Do you think all men are like that?"

The next few days broke gloriously with sun, the snow-covered mountains encircling the Peninsula so close it seemed you could reach out and touch them. I was returning to the cabin with Caitlin at night to sleep with Patrick, mainly so as not to have to deal with his guilt tripping and my hurt, but leaving early every morning. I did not move anything back in. She was now barred from Atwood's workshop, so was involved in other adventures, mainly exploring the Peninsula. I worked all day at the beach. I let Wyoming go for a while, to get distance, worked now on the small poem, "White Deer in a Field," the only thing I'd managed to salvage from six months of writing The Pornographer. *"Why// when you found me bathing in the pool/did you look at me and not see/the world and your land, sacred/genital to holy mouth, why/your need to haul my body/into property, your land/into pornography, why/your fantasy to love things/to death?"* With regret I scratched the line *"your buttock in my hand."* I loved the active eroticism of the female narrator but it screwed up the rhythm. I worked on the main image of the poem, a couple I once saw, briefly, from a speeding train, in a dark cabin in the redwoods, making love in the stand-up position.

One night after dancing I slept in Roses on the street behind the bank. In the morning I woke to Frank Herbert, the famous science fiction writer of *Dune,* who also lived out on Hastings, walking into the bank. I laughed out loud thinking of all the money I won't ever make as a poet. Then I laughed at laughing out loud all alone. Moonlight, my fantastic creature, joined in.

Because I wasn't hanging out, except to attend the readings and craft lectures, and my main gossip source was now barred from the place, I was only vaguely aware of the controversy brewing back at the Fort over Atwood's reading. William Stafford was said to be the most offended, and of course Matthews, Anderson and Hass, and Sam, too, the publisher of the local press. The rumor was that Sam was going to attack Atwood in his craft lecture.

By Wednesday, the second week of the conference, I'd gone as long as I could without money, my return trip having wrecked my strict budget. I was hungry. I called Sam and asked him if I could borrow $10.00 until Friday when my $42.00 unemployment check would arrive. "Meet me at the Schoolhouse at 1:30," he said, "for my translation workshop." As the afternoon came on, Mt. Baker spewed a column of steam and ash. The mountains seemed to be closing in on us.

I was listening with one ear, working on my poem, about the herd of white deer I saw on that same train journey, when Robert Hass said something that caught my attention.

"It was Pound's translating Chinese poetry that freed him and all of us from iambic pentameter. Images haunt." Then he was speaking of "the whole mythology built on this fact, of Cezanne painting until his eyes bled, Wordsworth wandering the Lake Country hills in an impassioned daze. Tu Fu said 'Images, they're like being alive twice.' Images are not like ideas, they are stiller than that. And they are not myth, they don't have explanatory power. They are nearer to pure story." He summed up, "They do not say this is that, they say *this is*."

Afterwards, Sam said he forgot the ten, he'd bring it to his craft lecture scheduled in an hour. I sat in the dark, empty theater, hungry, a bit crampy, working on the line *"holy and helpless with each other,"* worrying that it was too romantic. I hardly realized when the theater filled and Sam was on stage.

He was dressed in his best Western clothes, his anteater boots, rawhide vest, turquoise and silver Navajo jewelry. He introduced himself as a Buddhist pacifist, and then began reading from Susan Griffin's *Silence and Pornography,* the part where Acteon, the hunter, "the controller of nature," sees Diana bathing in the pool and is turned into a stag and eaten by his own hunting dogs. Wow, that's my poem, "White Deer," *"Why// when you found me bathing in the pool/did you look at me and not see...."*

"This idea that the sight of a woman's body calls a man back to his own animal nature and this animal nature soon destroys him reverberates throughout our culture. And in the reverberation lies the purpose and meaning of pornography: to rob the female body of its natural power and its spiritual power.'"

Sam read in his usual macho strut. He'd always called himself a Buddhist pacifist, but these days, wonderfully, he was calling himself a feminist. Even so, nothing in his body language had changed from the tough Utah orphan.

"Pornography," he continued reading, authoritatively, "is not an expression of human erotic feeling and desire and not of love of the life of the body, but of fear of bodily knowledge, and a desire to silence Eros…. Pornography is the poetry of oppression!" He guffawed at this use of his favorite word, the favorite word of many of us. Poetry.

"'The fear of the body is the fear of nature; the fear of death. To acknowledge the body, to acknowledge nature is to acknowledge one's vulnerability and mortality, one's own physical death…. In fact, like the Jew in anti-Semitism and the Black in racism, the woman is simply a lost part of the soul…. To have knowledge of this forbidden part of the soul is to have Eros….

"The fear the voyeur voluntarily engages, that he will die like Acteon of his own desire is a controlled way of touching his own mortality and the soul within the self. This perverted form of sexuality is fed by the sacred longing to touch the lost part of the soul."

But after quoting Griffin, Sam's talk slowly unraveled. "This stuff is the most important issue confronting the age," he declared, but then hemmed and hawed, making awkward leaps of reason. Another time, a different subject, he'd be up there breezing along, pontificating in his cock-of-the-walk strut. I recognized only too well my own lack of fluency when hitting this taboo. Something had crossed his lines; he was dyslexic, he was close to the forbidden, to dumbness. He'd fallen in the hole.

"This stuff is real. Copper Canyon Press began in a rat-infested slum building in Denver with me and Bill Daly distributing porno books to the stores.

"I don't know what to say about that," he stammered on. "Except that I would defend to the death anyone's right to print anything. Remember snuff movies a few years ago? They'd kidnap young women here in the States and take them to South America and torture them slowly, sexually, and then kill them, all for the camera."

An attack on Atwood didn't seem to be happening.

"What about the boy-man? What about fathers? Lovers? A husband you respect with whom you have been in close and good relationship begins to confess after five years that every time you've made love since the first time he's been imaging you as someone else, and even himself as someone else?"

I kept sending him good energy, running my eyes up his meridians, trying to help him pull it off. He's the only man I know who calls himself a feminist.

"And then there are silly women who write life style columns or run boutiques of Fifties clothes." That character in Atwood's story. Here comes the attack, I thought. But not of her writing. Of her characters!

"How would you like to look like Farrah Fawcett?" he interrupted himself again. I may have laughed out loud. Last month, the acclaimed Native American novelist Janet Campbell Hale meeting me on the dance floor clapped, "You must be the Farrah Fawcett of the poetry crowd."

"Whenever you wear lipstick or dye your hair you are a part of this thing." His Navajo jewelry flashed across the audience. Then he was talking of Olga Broumas' poem "Imogene Knode." The poem had originally been printed on his hand press and distributed at last year's controversial conference, and is now reprinted in her second book. "I had hoped," he said now, as I'd heard him say before so that it seemed her real trespass was in not following his orders, "that she would never print it in a book of poetry."

He read Olga's epigraph that explains that Imogene Knode, 25, who'd been beaten regularly by her husband, had the week before repeatedly begged the police to help her, that her husband was going to kill her. But they could do nothing. He killed her.

"I want this poem to be like razor blades down his throat, to pour like

Drano down his throat.

I call this poem to be a weapon.

I give this poem authority to kill."

I remember Olga saying in her craft lecture, "'Imogene Knode' was important to me. When I say those last two lines I mean it. I was not able to say that when I started the poem. It was a powerful process."

"This is the same old shit," Sam was saying now, "an eye for an eye, the same system. Remember Martin Luther King? 'I will not give you the power to make me hate.' He held up a piece of paper. "I have written here, 'Faith, Hope and Charity,' my only notes for this whole craft lecture." He seemed to be apologizing for, or explaining, his stammering.

Sam was the first to read *Hard Country*, my book-length poem, long before it was finished, and one of the few poets to encourage me. He said Copper Canyon would publish it. But a few months after that he'd suddenly showed up on my doorstep on Navarro Bluff and, as he would say more than once through the years, "you understand, I drove 700 miles to sleep with you and you would not have me."

I had not agreed to sleep with him, I had not invited him, though I welcomed him as a guest. And then invited all the local Mendocino poets to my house for him to meet. He fell asleep on my front room bed and snored through the whole reading.

I'm incapable of sex or romance as a commodity of exchange. I don't have sexual exchange with married men. Most basically I was not sexually or romantically attracted to Sam. Even so, given all this, and my lifelong horror of the stories of Hollywood producers demanding the same thing, fuck or you don't go, my experiences with college professors, fuck or fail, there seemed genuine exchange between Sam and me. Maybe it was the poetry and our rural western backgrounds. Faith, hope and charity, I loved him despite all his screw-ups, was glad to know him. And as everyone knew, the origin of his feminism, not considering the ego in calling himself the first male feminist, was that he was in love with Olga, a lesbian. And, as he readily told about lecturing inmates in his prison poetry workshops, "my feminism is no doubt from being raped in juvenile detention."

"There's probably no one in this room who has not been affected by domestic violence." I was still hoping that he'd make the connection with writing, the classism and sadomasochism of traditional craft, grammar, and poetry. When in conclusion he mentioned Dante's eighth ring of hell for pornographers "because they violate both nature and art," I cringed. The archetype of Beatrice, the so-called Muse of *The Inferno*, the "ideal woman," has been as responsible as any in our culture for the objectification of women. I was falling deep into my own old hole of muteness.

Then Sam was gone from the stage, his anteaters turning on their heels, descending the steps to the polite clapping. I sat there, paralyzed.

Then I remembered the ten dollars. I hadn't eaten since the day before. Everyone was gone when I finally walked up the aisle of the dark cool cave that was the theater. Past Sam, Margaret Atwood, Denise Levertov and Abby Niebauer gesticulating wildly in the lobby.

The sun hit my eyes like the car's headlights on North

Beach. Under the nearby fir Chris and Laura were carrying on excitedly too, their dyke-ish, female beauty a bit hallucinatory. When I joined them Laura was ranting about Sam's phony non-violence trip.

"I just wish he was more intelligent."

That was hardly a failure of intelligence, I wanted to say, despairing over the oldest prejudice, that to be inarticulate is to be stupid. I wanted to cite H.D.'s line, our intelligence renders us dumb, but the words wouldn't have come out straight and besides she was off then about a man in Oregon, a habitual rapist who was to be released from prison next week and I wanted to say, as Sam had said, but prisons are the other side of the same shit. Now she was ranting about Reagan's administration taking the money back from programs for teenagers about sex and birth control and abortion and putting it instead in programs for teaching them not to have sex. I'd become completely dumb.

"I feel like giving him my book," Laura declared. "I wrote a book on the subject. *The Violent Sex.*"

I'd read this book during last year's conference. Its subtitle is "*A Psychobiological Study of the Human Male.*" Her premise is that violence is innate in the male chromosome. All men are innately, inevitably violent. The last chapter of Laura's book is "How To Birth A Female."

I ached to defend Sam. And all men. My son. But Chris of all people began to do that for me.

"When I first knew Sam I hated him. An unmitigated hatred for him. He was a macho redneck, absolutely untenable. But Laura, I swear, he's a man who's grown. You have to give him credit at least for bringing up the whole issue."

I was trying not to think that Chris wanted to be published by Sam. I wanted to say but Sam doesn't understand that for women passivity and nonviolence are the same old shit, the position we've always been in, have always known as mothers, as the higher truth. I wanted to say maybe we have to trade places, and then from our reversed psychobiologies we will learn, we will change. I wanted to quote Olga, "I was not able to say that when I started writing the poem," and what that process must have been. Everything has to change, the dilemma, yes, is in seeing this stuff, say it without becoming what we hate.

"As a man he doesn't deserve my credit," Laura snapped, and then was saying that once she too was inarticulate. "My father was always jamming his cock down my throat so of course I couldn't speak."

"My father too." That broke the spell, I was finally speaking. "Well, he never did that, but…. I saw a woman on Donahue last week at my parents' in Oregon. Thirty-seven, serving a life term for killing her husband. She'd married him at fifteen, had two children, had been all those years a prisoner in her suburban home. She wasn't allowed to have a phone, to go shopping, to know her neighbors. He beat her before they were married. She thought after they were married he'd stop. They showed a photo of her at fifteen. She looked nine. He beat her all the time. He beat their children. He sexually molested her daughter for years. Finally she contracted a teenage boy, a friend of her son, to kill him. He shot him while he slept, she called her daughter, now twenty-two, living in California. The daughter said, Mother, you sound sad. This should be the happiest day of your life. From prison she said I don't regret it. At all. I'm free now. Donahue asked, Why didn't *you* kill him? The camera showed her pondering this, as if for the first time. She said I don't know why. I just couldn't.

"Which is the point I'm trying to make," I said to my fierce friends. "In that killing moment she was even then, after years of being passive with him and her children, still passive. She had an innocent boy do her killing. She ruined an innocent boy. Passivity is what women are guilty of."

At that moment Margaret Atwood came sauntering out of the theater. As she walked by us in the direction of Officers

Quarters where the instructors were staying, she quipped, "What are you ladies doing? Displaying your charms?"

"It's a verifiable statistic," she added, "that rapists will rape anything."

Denise and Abby came out a minute behind her. Denise too headed toward the Officers Quarters. Abby got in her little car, headed toward her new home, Rose Garden on Quimper Point. Beautiful Abby who would be dead in the not too distant future of her husband's gun. On the eve of the publication of her first book.

Then Sam came out. Laura sneered, taking off for the Main Gate. "See you two."

"Well," Sam said. "I said I was going to let the worm out of the can. I guess I did that." He seemed hurt. I loved him for that.

We sat on the steps of his print shop. We sat in the sun, the three of us silent.

The first time I saw Chris was at my first conference, near the beginning of the long process of writing my book-length poem. I had a good draft, Sam said he was going to publish it, and so now it seemed I could allow myself to learn from the academic poets of my generation. Tess Gallagher's *Instructions to the Double* had just been printed by the new press in town, Graywolf. I'd glanced through it and knew I needed her *Instructions*, knew she was somehow my *Double*. She'd been privileged to be in the last class of Theodore Roethke's at the University of Washington, had gone through the University of Iowa's renowned writing program, was published and then read by just about every poet in the country. Was female. Was somewhere around my age. Was from the rural working class too—from here, from the Olympic Peninsula. This was my first and only "shoplifting." Well, sometimes when I'm penniless I've taken the roll of toilet paper on the backs of public toilets, mainly because of the dangers of newsprint to the most delicate, vulnerable tissues of the human body, which my mother had us use when we were broke, and yes, I "stole" Joseph Campbell's 1948 *Hero With A Thousand Faces* from my college library for the Joyce book I was writing long before I became a poet, by not returning it. I thought about taking Tess's book from the book sale room for days, thought about it in terms of American Literature and my book poem, my contribution, rationalized that my poem justified the crime (not to even consider what she made as a university professor). I needed it. I still have it.

Now Chris was telling Sam the story I'd just told her and Laura about the woman prisoner on Donahue, about women and passivity. I was surprised to hear that she'd understood me. Sam just shrugged. I watched her with him, how easily she talked to him, without difficulty, with seeming passion and pleasure. Did her father not ever jam his thing down her throat? I'm unable to even hang out on the front steps. Chat. Network. Kiss up. Opportune in the sun. Learn what's going on. Wow, here we are with still another roiling gender controversy.

"I thought," Sam was saying adamantly, "that Atwood's bimbo answered her husband's question 'do you think all men are like that?' with 'I don't know.'"

"Speaking of pornography, Sam," I said. "Will you please the fuck give me the ten dollars?"

"I'm her banker," he laughed to Chris, digging into the right front pocket of his Levi's.

Chris caught up with me tearing toward Roses.

"I just wish Laura wasn't so hard," she said.

I was trying to breathe.

"Hold a baby boy in your arms," Chris said, "and you know the male isn't innately violent."

I sort of came undone then, in gratitude, swung around the only redwood on the Olympic Peninsula, singing the song I sang to my baby boy at my breast. "Oh Danny Boy…. Did you know, Chris, it's the oldest recorded tune in the world?"

"Yes," she said. "But those words are from the potato famine in Ireland."

Now I was about to cry. "I can't even afford Tampax!" I laughed instead, waving Sam's ten in the air. "And my three little sponges? Well, I got only one pair of Levi's and I keep leaking blood all over them."

I'd bought the sponges in Mendocino from a woman's collective. They were from the coral reefs of the Caribbean, from under the sea. How much I wanted them to work. The doctor had used seaweed to dilate me, the nightmare abortion. How much I hate the tampax companies, their chemicals, toxic shock, cutting down the trees, their capitalism of the most fundamental human fact of life. And the image that will haunt me forever: bleeding on el buso down the coast of Peru, the problem of washing out the sponge in a public bathroom, forty Indian women around me waiting to wash their hands.

"You have to figure out," Chris said, in the infinite authority of her Libra/Capricorn soul, "the shape of your vaginal cavity. It's a matter of form. Don't ask me how my vagina told me, but it did. That I needed a heart-shaped sponge."

We were at Roses, and Moonlight so happy to see us.

"Most women, I've found, don't put it up high enough inside."

I wanted to collapse in gratitude, to cry. "I bet you're right!"

I got down to the Sea Galley. The deep hole was drilling deeper, my past too stirred. Daddy. Brandy rather than dinner. Brandy in hot coffee with whipped cream would pull me out of my father. Besides, I laughed to myself, I love getting skinny.

As I plunged through the front door I got a glimpse of my old boss, Andrew, pretending not to see me. I remembered that time I was bartending here and he didn't back me up when I called for his help with two drunk whale killers threatening to rape me, how he poured each of them another drink scoffing that female bartenders can't take it. Later he actually apologized to Patrick, though never to me.

I sat down at the head of the horseshoe, the empty seat next to the silver-bearded older man I remember liking. I don't remember what he drank but once he told me of his flowers, of being retired and raising flowers, how he considered retiring to San Diego and other such sun places to grow flowers, but had decided, after Alaska, that this, as far north as it is, was as good a place as any.

I dropped Wyoming on the counter, ordered a Coffee Special. Two shots of brandy for $1.95, though I knew it was only a shot and a half. There was a tradition here of female writer bartenders, I'd replaced the novelist Maggie Crumbly. Now Sue, the writer who'd replaced me, asked as she made it, "How do you feel about the conference this year? Do you like those people?"

"It's so quiet and intellectual this year," a poet from the conference filled in my speechlessness as she entered the room with others.

The man asked why I looked familiar to him and if I was a writer. I told him I was the bartender here until March 3 when I got the phone call that my book was going to be published. I laughed, patting Wyoming. "July. And I'm still working on it."

I looked at his silver beard, the deep crevices beneath it, and thought of how difficult it would be to shave such a face. I wondered if the beard was hiding something. How different men are from women, thick long hair grows out of their faces.

"Anyone ever tell you?" a man called across the horseshoe, "you look just like Farrah Fawcett!"

Had he been at Sam's lecture? I laughed, remembering Farrah Fawcett on the mud walls of remote Peruvian villages when my daughter and I were on our bus trip to South America, and on the "houses" in Lima, the blocks of shelters constructed of posters of Farrah Fawcett.

"When I was the bartender here," I told the bearded man,

"I specialized in Drinks of the Writers. I did the research. A Hemingway Libre. A Kafka Vodka. A Sappho Ambrosia."

The man and I were talking then, the words between us easy and pleasant. I bought another Special, and then he bought me another, which I never touched, the whipped cream melting like the white clouds of the sun setting. I apologized but a third one was too much. I had five dollars left, after the dollar tip. I was thinking I should write a poem about my brother, Clarke. A letter to him. Why he and I can't talk. It's because of Daddy, Clarke. I was getting dirty looks from across the room from Jane's husband, probably because of Caitlin, but that's not my responsibility, butterflies are free, that was the song that was playing, fly away, fly away, Elton John's Norma Jean. I was thinking how Patrick's soul is like a butterfly, like Marilyn Monroe's.

The sun dropped behind the Olympics. In the last flash on the water I saw the rapist being mowed down by the police as he hits the San Francisco street. "The water has no mind to receive the images," it says on the Ladies' wall. And oh twilight in this beautiful place, it'll be a long time before dark.

"You have flowers, don't you."

What he shared with me then was so perfect, so beautiful, so genuine, so refreshing, so wise and calm, so to the issues of the Writers' Conference, pornography and silence, pornography and erotica and sexism, Patrick and rats in vaginas and domestic violence and blood and men and women and pregnancy and babies and commitment and freedom and selling-out, so of faith, hope and charity with the confusions of craft and politics, it felt like food.

But I had to leave. My job this year for free admittance to the readings and lectures was to sit an hour at the book table every night of the second week, from seven to eight. On my way back to the Fort I took the Quimper Point route, around the man's glorious yard of flowers high over the water, wild in the twilight with colors, smells, unbelievable shapes. For the next two days I held his words, or rather, more accurately, his words held me until I could get the chance to write them down. I have a kind of aural memory, like photographic memory, in which I can replay what someone has said, for about two days.

At the bookstore set up in the barracks there was an angry-seeming note on the counter, beneath the mailbox: WHO IS CAITLIN O'ROURKE?

When I got back to the cabin after the night's forgettable reading, besides Caitlin, Tim and Mary were there. Tim was Patrick's oldest friend, they'd become poets together in Boston, came to the town together. I made a bed for them in the living room, another for Caitlin in my so-called writing room, sharing some of the conference gossip, shining-on what I knew was their disapproval of my being involved. Caitlin had spent the day hiking Mt. Olympus, "twenty-seven miles up and back!" she exclaimed. All in all, things were jovial. We discussed Empty Bowl, our poet/tree planters' collective press, our future publications and possibilities. I ripped up the angry note I'd written Patrick. Giggled and pounded and played with him in the loft. "If Stafford really did react negatively to Atwood," I huffed, "then my estimation of him as a poet drops."

He laughed about his latest rejection slip: "Keep on being influenced by Stafford!"

Leslie Marmon Silko's craft lecture was on Thursday afternoon. I was hearing now from everyone the controversy. Stafford, Matthews, and Hass had gone on record in vehement disapproval of Margaret Atwood's reading. As I sat in my usual seat, Bill Bradd, my poet friend from Mendocino, was suddenly there. Jauntily, he removed his hat, bowed, acknowledging my surprise, climbed over me, leaving the smell of marijuana in his wake, and took the seat on my right.

"I've thought a lot about fiction and morality," Leslie began. "But I can't give a lecture on it. I can't. So I thought I'd read a story from my book, *Storyteller*."

The story was long, told by a woman in jail. This is Alaska. She's an orphan, a Native. She has an affair with a white oil driller she meets in the store. Every time he lies on top of her he tacks a picture over her head and looks at it as he's fucking her. Finally, one time when he's just come, she rolls out from under him quickly and looks. It's a picture of a dog fucking a woman.

Bill got up and left. Back at the cabin he'll explain, "It was too predictable, not good language. If it had been a picture of his mother, well, that would have been interesting." Bill's Canadian mother died when he was two.

Leslie's story slowly unfolds. The white store owner had traded her parents alcohol for a rifle. The alcohol was bad, it killed them. He attempts to rape her. She gets away. It's sixty below outside. She runs with her mittens in front of her mouth to protect her lungs. He runs out without jacket or mittens. He falls in a creek, into water and ice just as he is about to catch her.

She's in jail. She will not plead innocent as her attorneys plead with her to do, calling her crazy. She says, "I cannot tell a lie. I killed him. I wanted him dead. That's the story. I killed him."

Olga's poem, Margaret's story, the problem with the passivity of women, the woman in prison contracting the boy to do her killing, Sam's barely articulated feminism and now Leslie's story—it was all here. Stunning, the issues of this conference were coalescing.

That night Sam gave his reading, accompanied by music and a dancer. It had started raining. Some of us were wet in our seats. He read a poem, she danced it, behind and beside him in her leotard and skinny white legs and arms. Jennie was a local poet who'd spent all spring and summer practicing for this, working with him, dreaming of bridging the gap between him and the town, its resentment of him and his powerful press. But now something awful was happening.

"This was her idea, believe me," he guffawed, "not mine."

He deserted her, right there on stage! In that moment I hated him. A poet from Cannon Beach who'd walked out on his lecture yesterday noisily got up and walked out again. I was relieved someone had the cojones to do the right thing.

In the morning after everyone left, Patrick and I had a horrible fight. His disdain for Caitlin, now for Bill, his habitual putdown of everyone not of his own little tribe—I was so tired of it. I was in the loft, he was down on the kitchen floor, he was scolding me again for wasting my time with the conference. Why wasn't I writing? My screams raining down on him from that beautiful loft is a memory that still surfaces.

At the Lighthouse Café where I ran for coffee, a Seattle writer whose theme was virgins, said in the same tone of contempt as Patrick, "poets are the most boring."

Then, in my passenger seat on the beach at Point Wilson, typewriter in my lap, just as I rolled in the paper a young man tapped on Rose's window. His snazzy car purred behind mine, the sun ablaze now across the water. I was needed to tend the bookstore for the whole afternoon.

Sure, I told the intern.

They knew where I was!

Now to the note, WHO IS CAITLIN O'ROURKE? was the added line: THERE'S BEEN MAIL FOR HER EVERYDAY IN THE BOX!

It was hot in the bookstore. Near the end of my work time, Patrick, Tim and Mary came in to look at the books. My delight in seeing Patrick was big. I kept touching him, and kissing him. He looked good, so much better, his skin sun-warmed and calm now. We were both embarrassed by my effusiveness. I couldn't help it anymore than I'd been able to help this morning's screaming.

"I feel like I've been through a huge emotional trauma," he said. "In Nepal, words are written on flags, put out in the wind so that the words blow to the gods. That's how you pray."

"Yes, prayer wheels," Tim said. "In Hebrew, too, it's similar. Writing is holy."

"I felt like that's what I was doing. Wandering the bluffs all hours was holy. But all of it would have been easier if I could have flown my words on flags."

After they left, as I closed the store, I decided not to follow them to Happy Hour as I'd promised. I was losing the flower man's words.

But descending the stairs of the old barracks, Bill was waiting for me. I realized how far he'd come, this is a poet's quest. I should introduce him around, to more folks, to more of the scene. On the way to the Tavern we went by the post office. My check hadn't come.

They had the big round table at the Tavern's window, with other poets and the poet-dancer Jenny. They made room for us.

Then Patrick was saying directly at me. "I think Stafford is right, Atwood's story was in poor taste."

Across the street Margaret Atwood was walking by, holding the hand of her six year old daughter whose thick curly blond hair was like a halo around her face. Like the blond hair halo around my children. Mary laughed, mouthed exaggeratedly to her through the glass, "But what about my mother, Margaret Atwood? You embarrassed my mother!"

Margaret, not hearing, stopped in the walk, bent and kissed her daughter on the mouth.

"It was in poor taste," Tim agreed.

"What about the writing?" Jennie asked, trying to dance the gap. "Did you think the writing was good?"

I tried to ignore all this, worked at not exploding "what about that daughter?" Suddenly I was back in the hole. I couldn't open my mouth for fear of what would come out. If I could just get alone and write the flower man's words. I was beginning to know them more than words. My friends' insensitivity, or over-sensitivity, was galling. Had they objected in their lives when men had written such? "Yes," Patrick will say in the next argument, "I think Henry Miller is in poor taste."

The pizza came. I wasn't hungry, but crammed my piece down to keep from screaming. All I had to do was get up, say I'm going to write. It was seven. I had an hour before the reading. But I felt so pulled by Patrick. To utter a word, even those words to these writers, might be offensive.

Finally I rose. I bent down and kissed him on the mouth. "I need to write." He slipped from beneath me and was out the door before I'd fully risen, leaving me kissing the air, stranded there so publicly. Embarrassed, humiliated actually, I followed him out without saying goodbye to the table.

He was parked in front of Roses across from the police station down from The Tavern.

I got in Roses. Suddenly he was getting in.

"Well, once again it's Friday" he snarled, "and we are having problems." Then he had his big hands on my shoulders, shaking me. "Why can't I express my opinion?"

He accused me of censoring him.

I saw myself as a girl walking Industrial Avenue every day to the store to get bread for my mother, the old men in the bushes calling me, "looky here little girl!" And much younger, three or four, down in the hole with the teenage boys playing doctor. Giving birth to a rat. And Daddy. He was still shaking me.

My father, my father. Who I don't want to hurt, don't want revenge. Nor for my mother. No words can be uttered, words are not possible, words will endanger us, just the longing, the ache for understanding and explanation and exchange and soul search and apology, my father for whom I've vowed never to write until both my parents are gone. If I live that long.

"Talk to me!"

If only I could. If I could just cry. If I could just understand your resistance to this. Atwood's story wasn't shocking. It's the most common story on the planet, every day some version of it in this town, all towns, Patrick, it's the oldest story in the world.

"You think all men are like that, don't you!" he screamed.

Then he was trying to calm down, sitting back in the passenger seat, staring out at the street, growing dark.

"I'm not!"

Were they watching us from the Tavern? From the police station?

"I just don't want to think about such things. That's why I live here. It doesn't seem real here. This place for me is like a sanctuary, like the Church was."

"You were raped in the Church, Patrick."

He reeled into the windshield. He gasped and sat back.

"I can't believe I told you that!"

He was playing ping pong with the Father. The Father came up behind him, nothing under his black robe but his erection, started moving it around his butt.

Now I was seeing his beautiful gold body bent over the ping pong table, the penis plunged into his baby rectum. I felt the organs explode, I saw the priest afterwards trying to knead his ripped and bleeding buttocks back together.

"I'm sorry Patrick. I don't know how to express what is happening inside me. I wish I could. The other day I heard this beautiful man, this sweet old local guy in the Sea Galley who raises flowers tell of his understanding of pornography. Most innocently, Patrick, he called it fornography—get it, *for* nography! And, fornication! I don't know how to tell you because I don't want to lay it on you, but I feel betrayed. I don't know how to articulate the depth of my horror. Do I think Atwood's writing is good? Well, she wasn't strident, right? She maintained magnificent control over the subject, her cute little story—isn't that everyone's criteria? That criteria drowns me, silences me! Yours and Stafford's and Hass's and Duncan's censorship. You can't go there because of your sexual fantasies. They'll collapse if you do, and there goes your one true pleasure in life. Laura Baldwin says you guys can't change, you can't go there because every man knows that under certain circumstances he's capable of all those things."

His rage at this point exploded like Mt. St. Helens. "You think I feel guilty?"

I could see the dope paraphernalia displayed in the window of the police station. Our friends in the Town Tavern could see us. I wanted to say but Patrick what about your mother and your sisters? Do you forget that all spring I've been trying to write "The Pornographer"? I'll finish Wyoming, but The Pornographer…? It's the missing poem in my book. But I can't do it, like Sam couldn't in his lecture, it's an ocean. I'm incapable, at least at this point. The Pornographer box is right there in the back next to Wyoming's, all those notes, drafts, attempts. *"This hurt has to do with you. Touch it, touch me…"* I've failed, but even so I know it's right to have tried. To not write for good taste, that it might offend Mary's mother, that's censorship. And Mary's mother, hey! Remember? Mary's father turned out to be gay, remember? Was that embarrassing? Hey Mom, was hubby's deception because you're such a prude? Time to wake up to reality, Mom, and your own complicity. To look at it all, to keep looking at it all, to not turn away.

"I've worried about being raped, Patrick, every day of my life, but I've worked not to let this interfere with my sex life, my love of life, my love of men. My son, my father. My life on the road. So yes, I feel betrayal that you resist all thinking about this. Not just of me, your lover, but you don't want anyone to speak or write of this."

I recited a line from my poem about being attacked by those guys that night here in Roses. "I wrote it last winter in the cabin, remember?"

"Now I have to worry," he exclaimed, "that you need protection just walking down the street. And you're sleeping in here? That alone is enough to do me in."

"Yeah, right. Better lock us up as in the old days and throw away the key."

Before the craft lecture in the afternoon of the last day of the conference, Chris suddenly appeared in front of the audience. Tall, sturdy, olive-complexioned, her man's haircut in contrast to most men now with long hair, she smoked a corncob pipe, the smoke of which rose from her square face and lacquered black pompadour, evoking in me again the Mexican term from childhood, wow, now there's cojones.

"SOMEONE," she screamed, "HAS STOLEN TESS GALAHGER'S '*INSTRUCTIONS TO THE DOUBLE!*'"

She puffed on the pipe, her razored square face in shadow and gleaming light. "I want you to know I know who you are. I see exactly you, exactly where you are sitting in this audience."

I believed her.

"PUT IT BACK!" she boomed, and right before our eyes performed a witch ritual, invoking the gods' curses down on the thief. Then, in the sweetest of voices, "That's all we're saying. Please put it back."

The last night of the conference was Robert Sund's performance with the Cosmic Kelp Choir. They came down the aisle, men dressed in seaweed, blowing the long green tubes washed up on every beach of my life.

Afterwards William Matthews called Robert Sund cultish.

When I walked out of the theatre a teenage boy in a car full of other teenagers whizzed by and burped at me. He must have had some instrument, a horn, maybe even kelp, some technology that amplified it, that caused me to jump, scream. The poets coming out of the theater behind me laughed. I wanted to say to Bill Matthews, darling, *that's* cultish.

The local poets left immediately for Mt. Zion, to camp the night out under the lunar eclipse, Patrick and Bill with them. I ached to go, but stayed to have the cabin to myself, to finish my book.

I sat at Roses' wheel. The moon rose in Capricorn, slowly eclipsed by the earth. Moonlight turned in circles in the back, whimpering. I sat in the awesome sight, trying to come up from the hole. Lines of Patrick's beautiful poetry washed through all my holes. Three dim figures played tennis under the lights. The cars came and went, the red tail lights of the campers, the fishermen arriving for the weekend. Patrick up on the mountain. If I could howl, I would. I vowed in Moonlight's ear that I was going to have the moon tattooed on my belly.

I left Roses and Moonlight, walked across the 1910 parade grounds to the Victorian mansion, the General's house, for the End-of-the-Conference party, remembering Carson McCullers' story of the enlisted men and officers in housing on either side of the parade grounds, facing each other, as in a standoff. Moonlight, so unlike him, barked after me from the back window. On my left a group was taking photos of the eclipse. The problem was a cloud moving across it.

I was the first guest. The hostess, her back to me, was bending to the fireplace, trying to light it. I heard the first howl. She never knew I was there. I got back to Roses, held my dog. My period started again. I wrote the flower man's words.

Fornography

I'm a simple man. I remember trying to read Hawthorne's House of Seven Gables. *The sentences were so long, with many phrases, sayings and asides that in the middle of a sentence I wouldn't know what was going on. My mind would be thinking of something else. About fifteen years ago a neighbor gave me* Tropic of Cancer *by Henry Miller. Now. I don't know if I approve of everything he was saying, but the language was so clear and strong and direct, and his message so positive, you felt glad to be alive, somehow better about life. My neighbor was a teacher and a family man, three kids, and he gave me that book to read. I couldn't get over it. Alliteration? Onomatopoeia? Is that the word where words sound like their meaning? Like piss instead of urinate? I enjoyed that book.*

Someone showed me some fornography lately. It was two men and a woman. I was pretty shocked, though I've studied erotic art. I just ordered a book from the bookstore, Erotic Art and The 20th Century. *For years I've had books on Chinese erotic art. I've always thought fornography was for when you have a hard-on. Like a sexual aid. Or I always thought fornography is like the graffiti on the walls of men's bathrooms.*

I'm 67, I was born in Bellingham Washington and I lived in Alaska for 25 years. I got a degree in Ornamental Horticulture. I've never married. I'm a bachelor. Artists, it seems, are free thinkers so I try to read what they're reading and writing. It seems to me that printers and publishers produce work for people with families. Most publishers print for the family man, a man with wife and kids.

And so I read the Kinsey Report, the sexual behavior of the human male. Now that was very important. It changed everything. It said in there that all sorts of men—family men, men who have intercourse regularly with their wives, masturbate. Well, that was good to know. They had taught us that masturbation would make you crazy. Sometimes to this day I wonder if that's not true. You know, someone's on the borderline, it could flip them on over.

How did I get into flowers? Well, my father was in construction in Bellingham. I was the second son, so I was left alone a lot. I got into climbing mountains and I'd come into an alpine meadow and the flowers were so beautiful, it would tear you apart. Bending down to smell them, you just had to. I graduated from high school in 1934, right in the middle of the Depression. Well, what we thought was a depression, and I went to work in the woods. I didn't like that very much. When World War II came I was sent to Alaska to supervise the shipping of wood. After the war I thought I'd take advantage of the GI Bill. I went to Ohio to study Ornamental Horticulture. Then I went back to Alaska. My job was planning lawns for Anchorage. In the Sixties I got into doing this with computers. That wasn't very satisfying. My interest has always been flowers. So now I'm retired and I work on my lawn. My sister comes over from Bellingham and tells me I must shave. But I figure I'm retired now.

Do I regret not marrying? Well, I've had intercourse in my life with less women than I can count on my hands, but it has always been so extraordinary that I think it must be as good as doing it every night with a wife and growing used to it. It's always been a very heightened experience. And I have my books on erotic art.

Flowers, yes. They're something I can control, though occasionally one will die. You can't help that.

Trident

We've been waiting all spring and early summer. The date is a secret. Scouts are stationed on both sides of the Strait. Our assignment is to patrol Admiralty Inlet, the west side of Hood Canal, Marrowstone and Indian Islands. He's reading *Justine*. Our relationship continues to unravel.

We drift where the tides take us, our eyes on the water. We are looking for a submarine, the black fin, the thirty foot wake. It was coming through the Panama Canal the last time it was spotted. There are rumors. "It's here!" "Submerged just west of Port Angeles!"

If so, it too is waiting. By international law it doesn't have to surface until east of Port Angeles. It can go along the Canada side until then.

All summer there's been a Soviet spy ship, the *Gavril Sarychev*, ten miles off Cape Flattery, waiting for it too.

The large black circle with Trident in the center crossed with a red stripe of humans like paper dolls, their outstretched arms linked, is everywhere we wander, in windows, on banners flying from shops, on vehicle bumpers, on tee shirts. All six members of Eddie and the Atlantics wear the tee shirt when they play at the Town Tavern.

The dread, coming and going like the summer fog, the tides, that something terrible is about to happen. To the water. Albion Moonlight is as watchful as we are. How many men are under the water?

The pain of my love for him, for us, feels like drowning.

Sunday, August 1, Jerry Garcia, 1942
We go to Seattle to pick up the wet suits for the ones who are going to try to stop Trident, forty-five in all who face up

to ten year jail sentences, fifteen of whom have declared they are willing to die in the attempt. It's Jerry Garcia's fortieth, the Grateful Dead trucking out so sweetly from the cars on the ferry. I follow him through the drunk Indians in Pioneer Square, then through the Army surplus store on 1st Avenue. On every corner is the headline **3 Slain Women Linked For First Time**. Two women and a sixteen year old found dead in the Green River area south of the airport. We stay at a collective's house on Capitol Hill. My period starts in the night, bright crimson blood on our host's white flannel sheets, a brand new futon beneath. I sponge and sponge it with cold water but the stain won't come out. Tears spilling out. Falling into my blood like falling into the water. Ten minutes without a wet suit and you're a gonner. But our love-making is so good. Why did I have to spoil it by asking afterwards, "Are you glad I'm back?"

Crying again on the return ferry. Down in the dark car place he pleads "Let's just be friends, I'm just very tired."

"We were very tired, we were very merry," I laugh through my tears, quoting Edna St. Vincent Millay. *"We had gone back and forth all night on the ferry."*

Departing at Suquamish I take him to Seattle's grave. He, the deep ecologist/ bioregionalist/historian/editor/poet of the Peninsula seems stunned as we climb the hill. "No one else I know has been here."

Here lies the body of Jim Boss, or DABZOUTAL, a friend of Captain Reno while establishing his mill at Alki Point in 1853.

And O Love, I wouldn't have brought anyone else here.

Nancy Du-Du Hamish. Chas Ha-O-Dah. Kidbulitz.

Unknown. Unknown. Unknown. Qual-Qual-Blue.

He's standing under Seattle's canoes arched over one of his wives, looking at me in the strangest way coming up the hill reading aloud the stones. I'm wearing a dress, my only one, my wine purple 1940s threadbare but still elegant thing, a sliver of a silver belt, and pleats across my rear.

Unknown. Unknown. Unknown. Mary DeShow.

Coming back down, taking my hand he says, "I haven't been in a graveyard since I left the seminary. I'm very moved that Seattle became a Catholic."

I keep myself from screaming the Catholic Church, Patrick, was their Trident submarine.

George Clafruka died September 17, 1914, age 108 years.

Unknown. Unknown. Unknown.

"His name is Sealth, Patrick. Not Seattle."

"It doesn't matter that we are so beautiful," he answers.

Ground Zero is three and half acres adjacent to Bangor Military Base twenty miles west of Seattle on Hood Canal. It was purchased by peace workers. Near the end of May the Peace Pagoda at Ground Zero was burned to the ground by unknown arsonists. The same night libraries throughout the area were raided, the books of our small press collective disappeared. All summer my mail, which shares the Port Townsend Post Office box with Empty Bowl Press and Dalmo'ma Magazine, was diverted to the IRS, *Opened by mistake* stamped on the envelopes. Three times the mail in the box was delivered in shreds. The wide-eyed postal employees just shrugged their shoulders. There was a mysterious call from the Bureau of Alcohol, Tobacco and Firearms in Florida, a man saying I want to speak to her. Me? I laughed when I called back. I wrote the poem, "If I Am Killed," out of the paranoia that I was being followed crossing on the ferry to Vancouver for a reading. "Fear is the correct word," Patrick said. "Paranoia is for unfounded fear."

The bronze Buddha found in the ashes of the Peace Pagoda Zero had been smashed before the fire.

"I assume there will be no arrest," Fujii said. "This was an act of government."

Fujii Guruji was born August 6, 1885 in Kumamoto, Kyushu,

Japan. On his sixtieth birthday the United States dropped the atom bomb on Hiroshima, then three days later on Nagasaki. An ordained Buddhist priest Fujii began walking, beating a celestial drum and chanting the Lotus Sutra "Odaimoku"—*Na-mu Myo-ho-ren-ge-kyo*—the prayer for peace. It was the only thing he knew to do. He has walked around the world for peace many times, constructing peace pagodas in India, Sri Lanka, England, and other places. This year with his band of drumming monks he walked from New York to Seattle to Bangor on Hood Canal, for the arrival of the USS *Ohio*, the United States' first nuclear submarine of the planned Trident fleet.

When Fujii and Jim Douglass, leader of the Ground Zero Center for Nonviolent Action met they suffered a fundamental disagreement. Douglass, a Gandhian Catholic, had led the direct action a few years before, known as the Bangor 50—though a total of a hundred and twelve people actually climbed the high fence around the Bangor Naval Military Base, including his wife and five children.

"We feel it would be very powerful," the Catholic petitioned the Buddhist, "to have different religious traditions represented in the Peace Pagoda, such as Native American, Buddhist, Hindu, Jew and Christian."

"This cannot be!" Fujii objected. "The Peace Pagoda is not a *structure* but a representation of the Lord Buddha himself. Just as a head or legs belong to a single human being, all the composing elements of a peace pagoda, starting with the reliefs, roof, corridor, etcetera, should be enshrined as a representation of a single Buddha."

"There was a woman," Jim Douglass countered, "a Vietnamese Buddhist named Nhat Chi Mai who immolated herself in non-violent response to the oppression and killings in Vietnam in the 1960s. When she died she had two symbols, St. Mary, the mother of Jesus Christ, and Kuan-yin, the bodhisattva of Great Compassion, Mercy and Love, arranged on either side of her.

This was a deep symbol for me and for many people of the unity expressed in non-violent action. I think we hope here through our non-violent actions to express our unity coming from the many different religions of humanity, and if possible, for that to be reflected in some way in the Pagoda. I don't know just what way, but this would be very important to the people here."

"Self-immolation is non-violent action?" I gasp to Patrick as I read to him this exchange.

Fujii cited the assassination of his Hindu friend Gandhi by a fanatic Hindu. "He was affronted by Gandhi's inclusion of a Buddhist prayer in his morning and evening prayers. There exists a dangerous line. A peace pagoda is a stupa. When a peace pagoda is personified it is the figure of the Buddha. The Lord Buddha's right hand cannot be that of another person, his left hand cannot be that of still another person.

"On June 26, 1945," Fujii continued, "the United Nations Charter was signed at San Francisco. On August 6 and August 9 the United States dropped the Atom bomb on Hiroshima and Nagasaki. The United States used nuclear weapons. At least 125,000, probably more than a million people were killed. This is the greatest crime ever committed against humanity.

"If the United States President and the Army General had been executed then the world could have realized that nuclear weapons are only detrimental to humanity, and this issue would have been resolved then without bringing about the present danger."

And this too is labeled non-violence.

"Thou shalt not kill, Patrick," I mutter. "All life is sacred. Even genociders. How can people not know that?"

A broken statue of Jesus was found in the ashes too.

There was the day James Edwards, the U.S. Secretary of Energy thanked God for our nuclear weapons. "I want to be number 1, not number 2 in the nuclear war."

There was a day we gathered on the Port Gamble Reservation

beach near Ground Zero, the tribe having invited us. Their faces, their bodies, their drumming. Why do I feel so drawn, so joyful and rooted among Indians? The Revolutionary Communist Army folks were a total turn off. Her angry conspiring barking face in that beautiful crowd of S'Klallam, Christians, Buddhists, hippies, and pacifist peace workers.

One night the northern lights swirled through the sky. The moon, surrounded by the bright constellations above the firs and pines, shone orange and full in Aquarius. The milky bands of ghost light danced and swirled, hung in vertical streaks down through the dark.

On August 6, Fujii, on his ninety-seventh birthday, visited the blockaders.

Friday, August 6, Andy Warhol, 1927. The 37th Anniversary of the Bombing of Hiroshima. The cabin

I write to Leonard, my close poet friend in Albion.

Dear Leonard, Patrick is fine, asleep here beside me. Basically he wants to be alone. Basically he is a loner, loner not lover. Basically I don't feel loved, basically I am trying to draw away as basically I'm not a casual lover. Basically we are twins. Basically it has been fifteen months wonderful and I will miss him most basically of all as I know he will miss me. Basically I'm terrified of where I'm going but basically I won't let that stop me.

I kept leaving. I'd been doing it now since Mendocino, two years before. My kids left home, my love left me, so I left. My parents gave me a 1978 Slant Six Dodge baby blue van. I named her Psyche the instant I saw her in their Florence Oregon driveway. "You must accept this," they said, handing me the keys, "we didn't pay for your college education." They were hoping a van would help me get on my feet. Patrick would ask me to leave—I had Psyche to live in—and then he'd beg me to return. He'd catch freight trains across states, east and south, huddle in the dangerous space between box cars, to beg me to return. He needed me. Then three days (always three days) after my return he'd ask me to leave again. "Something's wrong with me," he'd say, a slight banner of red crossing his noble white nose under his blue eyes "I love you, I've never loved anyone like I love you, I want to marry you, have babies with you, but I can't make the commitment."

And my heart would break all over again.

I was living on forty-two dollars a week—Unemployment. I kept getting extensions, a great boon. This was because of the collapse of the logging industry, twenty-five percent unemployment on the Peninsula, some slick maneuver by the new Reagan administration to appease us. It enabled me to write. The unemployment checks went on from 1981 through 1983, then extended four months into 1984 by the jobs I did take, like the four months of waitressing and bartending in Park City, Utah.

Living on the road, living in Psyche—at times I was ragged and frightened. But the longer I did it and the more ragged I became, the more alive I became, the younger I grew, the healthier, and others said the more beautiful. And the more magical the world became. Synchronistic things kept happening. Carry no a purse, Jesus said, nor two tunics. There were times it seemed I had moved out of the artifice of civilization which blocks the connections, into the natural rhythms of the cosmos, into the true stories.

But why did I keep falling in love with men who didn't love me? I worked at being interested in men who were insistently interested in me, even if the chemistry wasn't there for me. In the two years since I'd met Johnny Dark one night in San Francisco he'd written me passionate letters several times a week. Besides the ongoing great avowal of love for me, though we'd not seen each other again, these letters were interestingly literary, and shared among other stunning things, his daily and nightly carousing with his famous son-in-law, the playwright and actor, Sam Shepard. Son-in-law: Johnny was married to Scarlett, the mother of Sam's wife, O-lan, though he was only two years older than Sam. The two couples and Jesse, the Shepard's son, lived together in Mill Valley. In minute detail the letters described the household which included the daily care and therapy of stroke-damaged Scarlett, their serious involvement with the Gurdjieff Society, their ongoing reading and journaling to each other, and photographing, videoing, film-watching, music-making, and the writing of Sam's plays, Gurdjieff's influence being his big secret. As Sam began the male starring role of the film *Frances* in Seattle, the letters became more and more about the secret affair he was having with his co-star, Jessica Lange.

For me the correspondence was an escape, part of my vow to change myself. The first time I was kicked out by Patrick I wrote back to Johnny from Psyche's bed, parked outside the Port Townsend Post Office, trying to hang on for dear life, as my mother would put it. But for all my willful efforts I didn't trust Johnny Dark's exuberant attention to me. Even through his letters I felt a pressure that was a bit like stalker energy. He assured me repeatedly that Scarlett was all for his having an affair with me, she'd lost her ego with head surgery to prevent another stroke and would never be interested in sex again. What about O-lan? I wrote, you're her stepfather, the man who raised her, how can you be in cahoots with Sam's infidelity, his betrayal of her and of their son, Jesse, too? He responded that he and O-lan, who was eight when he married her mother, had never liked each other. From the beginning I could see that Johnny Dark was the dark sidekick of the two men Sam repeatedly depicted in his plays. How could I be involved with such a man? Well, I was questioning everything about my old patterns.

Whenever I was back in Port Townsend I had the surprising desire to ride a horse. I hadn't felt this desire since girlhood. I credited it to the beautiful green rolling hills, the horse ranch I passed on Hastings, the wanting to know the land in ways you can't by vehicle, the feel of it, the deep cedar forests, the spectacular mountains, bays and seas. And the longing I couldn't sustain with a man, to be in physical and psychic oneness with a magnificent creature of this earth, in this case, a horse.

Shelly, the wife of one of Patrick's close friends, told me to visit Jane, "my best friend since 7th grade. She's your nearest neighbor, through the woods west of you. She raises horses, rides daily."

I found my way through the dense, wet cedars, then walked an old fire trail. Sure enough I came out to a picturesque ranch, thoroughbreds grazing in the fenced meadow in front of a modern ranch house.

She was in the early stages of pregnancy, so no horseback riding, but Jane and I became friends for a short period; there was something, a real feeling between us. She was the wife of Miguel Hernandez, had had their first daughter, now thirteen, on their sailboat, the *Edith Rose*, in Baja's Bay of Conception, had raised her on the boat all over the world. But Jane was tired of the life and her daughter wanted to go to middle school. Miguel had bought them this beautiful place, rather than lose them. But he was still on the boat, down in Baja somewhere.

There was the moment in July during the annual Writer's Conference. Carolyn was here again this year, one of the superstar poets and a friend of mine. There were Maoris in the Boat Haven; everybody wondered about them. I was in the phone booth in the Boat Haven staying on Maryna's boat in dry dock, talking with Johnny Dark. He'd pleaded with me for a month to call him. Jessica Lange's sister lives in Port Townsend, did you know that? No, I didn't. Her name is Jane, she has a horse ranch, but don't tell anyone. It's a secret. We're all coming to her house for the week of August 11. They've invited me because you're there.

Jane was Jessica Lange's sister! As we talked a giant column of dark smoke rose from downtown. The historic Town Tavern was on fire! When I got there Carolyn was there, pushing through the crowd to get closer, taking notes. "It's true what the critics say about me, I'm a voyeur, I get off on witnessing calamity!"

Amazing! Jane, the cabin's nearest neighbor, was Jessica Lange's sister. Our cabin with a box full of Johnny's letters about her sister's secret affair with Sam Shepard. Amazing.

At the end of *Frances* there's a hallucinatory scene of Frances hitchhiking away from the insane asylum, having escaped. The slight alternation of her body and face is to depict the damage from the shock treatments—from everything, the fascist state that the country had become, the betrayals by her mother and her sister. I recognized that the actress, to depict the results of the shock treatment, was Jane, not Jessica.

Sunday, August 8, LoFall, the 37th Anniversary of the Bombing of Nagasaki

"Excuse me. Is that white cement structure Bangor?" a man on the ferry deck asks us.

Looking down the long canal through the rain.

"Looks a lot like an airplane hangar, doesn't it?" I answer, remembering the giant blimp hangars in Orange County, California when I was a girl. Remembering Bangor 50. "To think, Trident will be right there."

We share two beers, an Oly and a Rainier, between the three of us, Barbara on the bed in the back with a headache. *"It's the water...."* Last night sleeping with Patrick, unable to sleep, I started reading a book entitled *GynEcology*, about the patriarchy's love of death. Around three in the morning a small plane droned overhead, flying west down the Strait. An hour later it came back. The loneliness of that sound. Me lying on the lawn, a girl in Southern California, listening to the planes, thinking that's the sound of time passing. Daddy working at Douglas making airplanes. Listening to them break the sound barrier. Waking at dawn now to helicopters and rain. The day sort of melted looking. Yesterday was hot, bright and clear. I wrote all afternoon on the deck, Tales of the Bomb, my girlhood memories of it. A yacht on the water seemed to be watching me. I can't leave yet. I want to be here when it comes in. I walked the mile through the woods, gazed at Jane's magnificent horses. How long it takes to make a human being, how sad I won't be here when she births it and can ride again. In town behind Family Market the boats are lined up in the watery sunshine. Boats from all over the world waiting for Trident, a two billion dollar machine possessing more destructive power than two thousand Hiroshimas. Waiting for Evil.

Now crossing LoFall. The waves fast and hard from the ferry. The sound of the cars starting up all at once. The rattle and shake leaving the ferry, this land we come to. Barbara sits up to watch, tells her dream that we are aliens, our generation. This is why we have the highest pain tolerance ever known. Nuclear war? We don't die no matter what they do.

Patrick keeps watching for the archbishop of Seattle, Archbishop Raymond Hunthausen, who has promised the blockaders moral and spiritual support. Last year Hunthausen withheld half his federal taxes to protest tax dollars for nuclear weapons, calling the Bangor Trident base "the Auschwitz of Puget Sound." "I feel sad inside," he said, "because if one examines who the blockaders are and what they're about, you have to acknowledge they are not in it for themselves. How could they be? They're putting themselves out there at great risk to their lives. From my Christian perspective this is the ultimate in the Gospel, when one is willing to offer one's life for others. What greater love is there?"

*Tuesday, August 10, Oak Bay, 5 p.m. The blockaders'
encampment*

There are six trailers, some campers, all retired old folks
camped here for their summer vacations. We spend the nights
here in Psyche now. Each morning there are more Naval and
Coast Guard ships on the water and more blockaders in the
encampment.

Small planes shoot over. Helicopter, *Channel 5*, circling,
chop! chop! chop! We walk down to the cooking yurt they've
built on the lagoon for dinner. They give us vegetables and rice.
A huge flock of seagulls circling the beach as one. Now landing.

"A number of cars belong to reporters," the Seattle Post-
Intelligencer reports on the front page, *"covering the protester's
planned attempt to stop the Navy's new Trident nuclear submarine
as it heads for its home port at the Naval Submarine Base at
Bangor, south of here on the Hood Canal."*

"It's really a fjord, not a canal," Patrick keeps saying. "It's a
shame it's called a canal. It's the only real fjord in the country."

"Hood Fjord," I try out. "And Birth Canal. And childhood.
Neighborhood. Priesthood. Hoodlum. Hood, a hood like a caul,
something hidden back in there. How bizarre to even imagine
such a large evil thing as Trident in such a tiny slit."

"Oak Bay is normally a place of stillness, the paper says,
*"lapping water on the beach, thick forests all around, passable
fishing, but great clamming.*

*'I expected some peace instead of the mob like this I got,' Bill
Shaw, 64, said, leaning against his house trailer. Only a few yards
away was the encampment's mess area, where demonstrators
hovered over bubbling pots, awaiting their evening meal of rice and
vegetables.*

*'To be honest, they've been peaceful but I was just camping here
and they came flying in.' Shaw lives in Hadlock, only five miles
away.*

He added he is pro-Trident because 'with four or five of those subs sitting out there, the Russians know they'll be wiped out same as we are.'"

Wednesday, August 11, Phil Ochs, 1931, Oak Bay

Waking in the middle of the night in Psyche's bed, he reaches for me. He says I reached for him. Well, whoever, we were fucking! Fast and hard, the waves building up one behind the other like ocean waves in a storm at high tide, then the riptide of returning water that comes after the crash.

Up at five. Hitting the beach. Looking for the thirty foot wake. Still more Coast Guard and Naval ships sitting out there. Rumors are wild again of the *Ohio* emerging east of Port Angeles. Port Townsend over there in the foggy glare on the tip of Quimper Peninsula. Quimper, the clitoris of the Olympic Peninsula, someone says in a poem. The patriarch's phallus entering her holy waters. I see Jonah I found almost four years ago, o.d'd on the horizon, sprawled in all four directions, the bay, the mountains, the city and Canada. This is our body, a stupa like the Buddha. I'm trying to understand what a stupa is. And a sutra.

Lotus Sutra?

We climb the hill to Beth's house for showers, breakfast, phone calls, maybe most of all, shelter, relief from the beach. Walking past cottages from the Forties and Fifties, homemade A-frames built from do-it-yourself kits. One has an enormous banner on its deck beneath the American flag hanging limply in the drizzle, WELCOME OHIO! Tomorrow the owner will be standing by this banner on the front page, above the fold. His name is Jack Daniels, 73. His ice plant, his landscaping, his pest control business in Seattle. His words in the paper: "*If it came to a choice of being killed or being enslaved in a communist nation, I think I'd prefer death.*"

Sharing the front page will be the headline "*Another Green River Murder?*" The speculation now is that the fifty unsolved murders in the Seattle area are the work of one man.

Inside Beth's the TV blinks 8:20. My mother used to point out that clocks depicted in catalogs and for sale in the stores are always set at 8:20. "The time Lincoln was assassinated," she'd say. Lately 8: 20 seems to be the time whenever I look at a clock, a.m. or p.m.

From Beth's big bay view window—she's working the breakfast shift at the Salal, Port Townsend's collectively owned café—I can see Jack Daniels sitting in his living room watching both television and the scene, his hands folded in his lap like a good boy. Like a bad boy sent to the corner. Like a boy who'd rather be dead. Like a dead boy.

Today we are to connect with our witness boat.

Back down on the beach we meet the legendary John Shields. He's 64, on the forty-fifth day of a hunger strike. One cup of coffee at 4 a.m. He poured his own blood on the White House steps, in the name of the Motherland, in the name of Uncle Sam.

"Merton says you have to get away, let yourself emerge, come up from inside. You can neglect your spirit so long then it'll dry up. A vacuum comes in, you're on empty.

"I'm aboard the *Cash Flow*. I don't have a penny. Have to hitchhike back to New York."

We drive toward town—I think. My sense of direction gets turned around in these inlets, coves, fjords, canals, the land convoluted by the glaciers. "The Vashon Glaciation," Patrick explains again. "Ice three thousand feet deep over Seattle just 14,000 years ago. That ice was here for fifteen hundred years and went as far south as Olympia. It caused the hills of Seattle and the depths of Puget Sound and Hood Canal. Thank god for the Strait. A straight, narrow waterway."

We come to a little bay I've never been on, have no idea

where we are. There's a large outrageous looking structure being constructed on the beach. Gothic, Arabic, Victorian, Modern, a combination of all of those. Maybe that's postmodern. The right hand of the Buddha, the left hand of Geronimo. A long pier extends from it. Phallic.

"Some sort of cult or religious endeavor," Patrick says. "But there's not a soul here, not a human in sight. Maybe a resort," he jokes.

Right then, a big black, two-mast ship comes around the pier, silhouetted too large on the silver water, the black line of the horizon, as archetypal-looking against the silver sky as the mausoleum/temple/castle/resort. A black stupa. Maybe this is Point-No-Point I keep hearing about in the poems, where the S'Klallam signed away most of their land. Suddenly the menacing-looking ship turns, bores straight for us. "Our witness boat?" Patrick mutters. We're walking out the long pier. We feel like silhouettes too. Besides Trident I'm expecting Johnny Dark. Suddenly I just know he's on this boat coming at us. We're at the end of the silhouetted pier, the sea a mirror beneath us.

"I just read in *Justine*," Patrick goes on, as if in explanation of something, "that amoral and amor have the same root."

The *Edith Rose* pulls up to us.

"You called, Madam?"

It wasn't a silhouette, the entire ketch, the two huge sails, the whole ship is black. The handsome buccaneer, dressed all in black, bows to us from his shiny poop, swinging his captain's hat down through the air, across his front.

"Miguel Hernandez at your service."

Jane's husband! Her daughter's father. I'm more than certain now that Johnny Dark is on it, this is the 11th, the day they're coming.

I wait for him to emerge, suddenly panicky about how I'm going to deal with him and Patrick together at this crucial moment when we must not be distracted. I wait in surety because after a few synchronistic turns with Johnny Dark they barely surprise me anymore. Maybe Sam and Jessica are on board too.

First out of the bottom emerge Bonnie and Duke and their two little daughters, Vadra, four and Luna, two and a half months. What a surprise. Duke is another old friend of Patrick's from the original commune. I wait for Johnny next.

Now we float out on the water watching for the *Ohio*, the haunting protest songs of Phil Ochs over everything. We float around Admiralty Inlet, out almost into Puget Sound, back to the Strait of Juan de Fuca, back down Hood Canal. Around the southern tip of Marrowstone, back up Indian Island. Where does one body of water begin, the other let off? I'm shaking inside, waiting for Johnny. Luna is propped now in her car seat at the helm, a miniature masthead. Naked, sitting in vulva reality. I can't take my eyes off her or her mother, Bonnie, it's like hypnosis. I always get caught in the aura of pregnant and lactating women. It must be the hormones, like a contact high. Maybe that's why I'm so drawn to Jane.

Finally I dare to ask Miguel, "Is Johnny Dark here?"

"It's been on Steward Island all winter," he answers, pretending not to know what I'm asking.

Vadra is named for a mountain in Spain where she was conceived, blond and chunky, Luna for somewhere in Baja. Duke and Bonnie both take their eyes off Vadra running madly between stern and bow. I'm terrified she'll tumble over. Last month in the Boat Haven an Oregon boy fell in and drowned. I'm waiting for Johnny, I'm looking deep into the water, to the mind of water, to the fish. All the water that ever was, Socrates' pee, Jesus' pee, Sealth's. The strength of water, Fujii says, is that it has no beginning, no end, it flows as one body. One must accomplish the relationship of water and fish, eliminating the mind that distinguishes one self from the other. We must become one with others. I become the Mendocino woman in the 1860s off the Big River headland in her storm-tossed ship. The town's people gather on the headland. She waves and waves her baby at them, tied to a wood plank. They wave back. Then, turning once more to make sure they are following her horizon pantomime, she throws the baby into the monster wave. All go down with the ship, only the baby survives, surfing into shore.

But no Johnny Dark, and no Trident either. I'm relieved, it feels like luck, it didn't feel good, the dread for Patrick, but after all Johnny's clamor, that he didn't let me know he won't be coming, not even a note of explanation or apology. Of course, when I was finally willing to meet him, he doesn't show. That's the story of my life with men.

But Archbishop Hunthausen is here, according to the radio, on a big white yacht. Also local heads of the Lutherans, American Baptists, United Churches of Christ, Washington Association of Churches, and Washington State Catholic Conference, as well as a nationally prominent rabbi. The University of Washington's campus minister, John Nelson, has sanctioned civil disobedience against atomic weapons. Nelson has received the backing of local Lutherans and the five-state Northwest Synod.

And maybe at Miguel Hernandez and Jane's house, Sam and Jessica taking a break from the film of Frances Farmer and the reporter who fell in love with her, Frances whose little sister lives right over there on that sunlit bluff of Sequim, Edith Eliot just west down the bluff from Jane's, the sister who signed with their mother and the judge to have Frances lobotomized and has written the book, *Look Back in Love,* defending this. Frances was brilliant, but a leftist, she visited the Soviet Union. From the moment I became a poet I started taking notes on Frances Farmer. I don't know why, it'll be years before I understand why.

Betrayal. My father. My mother. My sister. My sister like Frances' sister.

"We need to go in for mail," he says, late in the afternoon. This means we'll miss dinner, our plate of vegetables and rice. I realize I'm hungry. We are both broke.

At Pat and Finn's Pat reports that there's a bunch of rednecks out at Oak Bay now, they've blocked off the bathrooms, they're yelling obscenities, looking for fights. And then, most wonderfully, she feeds us cheese enchilada left-overs from the Salal.

"In *Finnegan's Wake*," I offer the group. "Joyce says Nostradamus predicted Trident Submarine. In the fifteenth century!"

Patrick gives me his most withering, brow-rising look.

"I didn't say it. James Joyce said it."

At the Town Tavern, newly opened for business, though you can see the burned-out apartments in the high windows above the bar, the energy is roaring, talks of the fights with the rednecks and where the sub is. *"What to do about Trident?"* is scrawled on the Women's blackboard. *" Sleep with the crew!"* *"Mutate now to Bangor & avoid the rush!"* I dance the whole time to the juke box, the only dancer, wearing my gold Emma Goldman tee shirt, *"If I can't dance I don't want to be part of your revolution,"* while Patrick talks with Marilyn, the girl he fucked in our bed. Her beautiful gold red hair all the way down to her butt.

It's late when we drive back to Oak Bay. The moon is in its last quarter in Taurus. My cramps worsen. Mid-month ovulation. I crawl in the back, curl into the fetal position, cheer myself on. Then I see Roque Dalton being shot in the back by his own comrades.

Patrick stops for a hitchhiker, a young sailor on his way back to Indian Island. "Thanks. Forty cars musta passed me up." He's from Arkansas, just a baby, really. "My commander told me it's going to be okay," he says in his soft drawl. Patrick drives him right to the base entrance. They shake hands. He never knew I was back here.

We descend to Oak Bay, pull into the same spot in the line of trucks and cars and tents, as if reserved for us.

All night still rocking in the motion of the *Edith Rose.* "Hey! *You hippie slime!*" The drunk locals leaving their two a.m. taverns cruising by. At the windows of our vehicles hissing *"The Trident's coming. The Trident's coming. It's going to get you."*

And still later I wake to *"Hippie slimes! Hey, hippie slime!"*

Thursday August 12, Cecil B. DeMille, 1881

Wake at five to the incessant drone of helicopters. *Today.* Crawling out, peeing in the sand by the back tire, Moonlight waking under Psyche, seeing the beer cans and household trash they've thrown at us. Crawling back in over Patrick, falling far away to the most interesting dream, as he is dressing, leaving. "You're going to miss it!"

But I've finally fallen asleep, it's too early, there are too many motors in the sky, the sound of war, for hours it seems, falling back to oblivion. I always fall asleep at the crack of dawn, after the danger of the night, my father, has passed.

Patrick opening the door. "You're missing it! It's happening!"

The sea is cluttered with boats, all makes and sizes, the sky with churning, whirring motors and metal wings. I walk down the sandy road to the cooking yurt. A raised pickup rumbles by me with a huge banner flying high above its bed. **WELCOME OHIO, BUT HURRY UP. WE WANT OUR PEACE AND QUIET.**

In the bathroom one woman saying to another in the stall next to her. "Did you hear? The Lizard was water-cannoned. They've already been arrested."

In the cooking yurt there's no coffee left.

"God! I can't go out there without coffee."

"There's grounds left," he says, a small teenage boy with a wispy goatee. "I'll boil them for you."

I thank him profusely.

"It's off the north point of Marrowstone," he says, collecting the grounds from several pots.

I gather myself up in his yurt, watch the incredible theatre of war out there in the foggy, dribbling mist. Hundreds of ships it seems, people on the water. Most spectacular is the boat with the giant peace sign.

"The *Pacific Peacemaker*'s come all the way from Australia," the boy explains. "Inexperienced crew, ages sixty-three to three, a Shakespearean actress on board, a 1973 Mother of the Year, and two or three Maoris. The Captain has his mother, his wife and their four children on board!"

Those Maoris I saw in the Boat Haven in July. Maybe they were scouts.

"They've been twenty-nine days at sea, one of the roughest oceans in the world, twenty-one without a compass. The Captain's kids, three girls and a boy, were involved in everything as equals, including the deal that on the day of confrontation they'd have the option of participating in the protest or not. In the spirit of peaceful nonviolence, you know, non-authoritarianism, non-coercion. There'd be absolutely no pressure. Well, this morning they lined up on deck to give their answers, the grandmother cheering them on to each's deepest truth. One, then the two other girls opted to come ashore, to not confront Trident. The boy said, 'count me in.' I swear you could hear the roar of approval to here.

"The girls and the person who rowed them in were huddled here in the yurt all morning. They kept saying their father was so proud of his son."

The boy hands me a large metal cup of steaming hot coffee and shrugs. "Poor kid."

His wet stringy curls, his beads, his button of the world, *DON'T BLOW IT!* You're my hero, I want to say, I'm stunned that you get it.

But I just say, "poor *boy*." And then, "and poor *girls*."

Gender roles! These folks of great consciousness and conscience will go on telling this story all week like it's the most wonderful thing, maybe even relieved that the girls opted for passivity, that is femininity, not seeing that the gender roles allowed them this, that his, to be a successful male, demanded that he confront Trident. There was no choice, really, no matter what was mouthed about their so-called deepest truths.

Patrick is running down and across the silver beach from Psyche and the sea to me. Even in this moment I'm struck by his beauty. A rowboat, the *Love*, with two women is coming in to us.

"C'mon!" he shouts, grabbing my arm. "It's Annie. This is it!"

We plunge into the waves, Moonlight barking and barking.

Entering the cold water is like entering pain.

"You stay here, Moonlight. Guard the beach."

"You sit here," Annie, the rower says, indicating the end pointed to shore.

Trying to get a footing in the rocking thing. Patrick gallantly holds it for me. He takes the middle with her, takes up an oar. At the other end, her back to us, facing the open sea, is—I can't believe my eyes! Of all boats to get into. Naomi.

Against the horizon and sky in her pea-green foul-weather jacket, her blond hair cut like mine, wet with dew, curling up just like mine, she holds her small angry self with each hand clutching the sides of the rowboat. She doesn't greet us, speak, or acknowledge us. She will speak only once during the entire confrontation just beginning to unfold.

Naomi's husband, David, and I returned from the annual Midwest Book Fair in Minneapolis on different planes, having lost contact after the night I found him and Carolyn together and threw up in our host's bathroom. I attributed the rare vomiting to my dismay. That I was made witness to their betrayal of Naomi, that this was treated almost as if a privilege, I should be honored to know their secret. Prominent, political activist poets passionately fighting against the imperialist, annihilative powers of our government, the corruption and hypocrisy,— well, hey you two, what about the personal is the political? In my book amoral and amor do not have the same root. Of course I threw up. Returning home from the Book Fair David and I encountered each other on the ferry. I had no way of getting to Port Townsend from Winslow, was walking the line of cars hoping to see someone I knew, or if necessary, to be up front when the cars started unloading with my thumb out. And there was David.

We'd both just had books published by small presses, mine, a $19.95 paperback, 274 page epic poem by a politically radical one, his by Copper Canyon so fine each chapbook was priced at $200.

"Naomi is picking me up. In about forty-five minutes."

We wandered the dock sharing a little of the Book Fair. He talked of Carolyn, mostly. He'd been in love with her for five years. I could feel his hoping I'd share something about her. "I'd leave Naomi if she'd have me."

I was fairly certain that the feeling was not reciprocated with Carolyn, though how she felt about her many lovers, how she maneuvered and manipulated them for her causes, was a big mystery to me.

"Does Naomi know about her?"

"She knows, but not ever, *not ever!* that I was with her in Minneapolis."

No one spoke the hour drive home through the two-lane, emerald green landscape in twilight. David sat in the passenger side. I sat directly behind her so she couldn't see my face in the rearview, our eyes couldn't meet. I knew she was working on the cover illustration for an H.D. book that Copper Canyon was publishing, H. D. being my first poet, but I knew not to ask about even that. In Port Townsend she drove directly to their house on the dirt dead end behind Kai Tai Lagoon, slammed the car door shut, disappeared. I declined his offer to drive me the four miles to the cabin, even though it was dark and I had my luggage. "The walk will be great after the plane, after Minnesota." I left my luggage in the trunk.

Much later that night, trying to sleep in Psyche on Cape George beach, having flown the cabin after finally getting there, hanging on for my life again, my heart trying to break, to stop, to pound right out of my chest for finding Patrick fucking that girl in our bed. I saw again and again Naomi walking up to us at the ferry station, burning hatred for me. I was stunned by the fierceness of her intuition. "But it's not me," I wanted to cry (wanting to take her in my arms, somehow knowing, hey, I'm in the same boat as you.) But by association it was me, Carolyn being my friend. I witnessed her husband's infidelity with her. There are always exceptions, I suppose, situations that require deception, I'm certainly not a legitimist, an unbending extremist, a prude, there's Johnny with his stroke-damaged wife who, he says, encourages him to have sex with me, she who has no ego now and no desire for sex ever again. I was still in denial that my principles stem, at least in part, from the fact that as a little girl I'd been forced to betray my mother by my father's molestations, by my helpless muteness. I couldn't understand this most common of behaviors, all my lovers' betrayals, each and every one having devastated me. When do we stop lying to our so-called loved ones? When do we stop doing psychic violence to them, and therefore to ourselves? When do we live in truthfulness? "I would leave Naomi if Carolyn would have me," means you should leave Naomi right now. Period.

Now Naomi's small back to me vibrates with hatred. The armada of the Coast Guard is ahead of her and six helicopters are above her. How would I have handled it if that girl had picked us up? Slowly, as Patrick and Annie row, teenage boys with enormous guns come into focus beyond Naomi. The noise is deafening. I wash between her hate and theirs. I should jump out, swim back.

Surprisingly, David has emerged from the training camps as one of the leaders of the blockade. Surprising? He was in the Bangor 50 in 1979. He told me once on the dance floor of the poster that greeted him when he climbed the fence. He came to a pair of double doors marked off-limits and on each door was a poster of Poseidon, God of the Sea, standing in water up to his waist, holding a trident in his hand, a crown of kelp on his head, and a missile coming out of the water from where his penis would be. David had also founded Poets for Peace, had signed up over five hundred poets all over the U.S. to vow their skills as poets to help prevent nuclear war. None of this meshed with his aristocratic, removed, yuppie personality and looks. Everyone said this. He said it of himself, said he was trying to change himself, find his real self, trying to enter the world, be responsible for it. And, I'm sure, to impress Carolyn, to win her love.

They row us in and out of the traffic—speed boats, cabin cruisers, sailboats, yachts, catamarans, dinghies, fishing vessels, ketches, crabbers here for the event—heading for the *Shamrock*, Annie's classic, emerald green sailboat with the maroon sail that's been my favorite in the Boat Haven. *"A yawl, a ketch, a sloop and kayak,"* Patrick recites from one of his poems. Someone on the *Peacemaker* shouts across the water in a tone of delight "Annie!" We move deeper into the scene, into a Fifties war movie. The bridge to Indian Island is silhouetted starkly against the sky and the shore we have left is becoming clearer, sharper in the perspective of the whole inlet. Our crummies, vans, campers, tents. And the daughters of the Captain playing hopscotch with Moonlight along the length of Oak Bay beach.

The four of us climb onto the green and maroon *Shamrock* one by one. "Remember when Pinocchio got swallowed by the whale?" Patrick laughs as he makes the step from the rowboat to the rope ladder.

Annie works at starting the motor. She is a small, tight, muscular woman, like most lesbians I know, and of great boyish beauty. Her tan biceps ripple in the sea light. She owns the sailmaking business in town, is, like Patrick, part of the original group of counterculture people who came here, who, for whatever reason, he seems to prevent me from knowing. Annie is beloved in his community.

We head toward the center of the action, through the churning copters, a huge pile-up of boats and humanity on the horizon. Patrick watches for the archbishop's yacht. "I didn't leave the seminary for political reasons," he explains. "I never rejected my faith. I never had a crisis of doubt. It is that I deserted it."

For good reason, I keep myself from saying, you were raped by a priest then you were thinking of becoming a rapist priest. That's why, you told me, you left the Church.

The scene passes, frame by frame, from warriors on a battlefield, from fascist military show and to something akin to a children's parade. It's like a past life battle I was killed in, the sky full of metal, motors. But I wasn't in Vietnam, Algeria, Korea, World War II, how can I feel such?

Up ahead we spot a couple on their knees in an aluminum canoe, *The Children*, bent to the water, paddling hard with bare hands.

"They're in trouble," Patrick shouts over the roar.

Annie guns the motor. We speed past orange-robed Buddhists on the *Gull*. "There's Fujii!" Patrick shouts, pointing to the old man at the high helm beating his drum, his profile silhouetted against the foggy sky, an enormous gold-toothed grin, his bald head shining. For a moment as we pass, the drumming is louder than the helicopters' incessant chop. We come alongside *The*

Children, tiny in the immense sea. "The Coast Guard took our oars!" they shout in unison. We give them ours. As they row determinedly away I throw her a kiss. Her eyes light up in the dim dribble. Later, they will be on the list of the missing.

We keep moving towards the heap on the horizon, the drums coming at us in waves like a collective human heart. Then we spot two heads, sleek black, bobbing in a wake of gasoline. At first I think they're seals surfaced to see the show. A little ways from them the triangular end tip of a rowboat bobs against the sky. Suddenly it goes under as if yanked by something below.

The three of us lean off the side and way out, reaching for them, an older couple. She's small and so gritty you could believe she came from the sea bottom.

"I never expected a scenario like that," she gasps as we pull her aboard, shaking cropped curly grey hair from the rubber cap. She turns to help the man. As soon as he's on board she's peeling off her wet suit, the black rubber from her small muscular burnt shoulders.

"I'm a realist," her green eyes flash. "But still…."

Stripped now to a bikini, her flesh is blue white with goosebumps, vulnerable-looking against the tons of metal of the scene. Annie throws her a bathrobe from below, puts the kettle on for tea.

"We were of the fifteen people willing to risk our lives."

The whistle of the teapot comes through all the cacophony.

Now the couple from the sea huddle over the steam rising from their cups, teeth chattering. Their names are Dot and John Fisher-Smith.

"They came alongside us with a pike pole and grappling hook, snagged our boat and rocked us until we capsized." She laughs. "I feel guilty at least for not getting arrested."

Her husband, John, handsome, maybe English, puts his arm around her tough shoulders. "Well, we put ourselves out there. If we didn't die…."

A flock of seagulls suddenly rises from under the front of the *Shamrock*, up and over us like a tidal wave. Like a blessing.

"But the ones on the *Lizard*, they were blown off by high pressure water hoses. That'd knock you out for a second."

Now the *Ploughshares* with mainly religious leaders, is sailing toward us at full speed. Dot and John jump up and down, waving. Pulling up beside us, someone aboard is yelling "The Coast Guard is ignoring our permits!"

"Where are you from?" I yell as they climb over.

"Ashland, Oregon!"

"Ashland?" I'm dumbstruck. They're pulling away. "Do you know my sister, Donna Eden, the healer, I mean, kinesiologist?"

"Donna's your sister?"

And they sail off.

The synchronicity again amazes me. To have pulled an Ashland couple from the Trident-infested sea, that they know my sister! Our worlds, my sister's and mine, never cross. She moved to Ashland two years ago, the same summer I came to Port Townsend; my daughter is there sometimes, but I never connect with other people there. On the California border, two states away, Ashland seems isolated to me, of another world, entirely separate from mine in its cute, nonpolitical, New Age, stage and moneyed consciousness. But many of these blockaders, I'll learn, are from Ashland, including the Shakespeare actress aboard the *Peacemaker*.

Now we search for the *Lizard of Woz* from Quadra Island, B.C. No one knows what's happened to it except for the rumor that everybody aboard was hosed into the water.

"We were ambushed," the newspaper will report. "We're a trimaran, forty-five feet. We carried six skiffs each named in honor of something sacred. I was on watch from two a.m.to four. Sixteen Coast Guard vehicles, four at a time, came through the cut in the dark. Getting terrified! We'd taken off first, before the *Peacemaker.* Sorry, we meant no insult but we're devout Christians, we just couldn't trust the bohemian imbibing crazies on the *Peacemaker.*

"The Canal was lined with patrol boats. What a surprise! Two large Coast Guard cutters greeted us, causing us to thrash around in the water. We watched a guy on the *Pt. Glass* assemble a huge machine gun on the bow. We were drenched and drenched again. Some of our small skiffs got in the water, then were hosed down. One of us swam, calling out all the international laws he could remember. Four or five of our members were kneeling, saying the Lord's Prayer. The Coast Guard seemed to become ever more frenzied. Our captain had a pistol put to his head and told to quit praying.

"We were outside the government's restricted zone where we're supposed to be protected. Civil disobedience is protected by the Constitution. We did exactly what we said we'd do, what we filed on, were granted permission to do, but the Coast Guard didn't believe us, I guess because our mode of behavior is so foreign to them. You get used to lying, you assume everyone else is lying.

"There were FBI, CIA, KGB, French Secret Agent boats out there. We were in Zone B. Then three cutters came on either side and from behind, and herded us down the Canal and then arrested us.

"Quit praying? Forgiveness and compassion is the only thing that's going to get us through this nuclear disaster."

Naomi continues looking through me as through the grey sky. One must accomplish the relationship of water and fish, Fujii says, eliminating the mind that distinguishes oneself from the other. We must become one with others. That's my girlhood Christianity!

No sign of the *Ohio* or the *Lizard.* We give up, turn back to the scene of action, begin circling the *Peacemaker* with the other witness boats in the soupy fog.

On its sail is that poster, a red sun which turns in the light to the peace sign, the black circle of Trident in the center, the red stripe of hands touching across the seas. The scene looks like a hippie dream, a medieval pageantry, an actor's fantasy, Chaplinesque, somehow comical. Little homemade orange rowboats are tied behind the *Peacemaker*, the ducklings they're called, each one with a rubber-suited rower, and then the *Ploughshares* and then the *Gull* with its orange-robed old men beating celestial drums. Words bob on the water: *Amazing Grace, Rosie Parks, Gandhi, Imagine, Blowing in the Wind, Rebellion, Redemption Song, Nuevo Mundo.* Every time I look at the *Peacemaker* something wells up inside, something trying to push out, like the images of a recurring dream, the images of something that really happened.

The Coast Guard, their ships a grey duller than fog has all of this loosely surrounded, just sitting there in their big cutters, their big guns. We, the witness boats, manage to circle outside all of it. All of us just waiting. For someone to make a move. From somewhere someone is playing *Major Tom.*

I'm slipping through the door and I'm floating in the most peculiar way. I miss the earth very much. I miss my wife.

Suddenly there's commotion. "Oh no, no, no, no, no, no, no, no...."

"They're charging!"

Mars ain't the kind of place to raise your kids.

The *Pt. Glass* is closing in on the *Peacemaker.* The drums beat over the rocket man, *"I'm not the man you think I am."*

The Coast Guard's smoke obscures everything.

"Oh no, no, no, no, no, no, no, no...."

"There it is there it is there it is!"

It's coming through the fog behind us only partially above the water. A long dark sliver with its little box on top, silently and slowly making its way around us, protesters as colorful and outrageous as an acid trip. The cacophony of choppers and drums, maybe I'm hallucinating. Smoke from the choppers and ships mixing with the fog, that's how L.A. smog was explained to me as a girl, my first etymology.

"Mother fucking dildo," Annie spits.

"It's heading towards the mouth of Hood Canal," Patrick gasps. "Look! They're sending the hospital boat out."

Trident is sneaking around our whole scene, slithering through the water. We're being detained here.

The Coast Guard boards the *Peacemaker*. We and the other witness boats, move in tighter. Another barely discernable tune is coming through the rhythmic beats of the drums and slaps of the water.

"Happy Birthday to you. Happy Birthday to you...."

Before our eyes, to *"Happy Birthday dear Ivy...,"* the mother of the captain, throws herself overboard. Her ten year old grandson is hysterical, running, screaming between those on their bellies, their hands cuffed behind their backs, singing louder, *"happy birthday to you."* Teenage boys, uniformed with machine guns, stand over them.

On the *Ploughshares* also boarded by the Coast Guard a young man can be seen on his stomach, his hands cuffed behind his back. The young man standing over him isn't holding a weapon but a ukulele, frantically strumming. We come around again. *"Onward Christian soldiers, marching as to war."*

The *Peacemaker*'s hull towers over us, we're that close. Suddenly, in a jutting back and forth motion, the stern of the *Gull* inserts itself between the *Pt. Glass* and the *Peacemaker*, Fujii at the top of the prow, silhouetted against the sky, gold-toothed smiling, beating away, chanting *"Na-mu Myo ho-ren-ge-kyo...."* *"Without possessions but my drum I enter."* Back and forth, in and out, the *Gull* comes.

"They say he got his name from Gandhi," Annie shouts. "He's ninety-seven."

"At nineteen, he was in the army," Patrick shouts back, "in

Japan's war against Russia, 1904. He got it. All Japanese wars are holy wars? Fuck! Fujii became a monk."

In Seattle two hundred protesters are lying down in the streets as if killed by a nuclear bomb. A die-in.

We circle and circle. The *Ohio* keeps slipping by. Now from somewhere comes *Pleased to meet you, hope you got my name!* We move around the starboard side, the beat of the drums lessen, the hands of the captives too tight behind their backs. As we come around the port side the drums are louder across their prone bodies. Around and around, the soundtrack lessening, increasing, *let me introduce myself.* The boys with Uzis, machine guns, M16s, *I hope you get the nature of my game!* The *Gull* gunning in and out, a staged opera except the guns are real, just one hair-triggered boy would cause them all to start shooting. *Who killed the Kennedys?* The women are handcuffed with plastic, the men with metal. On the *Lizard of Woz*, wherever it is, nine hours face down on the deck. Nothing to eat, no place to pee, unable to take your meds.

"Auschwitz!" Patrick exclaims. "This is organized violence all the way down the line."

"Hey *Peacemaker*, looky here!" The *Pt. Glass* is raising the anti-Trident flag. *After all it was me and you.*

The orange-robed Buddhists pound, sometimes eardrum-breaking loud, Fujii's bald head coming through the conflagration, his gold teeth grin in and out, up and down, the sound and rhythm almost too much. Like the spasms of an epileptic, the rhythm of a convulsion, Sealth and the Unknown rising. The Makah whalers at the mouth of the Strait entering the Pacific, the waves pounding in and out too fast, the whalers battling them too fast, the women dancing on shore too fast, everything speeded up in the way of early film. Like the way we made love last night.

I'm trying to understand what a stupa is. A Buddhist stupa.

"Sutra is the sound and stupa is the sight," Patrick explains.

"Stupa means to heap, to pile up. The Buddha heard the sutra from within the stupa and entered it."

"Was the end of the war and the dropping of the bomb on Japan the same event?" Annie asks.

"Yes!" Naomi gasps, breaking her silence.

"Japan surrendered instantly," Patrick rushes in to overcome the shock of Naomi having spoken.

"The vibration of sound, the sutra, opens you," he continues. "The birds sing in the tree so the blossoms open. The drums open you, the waves pounding the shore is the sutra. Everything is connected, sewn together. But now there are nuclear bombs in the temple, the *Ohio* is slipping through."

Just then, a small speedboat with three black silhouetted bodies, sort of meanders nonchalantly away from the scene, then speeds for the sub.

They are headed straight for Trident.

It's Sunshine and Renee Krisko, the two crazy nuns, and Turtle, a math teacher from Ashland. Sunshine has said all along, we're going, we are really going to Trident. They got kicked out of two boats this morning for going against the consensus.

"We're going to Trident. I'm very serious. We are going to get on Trident," Sunshine says. "We love this water. We don't want it atomized."

A Coast Guard cutter goes after them. They easily outmaneuver the big awkward thing, they're speeding toward the sub on the port side now. It's like we're watching a movie, the sound track is beating drums, the whirr-chop of copters, and *hung around St. Petersburg.*

The little boat, the *James Jordan*, with the three people is there now. The *Ohio* is going between six and ten knots. Then a helicopter is above them.

"GET BACK!"

"No. We're taxpayers! We want to see."

The updraft of water caused by the helicopter increases their speed. It's a storm. Trident is so close they feel its metallic evil. The spray and waves whip around the *Jordan* which suddenly zips out and around the front of the sub. Now it goes down the port side and across the wake. Then it comes back to the nose. The helicopter comes back, pushes the *Jordan* away from the sub. The *Jordan* turns around and heads back to the *Ohio*'s stern, away from the copter. Two patrol boats begin closing in. The *Jordan* again spins around, heads back to the bow.

Sunshine jumps in front of the USS *Ohio*. Her silhouette on the horizon. Unbelievable.

"I was floating around for ten minutes looking at it. I wanted to look at evil with my own eyes. Then Renee and Turtle were shouting, "over here, Sunshine, over here."

A stupa appears. They hear a voice from within the stupa, explaining the law. The Lord Buddha opens the stupa and enters it. Sunshine too. She enters it.

"We never saw a thing," the Captain of the *Ohio* will say. "We never saw a thing until those three in that speedboat...."

Everyone on the *Ploughshares* is arrested. No one knows what's happened to the *Lizard of Woz*.

Someone in a small boat is approaching the *Peacemaker* shaking out a wet white flag like a hankie. The ducklings, the manned orange rowboats, come undone from the *Peacemaker*, go off in all directions. The Coast Guard starts tipping them over with their long hooks.

Two men get back in the *Tao*, wedge it between the *Pt. Glass* and the *Peacemaker*, leap for the high ropes the *Pt. Glass* has tied to the *Peacemaker*, and hang from them. "This is not a question of peace," a Marshal roars on a bullhorn. "This is a question of authority." Then the hosing begins. The Coast Guard water-cannons them, torrents blasting their heads and necks as they hang from the ropes.

The water pressure increases. The *Pt. Glass* starts moving backwards, pulling at the ropes.

The two guys hang on.

"One of those guys could be David," Annie gasps.

"It *is* David!" Patrick shouts.

Two thin men in black wetsuits hang between two gigantic ships, their silhouette above the horizon.

The *Zodiac* passes under the lines the two are hanging from, the guy still waving the small white flag is almost decapitated. Zodiacs are medical boats honored by all sides, but it's a Coast Guard Zodiac and it cuts one of the lines. Three guys come along and throw a Peacemaker in the water. See you later! They didn't want another Bangor 50. The arrested are being let off on deserted roads. They increase the pressure. They're moving backwards. One hangs on for about five minutes. Then he can't hold on any longer, lets go.

David hangs on, tiny, being water cannoned, between the two enormous ships banging back and forth and the *Gull* rhythmically inserting itself. He's throwing kisses to Naomi!

Naomi stands, lowers herself down the side of the green *Shamrock*, reaches for an abandoned orange duckling, boards it, and rows toward shore, demonstrating to all her personal protest against our hero.

Since 1982 when this story takes place, Bangor, Washington has become the home port of sixteen Trident nuclear submarines.

Jerusalem Delivered: *An Italian epic poem by Torquato Tasso (1544-1595) about the siege of Jerusalem by the Crusaders. Clorinda is the pagan heroine, daughter of Senap'us of Ethiopia, a Christian. Because she was born white, her mother traded her for a black child.*

...thou Ethiopia com'st to me. Walt Whitman

April 11, 1984. On the bus, Oxford to Cincinnati

A small black man on the steps of the Campus Center Store outside of Oxford, Ohio. He takes the first empty seat, three in front of me.

At the next stop the scene beneath my window is emotional. High school kids black and white hugging and crying, "goodbye! goodbye!" Long deep embraces. "No babies!" A large boy yelling back down from the bus "We LO-OVE you!" Someone sobbing as we move out.

He sits very still the two hours south to Cincinnati.

I want to go to Cincinnati. I'm not sure why. Joe, my host who has been teaching my book in his American Lit class, offered to drive me to Dayton, "a free ride," the direct route to Columbus, the connection to Pittsburgh. I looked at the map. No thank you, Joe, I'm taking the south-by-way-of-Cincinnati bus."

> *home of the Shawnee*
> *born from the brain of God*
> *immigrants from another land*
> *divided into twelve tribes*
> *receivers of prophets who warn of impending doom*
> *who turn them to paths of righteousness*
> *who believe in the Fall of Man*

The Shawnee

the favored and chosen people of the Master
himself an Indian
and all other races

Inferiors

On the outskirts we come through a bombed-out district, old buildings near ruins, boarded up, trash flying around in the small winds, a woman's pale dress through her dark running legs. Desolate like South American cities. A little boy in diapers with rocks in the street before an old movie house. Piling them on the curb.

Inside the Cincinnati Greyhound Bus Station the black man is standing in front of me to the information booth. His bus to Chicago has just left and now he has to wait four hours. I have to wait an hour and a half for the bus to Columbus.

"You want to walk around Cincinnati?"

"Yes," he says.

We both get lockers, unload our things, go to the bathrooms. Then we hit the streets.

The sun's bright. We walk in what I hope is a southern direction, through high cool canyons of granite buildings. He says how boring the bus is. We turn up a street and he says how old the buildings are. Lots of sun-glary traffic at the corners. He says he's looking for a restaurant or café. Running across, weaving through the stopped cars, laughing. Coming down a street of enormous white marble pillars, outrageous statues of the Founding Fathers sitting on the roof. Three jivey black guys raising a ladder over the sidewalk up the granite building. Excuse us, I laugh, leading the way beneath the ladder. The guy on the ladder, shirtless, grinning down.

"That's oka-ay!" Singsong.

I feel strong and free, no longer pained with shyness and fear of new places as when mi hija and I went to South America, the dread I used to feel going anywhere I didn't belong, even to San Francisco, those journeys down from Mendocino. He's coming from Minneapolis, looked into the Ph.D. program at Miami University.

"In what?"

"Political Science."

"I want to see the river. I wrote a poem once about crossing the Ohio in Cincinnati.

The long knife flowing through time's green groin
the present
that never stops passing your window

The sky in the one direction seems like a river sky so I keep moving us that way. "So what does Cincinnati mean to you?" I ask.

"Well, it's the border—it's a border town. Between the North and the South."

What's his accent?

I keep seeing the signs, Queen City. I can't remember what this refers to. Queen Cincinnati?

"Cincinnati was the city furthest west for a long time," I exclaim as we cross another intersection. Joe said they thought it was going to be the major Midwest city, not Chicago. On the Serpent Mound he asked me if I was a shaman. The shaman doesn't choose. The shaman is one who has been dismembered, has died and come back and in the example, heals. There is the skeleton of death in the shaman, he said. I was becoming aware now of how we looked. Me in my thongs, Levi's, long, thick blond hair, Air Force leather flight jacket, with three political buttons. I thought even as I saw him on the brick steps of the store in Oxford: Africa. That delicate, reserved, tight constriction, so English, so educated, so formal in manner. Round glasses, a scholar. His brown leather jacket light as plastic, like skin pushed up to his elbows. I noticed others on the street with the similar jacket. Fashionable. Black pants and shoes.

"Cincinnati was originally a sanctuary for Revolutionary War widows and children." I continue as we walk another block.

"There was a revolution in my country too."

"What is your country?"

"Ethiopia."

"When was that? I'm sorry, I don't know."

"1974. Many many thousands were killed. There's still a military dictatorship now."

"I saw Haile Selassie in 1969."

"You did?"

We're on a busy corner waiting for the light.

"In Washington D.C. His helicopter landed on the White House lawn to a big turnout of the Ethiopian community. But I've never understood why the Rastafarians in Jamaica consider Haile Selassie God?"

"Haile Selassie is from the direct line of David." So proper his speech. "You know David?"

"David in the Bible?"

"Yes. Solomon was his son. You know, the Song of Solomon, I am the Rose of Sharon? Well, David met Sheba, the Queen of Ethiopia. She was going for water late one night and he caught her. And she went home and had a child. From that child the family ruled until 1974. 3500 years. Haile Selassie is considered of the line of God."

"Was Sheba willing or was she raped?" I sort of laugh this as we start into the next crosswalk.

"Well, you know," he sort of laughs. "In those days..."

We are in the middle of the crosswalk.

"And it came to pass," he cites, "in an evening tide, that David arose from off his bed, and walked upon the roof of the king's house: and from the roof he saw a woman washing herself; and the woman was very beautiful to look upon."

We walk awhile, in silence.

"What happened to Haile Selassie?"

"He was last seen being bundled out of the palace in the back of a green Volkswagen."

On down the block he says, "He died in detention but no one knows his final resting place. The Imperial Tomb stands empty."

"Do you know *Uncle Tom's Cabin?*" I ask after awhile, "by Harriet Beecher Stowe? Cincinnati is where Eliza and her son crossed the Ohio. They were being pursued by the slave owners
like Eliza and her son
who escaped the bloodhounds
by crossing the Ohio
on cakes of ice
She wrote much of it at Miami University. It was a woman's college then."

Joe pointed out the room she wrote it in. Later, sitting on that porch with another Lit professor who told me of her preacher-father beating her.

"Oh," he says. "The Deep South."

We turn down another street. I'm still trying to find the river but he says again he'd like to find a café. The Queen City Café is right here.

The place is full of businessmen having lunch. All eyes look up. White businessmen. I spot one black person, the woman cashier. Through the kitchen window the crew staring.

We sit at the only empty table, a small one in the center of the room. Order 60 cent cups of soup, vegetable. Me, milk. He, hot tea.

On the street I'd asked him about politics within his political science field. "International law," he'd said. And something about NICs and LDPs. Now he explains.

"NIC stands for New Industrial Countries, like Taiwan, Brazil, Portugal and Spain. LDC stands for Least Developed Countries. They used to say Third World Countries, but now there are Fourth and Fifth World Countries."

I didn't ask where Ethiopia stands in the classifications. He's applying also at the University of Ohio and somewhere else, maybe Chicago. But Miami could get him money, he thinks. And he thinks of going to law school too.

When I say Washington he says Seattle. He says Green River. Then he says The Green River Massacres. When I say California he says "Originally when I came to this country I was going to the University of Santa Barbara, but I stopped first at a friend's in Minneapolis who convinced me to stay. I never left. This is my first trip."

When he says Minneapolis I say Twin Cities, my book was published there. When he says friend I think girlfriend.

"I'm a native of Los Angeles," I say. "I was just there for the first time in a long time. How healthy it seemed! That's the word that kept coming to me, healthy! Over half minority now. Mostly Mexicans and Central Americans. People seemed so relaxed. Not Yuppie, you know, like most cities."

"I have an Aunt in LA," he says, sipping his soup. "She wants me to visit. I've never been to California. I've been afraid to travel. I work as a nurse at the university hospital. I like Minneapolis. But I can't get a Ph.D. there because the Political Science Department has a policy against getting both your undergraduate and Ph.D. degrees from the same school. In this field you need diversity. I've been afraid to move. But this fall I will go somewhere else to school."

His cup is still full. I start on a cracker. I tell him of my epic poem. I write the name and the name of the Minneapolis press on the napkin.

'Their office is on the corner of Chicago and Lake by the Old Sears Building. They do a lot of political poetry, you might be interested."

"Are you with a university?"

"No," I sigh. "No. I didn't study to be a poet. Well, I got an MA in English."

"Longfellow," he says. I jump a little in my seat in delight.

"It's called the Queen City because of Longfellow! He called Cincinnati "Queen City of the West. You know the poet Henry Wadsworth Longfellow?"

"By the shores of Geetchi Goomie," he laughs. "And the falls of Minnehaha. But I don't know American poetry. In my country I studied Homer in English and Tasso's *Jerusalem Delivered* in Italian. The Italians occupied my country in World War II."

The cashier is jovial, charges me for both soups.

"How do we get to the Ohio River?"

She looks back to the waitress.

"Don't ask me," the waitress shrugs.

"Just go down this street here," the cashier says, handing me back the change. "Two-three blocks, you'll come to it."

Out on the street he hands me two dollars.

"But yours was only $1.06," waving the bills away. "My treat!" But he's firm. This is important to him.

"I want to see the river. What time do you have?"

"You have a half an hour!" he shouts as we run across the street.

"Half an hour? What time is it?"

"1:30."

"I have forty-five minutes!"

"Well, yes," he laughs. "To be precise you have forty-five minutes."

The end of this street looks like a freeway dead end. Two huge stadiums in the sky on the other side. Maybe one's a court house. Again, he's hesitant.

We get to the end, to a grassy bank that overlooks a huge gulch of freeway interchanges.

"This morning I heard a great story about the Ohio. You know Mohammed Ali, the boxer? He won the Olympic Gold Medal when he was twenty. He was Cassius Clay then. He came home a hero to Louisville Kentucky from the Olympics in Rome, 1960.

He took his friends to the big restaurant downtown. The owner told him he had to leave. But I'm Cassius Clay, he said, showing the gold medal around his neck. The owner said I'm sorry, that makes no difference, you and your friends are not welcome here. Cassius Clay stormed out, walked over to the Ohio, yanked the medal from his neck and threw it into the Ohio."

"Well, let's go this way, since it seems in the direction back."

Everything in me wants to go the other way but I say okay. That wasn't such a great story to tell him.

Then I spot an historic marker on the long green flank. "First, I have to read that."

I dash between the cars, run up the steps.

A few blocks north of here was Fort Washington from which the Opening of the Great Northwest began.

A little map on the bronze plaque.

"The river should be right here."

Above me, over the freeways, a young tree loaded down with large white sweet-smelling flowers. So beautiful, so sweet-smelling I'm stunned. A real Southern tree. A symbol almost.

I pick one blossom. Velvet white.

Run back down.

"Can you remember what it's called?"

He puts his nose to it, but can't.

We head back.

"The Arabs say Solomon lost his magic ring while bathing in the Jordan and forgot his wisdom."

"Do you want to go back to your country?"

"Yes." He says this hesitantly. "My mother and my sister are still there."

"Is the military dictatorship strong? Could there be an overthrow?"

"They are strong. The Russians are supplying them."

"They are Communists?" Military dictatorship, I had automatically thought right-wing dictatorship.

"The military is the same everywhere, whether left or right. Ethiopia is Communist. Sudan, next door, is Capitalist. Under both systems people are starving. My uncle was prime minister."

We walk another block.

"Are the conditions of the poor people better now than before?"

"I didn't approve of my uncle's government."

"Would you go back with the new government in power?"

"I don't know. You see in my field, Political Science, and with my name, they would follow me as soon as I got off the plane and if I said anything they would arrest me."

We walk along.

"If I go to law school here, it would not be recognized there. Three years here. But I'd have to do two more years if I went back."

Now I'm worried about where we are. *The Shawnees were made of the brain of God, the French and English of his breasts. He's lost too. The Dutch were made of his feet, the Long Knives, the Americans, of his hands.*

"The real division is city and country. Both systems cheat the country people. There's a saying in my country, starve the city dwellers, they riot. Starve the country dwellers, they die."

I recognize the block of white pillars and then the huge granite building on top of them with eagles and angels and George Washington and Thomas Jefferson and Ben Franklyn sitting on the roof. No sign of those three jive-ass guys we passed under. I wanted to ask them what that building is. 800 Broadway. The plaque says Cincinnati was the dictator of Rome, 458 B.C.

"Thomas Jefferson said you have to have a revolution every seventeen years to keep democracy."

"Imagine," he says, "building these enormous elaborate structures in those days! In Minneapolis they have so many and they were all built in about a ten year stretch. 1880s. They didn't have heavy equipment in those days. And they were out here on the frontier."

I see his land then. Our cities are old to him. His excitement is delightful, the only time fear leaves him.

"I think the pioneers were Crazies. *Real* Crazies! Imagine bringing in this granite on horse and wagon!" Though I said wagon and horse, typical of the dyslexia I've had since my trip back to LA in February. I felt my left brain switch to the right as I went over Gaviota Pass.

"It must be terrible to be in exile from your land." Saying this I feel my land under me.

"Yes."

"What happened to your uncle?"

"He was put before the firing squad." He sort of laughs, making a submachine gun gesture. I feel the impact of the first bullet. "And my aunt. And my brother. And my cousins. Oh, many in my family…. Everyone." Moving his hand over the street. "Everyone."

The bullets keep hitting me one by one. I feel them hitting him one by one. We are walking by a block-size hole, fenced in. I see the bodies, I see ours falling in.

"They killed all the males," he says on the next corner, "of the royal family. They put most of the women in prison. In Akaki, it means *'end of the world.'* Selassie's daughter and granddaughter are there."

On the next corner he says, "At this point I have to decide what I'm going to do with the rest of my life. I've been afraid to move."

"What is your name?"

"Teshome."

"Teshome?"

"Teshome."

"How do you spell Teshome?" I ask half a block later. The skeleton of death is in the shaman.

"T-e-s-h-o-m-e."

"What does it mean?"

"The Appointed," he says. But in a few steps, corrects himself. "No. The Anointed."

We walk more blocks.

"Teshome, I'm sorry."

"Oh." He brushes it away. His exquisitely long black hand over the street.

In a rush I'm telling him how I'm on my roundabout way back to California where I left my dog and van. "My dog's never been without me. I have to call him tomorrow and see how he's doing." On the whole walk through Cincinnati I had been seeing Albion Moonlight running the streets ahead of us. Streaks of white lightning leading us.

He's telling me not for the first time about his dog, but I'm still lost at the firing squad wall, his family up against it. Does he tell me what kind of dog? I see a happy orange-and-white dog, a small shepherd mix running through the rooms of a marble palace.

"How strange it is, how dogs know what's happening. The morning I was to leave my dog started howling. He howled. Is that how you say it? I hadn't told him. I thought of that later on the plane.'

"You ought to go to California, Teshome."

"I am," he shook his head. "My aunt lives in LA. She owns two beauty salons. She must be doing well. She says she'll pay my ticket if I will come."

"Did you lose access to your family's money?"

"Oh, yes." We keep walking. "I haven't gone to see her because I've been afraid to move."

The first time he said this I laughed with him, told him how scared I was traveling in South America, how determined I was after that to learn how to go out. I'm a poet, I love the world. But how could I say that when it hurt so much? But now I see how different his fear.

The station is up ahead, we both see it now. The Greyhounds are pulled in diagonally, humming exhaust. He points to the top of the hills, says he thinks he'll visit the university since he has two more hours. I write my Washington PO address on the napkin I'd written the name of my book, pulling it from his jacket's breast pocket. *"Please write to me, Teshome. I'd like to know what you do with the rest of your life."*

We embrace.

For a long while we are in this embrace outside the swinging doors of the Cincinnati Greyhound Bus Station, the velvety-white, sweet-smelling Southern blossom in my right hand around his velvety-black neck, the skeleton of its death already turning a burnt color, a sort of heliotrope-night color. Magnolia.

"Magnolia! Teshome," I say laughing. "It's called magnolia."

That's how I say good-bye.

At the doors, the long, high-ceilinged Mediterranean-tiled room bustling with travelers, I pass a young black albino woman.

Our eyes meet in the turnstile.

Hers hit me like bullets.

There used to be a girl years ago in MacArthur Park at those antiwar demonstrations. A blond Negro girl more white than me.

Old Kentucky homes come over the horizon
four hundred feet above the Ohio

I never did see the river, the long knife flowing. But I saw your child, Sheba.

Black and comely
o ye daughters of Jerusalem
as the tents of Kedar
as the curtains of Solomon

On the last day of our marriage he was body-casting a young beautiful woman for a full-body bronze sculpture she'd commissioned as a gift for her husband, said to be the richest man in Oregon. Kiki had made two previous appointments in October but both times she canceled at the last minute. Each time I had to admit that I didn't want it to happen, which was something for me, the pliant wife who wanted to please her husband, the well-published poet who wanted to psychicly support her husband of lesser renown. Kiki's cancellations were like answers to my prayers. He had body cast several other young, rich women that summer and was making a reputation among them, this work a needed boost in our income—the summer my father was dying and I was gone much of the time nursing him.

There was the time I showed up from Florence Oregon, the five hour drive, unexpectedly. He met me at the door of the enormous barn that was his studio. "Be prepared. There's a naked woman in there."

She was long and thin, white skinned and black haired. Linda, an Olympic swimmer, he'd tell me later. She lay on her back on one of his work tables plastered to it, her middle a sharp concave, her black pubic hair flaring above it. Prepared, I greeted her. The dabs of white plaster in the shape of his fingertips coming down her shoulders, under her arms, just beginning to cover the small pointy dark-nippled breasts, the ribcage to her waist to her navel and dipping to the slight curve of her right hip—this was a partial body cast. Saran Wrap and Vaseline under the plaster. For the stuff to set you have to lie perfectly still. She lay perfectly still, delicately glowing in all the black grease, machinery, metal, the huge virgin beams, the big masculine mess of the barn, her eyes following me like a trapped animal. The image of Jesus nailed to the cross rose from deep within. And ever since her image plastered to his table has been one of the images that haunts me in love making. For the following week her plaster cast floated in the bath tub in cold water, forming. Every time I went in there I had to look down on her again. Later, I'd see in my mind the final bronze piece in the entryway of her Lake Oswego home over the Willamette River. I'm not a jealous person, but I see now I was breathless with his betrayals and cruelties, with my denial of them. Hurt for all he excluded me from. I wanted to accompany him to the installation in her home, see his final work there, the Willamette flowing by. I loved her too, and him, the sculptor. I'm not jealous, but that was his accusation.

Once something came out of me, maybe a gasp, a widening of my eyes to him in question. He railed that I could damage his art if I let out one more negative vibe.

Her two young daughters were there too, running around, playing in the dark fantastic place. Later we learned that she'd been pregnant, despite her concaved middle, adding still another ineffable dimension to it all.

Then that day in early December. My father had died eleven weeks earlier. Kiki called, she was in Tualatin, on her way.

Hunter at the time was doing what he considered his major life work, five bronze and neon pieces combining the shapes of high heels and irons. I teased him that this organic shape that repeatedly came out of him when he free-drew in search of his next creation must be from early childhood of watching from the playpen his mother iron in high heels. The Lounge, a small room in the barn with bed, TV, portable electric heater, computer, served as privacy from me in the bus, our living space. Displayed on a high shelf dominating everything was his collection of antique and/or otherwise bizarrely shaped high heels. I teased him that he had a foot fetish. I read to him a *Ms* Magazine article about Chinese foot binding, which upset him. That Kiki was a ballerina in the main Portland ballet company and married to the tennis shoe founder was no doubt part of my perplexity.

When she drove her shiny red thing into the wrecking yard, I was washing the breakfast dishes. Through the front window of the bus we lived in, above the steering wheel, I watched her red shoes, which was all I could see of her, coming down the gravel. Prepare yourself, wife. You have to take this.

I stood in the doorway of the bus above her, greeted her. Hunter came from the Lounge which he'd been heating for her, where she would soon be naked. Her red shoes below the bus door suggested, however slightly, the pli`e position. He explained to her the problem of a full body cast.

"The only way a full body cast can be made, with the wet plaster, is by your being in the prone position. Lying down means the breasts fall and flatten out. There is no way to plaster the breasts in an upright position. No way to get a true form of the actual woman, a true body cast as she actually is upright in bronze. You understand?"

"Yes, I understand."

She was sweet and nice to me below the bus door in her dainty red shoes, my husband in his heavy work boots. I watched them disappear into the barn.

Now I understand that he set this up to get rid of me.

I rushed to my trailer studio, heart pounding, drafted a story called "Stripper." The trailer was parallel to the barn wall right against the Lounge. Occasionally, I could hear the low hum of his voice talking to her. She was lying on the bed on her back. He was Vaselining her, wrapping her in Saran Wrap. It was my first experience in years of writing fiction. I wouldn't read it for eleven years, on the day after my mother died, though I threw notes into that file, *Stripper*, regularly. And regularly, at odd times, I remembered that fictitious story.

After four pages I met him back in the bus, our shared living quarters. He was out of Saran Wrap.

I was thrilled for the opportunity to be a part of the creation, to be a participant, for the project to be ours. I drove the several miles to Fred Meyers, bought boxes of Saran Wrap.

He greeted me at the barn door, a heavy sliding metal thing. He slammed it shut. "You can't go in."

And said something so deadly, so hurtful, so personally cruel I can't remember what it was. Except that I had to get out of the place, I was creating bad vibes.

It was about eleven that freezing Saturday morning. Through the metal gate of Aries Wrecking Yard. I turned right, sort of crazed, gunned up the muddy road, through patches of woods, beneath parts of hillsides not yet excavated, past the gravel pits, past the shooting range. This was the weirdest place I'd ever lived. The constant bang, pop, explosion of guns, the dynamiting, the grind of cement trucks, the roar of trains down the tracks that bordered the east fence, miles of vast holes with standing rain water, frogs, and at night a roaming, howling band of coyotes. It began to snow. Out to 99W, I turned east, sped past the Q-tee.

It was Saturday noon when I walked in.

Coming from even my home in Aries Wrecking Yard, there's no preparing for the sight of a naked woman playing pool and dancing among a bunch of dressed men. Or for drinking wine at that time of day which I proceeded to do.

I sat at the bar. Watched her work. In clothes she would be labeled fat. Without clothes her beautiful form and color were breathtaking. Bleached blonde but no doubt a true blonde— she was pearl, she was luminous. She wore clear plastic and rhinestone four inch high heels, and a sheer fuchsia-pink scarf that she flung and wavered as she danced through the smoky air. She bumped and grinded in the classic way to the juke box. Once she danced over to me, very friendly, which helped to relieve my self-consciousness. She said her gig is Saturday noon because she's the favorite of the Latino immigrant farm workers.

They were pulled up around three tables, about a dozen men. They were small, young, tired-looking and drunk. Glassy eyed in lust of her.

She played pool with them. There is nothing like the sight, it's hardly just a visual experience, of a big naked blonde woman wearing only clear plastic, glittering high heels, a cigarette in her mouth, playing pool with a bunch of dressed young men.

And then she danced again. Truly the Goddess. High heels necessitate arching the back, shift the pelvis and open the vagina.

This time when the tune came to an end she took the bar stool beside me.

She had her third baby six weeks ago, she still has her baby fat. Her body, well, depends on your tastes. These guys like her because she's fat, because she's lactating. Not many clubs in Portland would hire her now, in this shape, but these guys make it here all the way from Woodburn to see her just cuz she's lactating. The scarf is to sop up the dripping milk.

She assumed—and this made me feel better—me the old witch-bitch-wife of the artist with the beautiful models, Kiki on whose breasts in the prone position he was dabbing plaster this very moment—that I was there looking for a job. This explained to her my pen and paper. She proceeded to tell me the politics of the different clubs in Portland, the working conditions, the legal and sociological facts—the kinds of guys. There's only two places in the whole county that's tolerable anymore of the variety of shapes, the Q-tee and another place I didn't get the name of, just that it was in the Northeast area, out by the airport.

She drank gin and tonic and I drank white wine and the Mexicans drank Tecate and tequila and all this made my heart slow down, made it hurt less, made me understand more, and love more, my husband and his work, his beautiful fantastic art, his beautiful fantastic models, our beautiful fantastic artist world in Aries Wrecking Yard. He just has a hard time, I thought, because I'm more well-known as a poet than he is as a sculptor.

She had to go soon to nurse her baby, she pumped her milk into a bottle for her while she worked. She told one horror story about the place, in warning, in case I got the job. Something about being in the cubicle stall of the Women's and one of her bosses forcing cocaine up her nose, or something into her arm. But even then she didn't abort, just kept dancing into the eighth month. This was when her reputation began among the Latinos.

Something really bad was happening in my marriage which I was handling by denying it. My father had just died. I stopped bleeding the minute he stopped breathing. It'd been eleven weeks. I hadn't had a period since. I'd worried that it was menopause but this couldn't be, I was too young, I'd always assumed menopause wouldn't happen until I was in my fifties, like my mother (though she took the big hormone shots), and I've always loved my period, celebrated it, my fertility, so this possibility felt deadly. When we first met we talked of having a baby, that's why he wanted to get married. It must be sympathy with my father and his prostate cancer. It must be sympathy like men have sympathy labor pains. And I'd just completed a book-length poem and as always when completing a major project, the doors fly open again. I was wondering well, what next? I was yearning for something new, for something I'd never yearned for before. Fiction. So I was getting into it here on the bar stool next to this naked lactating blonde stripper, Latinos bent to the pool table, the bartender behind us looking for an application for me. In this Saturday noon middle-aged moment of my life I wanted to let in fiction! What the fuck.

I told her yeah, I was looking for a job, how much I missed the work, how there's nothing, nothing that can replace it. And I let her, so naked in her pearl white baby fat, see my naked truth: the profound weariness of my flesh. The Women's Clinic had diagnosed it as traumatic menopause, my estrogen count higher than most teenage girls, no doubt my period would start again. But in fact, in just a few hours, the moment he kicks me out, the very last drop of blood, ever, will trickle from me.

Driving back, down the potholed, deep-puddled five mile road, the application in Psyche's passenger seat, my period started. What a relief. And I'd drunk enough wine, also, to do the right thing, what I should do, what I must do. Just go home. It's my home too.

I slid open the enormous corrugated aluminum door. Walked down the long barn. It was once a pig barn, a slaughter house. When raining Aries smelled of pig urine.

I got to the little room, the Lounge with the irons and high heels. I knocked. The door opened.

He came out, pulled it shut quickly.

He needed toilet paper.

Yeah, sure. I'll go back to Freddy's, I'd love to. I was out of tampons.

The front part of her was floating in the cold water tub. The breasts not fallen as he had warned her, the breasts big and beautiful, with very large nipples. Must be silicone implants, I couldn't help but think.

Jiggles, a more upscale strip joint than the Q-Tee, blinked neon tits, arched back, and ballooned ass to 1-5's ten lanes below and to us in Fred Meyer's mall. The Mormon Temple towered behind it. For years there had been efforts to shut Jiggles down. I sat behind Psyche's wheel. How to understand the image that floated above the parking lot. *He's got me drugged, tied up in the back of a big diesel parked behind Jiggles. There's a line of men waiting outside. He's rounded them up, is charging them.* Maybe I should go to Jiggles next.

Now I think he was impotent. At least often enough that this was some of his issue. He'd never let me know that. That our sex life had diminished was my fault. When he kicks me out that night his last words will be "You're no longer erotic to me."

Back in Aries, it was no longer avoidable. No excuses, chores, errands, no getting rid of me, my getting rid of myself, no going into fiction, nothing was going to arrive now to stop me, no phone call canceling the appointment. There was nothing left to put itself in front of this moment, not even prayer. I made myself do it.

I stood at the small window of the door, stared in. She was pressed up against the wall, her beautiful behind billowing out. Both arms were up against the unpainted sheetrock. He was working, sullenly, waist level on her back. Dabbing, dabbing. Dabs like the schoolmarm angrily punctuating your sentences. She was maybe five feet two or three inches, but she was beautiful. In my aesthetics it's difficult for a small woman to be beautiful rather than cute but maybe that's about clothes. That's what I remember mostly, her dark tanned astounding naked beauty. (Why do we wear clothes?) Dark blonde, almost a redhead. I never saw her pubic hair; her front will always be bronze in my mind. Her flesh was taut, barely gave as he slowly came down with the dabs of plaster. Her butt seemed to bloom out even more as he meditatively, methodically, slightly sadistically, pushed the plaster into each square inch of each bronze-colored buttock, into each Pygmalion pressure point.

I stood there, paralyzed. This was art, not sex. Lately I'd been researching the model and the artist, the history, the archetype, the facts. Hunter left his first wife and baby boy for his first model, Beatrice. I remembered the Rodin sculptures at the Maryhill Museum on the Columbia River Gorge, right where it turns from sea forest to desert. The exhibit—the penciled handwriting beneath each sculpture and photograph seemingly in a woman's hand—told of his rage and disgust for a model's changing form, she being pregnant by him. I found the Henri Moore exhibit at the Portland Art Museum intolerable. Previously I had loved Moore's work but suddenly I was insane at his smooth round headless clumps of women, all so alike. I wanted to scream and never stop, I wanted to wreck his world-regarded, expensive art. We had a ferocious fight about it before we got out of the place. I was beginning to have impossible feelings that sculpture is a lowly art. Pygmalion hated women—that's the first statement about women in Western art. He sculpted women to perfect nature, God's work. Sex, not art. Sex as in pornography.

He will say of Kiki, "She acted so bravado, but I saw that she wasn't that sure of herself." That was one of the breakthroughs, seeing that his way with me was his way with other women. He searched for her weakness. He needed a sign of her weakness to feel like a man.

"There's the aspect," I sort of laughed, "in this gift to her husband, of his having to deal with the fact of another man's hands on her."

"Oh, yes," he said. I saw that he dug that, his power over one of the richest men in Oregon.

"Let's vow to keep it holy," he said our first night, after first sex. He regularly spoke of the Sacred, regularly insinuated that I was failing the Sacred.

"What do we do now?" She asked him when they went into the barn.

"Well," he said. "Take off your clothes."

When we fell in love, I returned to Port Townsend for a week to get my stuff and say goodbye to Patrick. When I returned there was a photo of his previous woman—just weeks before me—that had not been there before, over his desk, naked, on one of their trips to the Eastern Oregon desert where eventually we would honeymoon. She'd been pregnant, he'd insisted she have an abortion, then left her as soon as she had it. The photograph remained there for the three years I lived with him. When I opened my eyes in the morning, I opened them to her.

All this subtle, low-fever pain and a lot more—like Beatrice, his first model, coming to Aries one day when he was gone to inform me of the Hunter Sister Support Group, of the two dozen women she'd met with for years to heal from the devastation of him, assuring me that he's not malefic but a malefic force is in him to seek out powerful, beautiful women in order to destroy them, that no matter what I knew of love and feminism, it was inevitable, the exact same thing was going to happen to me, right down to the words he'll use to kick me out, "you're no longer erotic to me"—but I didn't even then suspect that he was having an affair with the photographer and assistant of the woman who married us. The girl he met at our wedding and fucked between our instructions and vows. Who photographed us taking our holy vows. Keeping it holy for me was a dream come true. I'd prayed all my life for such a man. So the more he questioned my love for him the more I loved him.

He lost his virginity when he was fourteen, in John Day, high up in Eastern Oregon. He and his father and crew were asphalting the Dixie Pass through the Blue Mountains. They were guests of a physician there, who showed him the knives he used in surgery. That night it happened in the front seat of his daughter's pickup, up that high mountain pass. She was old enough to drive. It was snowing. He hardly knew what happened but in the morning there was blood all over him, his cock, his thighs, his clothes, and forever after he saw the surgeon's knives when he had sex or just studied women. He never saw her again, didn't remember her name, but soon afterwards he hooked up with a hooker higher up in Sumpter and fucked all summer so incredibly that to this day he had in the barn a horseshoe-shaped bronze ashtray he'd taken from her cabin, as memento, to never forget.

On the day after my mother died, eleven years after my father died, also on the beautiful Oregon coast, I went straight to that fiction file, "Stripper," never opened before.

Hunter is working on the swimmer he cast that summer

my father was cast in a neck brace, the summer he was dying, the prostate cancer riddling his spine. She is cast on the table, Vaselined, Saran Wrapped and plastered, all the work of his hands, his fingers in a precise riveting punctuation to every part of her torso. He has the other guys in the wrecking yard come in to witness, he loves lording it over the outlaw redneck mechanics, the lowlife he managed to escape by becoming an artist. They hover over her, masturbating, he doing all the technical work. This for her own good, too. To make her come, too. His leather apron over his otherwise naked Herculean body, protecting, maybe concealing his small penis. (What if penises were fashioned as breasts are for all the world to know and judge?) In making her orgasm you have control. You are Pygmalion perfecting nature. He got Beatrice to leave her son.

Sometimes I'm the one in the Lounge being dabbed, sometimes it's Kiki, she's pressed against the wall and with his pinched-together fingers is sensuously pressing dabs of plaster into her behind, gesturing to me at the window in exasperation that now he must plaster up and under her buttocks. He's sorry, but of course he has to do this, for art's sake.

But mostly it's Linda, the other woman, the Olympic swimmer, pregnant in the deep cavern of his studio, metal and grease, blacksmith and welding tools, her boy and girl playing, sculptures and nude photos of his former women, the smell of pig urine, how he works on women in hopes of finding one he can perfect enough to love. Be the creator of even her desire.

Tsagalalah, She Who Watches

Tye and I walked home from the party through the dark fall streets of Denver. As we made love on the floor I found myself back in the Pendleton Oregon bed of the mother of my ex-husband.

Before Hunter and I went out for New Year's Eve, I lay on the bed waiting for him as he talked with his mother in the front room. His low sensuous voice hummed his ascendancy, the problem of father now, the drinking and gambling debts. Her voice hummed too, joy for the gift of conversation with her son, the unexpected gift of their conspiracy. We'd been married three months but he'd not consummated the union; this will be the first, and was probably the last time we made love. I was a page into a story from the year's best short stories, about a girl in Mexico on a kitchen stool, maybe twelve or nine, a man coming in, unbuttoning her shirt. When Hunter came to the bed and began to make love to me I came quickly. He pulled away, snarling "I hadn't even gotten inside you." I heard the oldest tone, my father questioning my integrity.

It wasn't that I was not with Tye in Denver, but suddenly the room was Hunter's mother's. Her room swept out of me from a place it was stranded as image, rose on a wave, was released by Tye's touch. After the separation from Hunter our scenes presented themselves in the new light of his betrayal. I was made to relive everything. With this new love in Denver I thought I was purged. I hadn't been thinking of my ex-husband, the memory was not erotic, it presented itself as warning. Each time the promise approached, the room of Hunter's mother approached. The lumpy two beds made as one, the ceramic knick-knacks, his first sculpture, an owl. The cute furniture, early American. And genuine relics, the black antique bag of little bottles, his preacher-physician grandfather's homeopathic remedies, the large black Bible on the bottom shelf. The sermons across its back pages sometimes floated the bed with the family trek from the West Virginia/Virginia border to pioneer the valley west of Mt. Saint Helens in Washington. The grandfather, long dead, who, it had just come out, raped Hunter's older sister, Eleanor. And maybe him, I dare to think now. Their mother too I can't help but think.

The next day, January One, they watched football. I took his car out the Cayuse River Road to the Umatilla Indian Reservation, climbed the Blue Mountains he hunted as a boy, hoping to find the source of the river. I stopped at the historical marker. Chief Old Joseph was *Twaeet Tuekakas*. He died in 1872. Chief Young Joseph was *Hinhamtuyalatkekat*, which means *Thunder Rolling in the Mountains*, or maybe *Thunder Strikes Out From The Water*. I didn't know why but I was driving to Thornhollow, the remote eastern corner of the reservation, to the cabin where the bodies of two women were found last week.

As always I felt shame—maybe the word is self-conscious—to be on a Reservation. Tourist. Voyeur. The shame, orders from everyone, but greater, my respect had always kept me from the people and places of my mother's Native American side, lost rivers running through me. This time, New Year's Day, I would not to be stopped. I held the story of the murdered women ripped from the paper beneath my right thigh, my map, the Blue Mountains like white hands cupping the round faces coming at me down the wet highway. Past the Yellowhawk Health Center, the mailbox of Red Elk.

I wasn't remembering any of this. Tye and I were walking home from the party through the dark Denver streets when I saw that the university was built on a rise, hard to detect in suburbia, but a rise which would have dominated everything on this river plain back then, two miles east of the South Platte.

It was a major burial ground, a poet student wrote, which is why the psychic happens here, why the shadow of an Indian kept appearing on her bedroom wall and in her poems. I wasn't remembering this but each time I came near, Hunter's mother's room came back, the orange and brown knitted squares of her afghan on top of us.

Up against the eastern flank and St. Andrews' Mission, *"Tutilla since 1847,"* where the Whitman Massacre occurred, one of the few times in Western U.S. history Anglo settlers were massacred rather than Native Americans, I realized I was on the wrong road, turned around and sped back down. The clouds circled the rolling hills like memory. I turned north, the Cayuse River so deep in loam, old cars and camper tops stacked to hold back its floods, only occasionally did its silver flash hit me.

I couldn't say I was lonely, that would be his sneer, "narcissistic," "romantic," "sentimental," but the gold fields of winter cut by bronze crevasses, the twisted strata of the mountains, gasped horror and grief. I felt like the moon probing the woods, the globed hills of wheat stub and snow patches, the seeded circles of farmers as far to the west as the five visible peaks, Jefferson, Hood, Adams, Saint Helens, Rainier. My elevated body felt as if it was entering the Ring of Fire. The demand that I drive until Sally became Salaha Owega again, Elly, E-Ahnee, and John Jackson, Saloli Wodi.

I descended the ravines he hunted as a boy. "No!" he'll cry when we separate. "I never thought of hunting from the perspective of my prey." His mother had been on those hunting trips killing too. His first break had been to sculpt the owl. "It's because I was a hunter," he said in shame of Pygmalion who sculpted Galatea to improve God's creation of women. I didn't hear those words until Denver. When it rose up, volcanic memory, I realized I'd been his target.

The road forked. I came to a dilapidated store deep in the sticks. An old white woman in there. As white as me. Alima. I bought lukewarm coffee, couldn't speak, though I wanted to. Back in the car, behind the steering wheel, I wanted to write, *"Yesterday on your mother's bed we made love like I was a girl."* On the page before this was a note I'd written on our visit to the Pendleton History Museum, *"Alima, a Umatilla Reservation word (Cayuse and French) meaning mixed-blood Indians, half breeds. Meaning "the people in between."*

After our attempt to make love, we went dancing at the Elks Club with Eleanor and her new love, Luke. Luke was a rodeo cowboy who'd just been released from prison for molesting young boys. A gifted story teller from his prison years, he entertained us. The orchestra played and retired couples danced romantically the forties and fifties around us. Weeks on the range tending and driving cattle—modern day wranglers with diesel rigs. Against the whole town, the State, his absolute stoicism, Eleanor believed him innocent.

When we first loved we planned a child. And so we married. In my fidelity I couldn't think the marriage would fail, that it was part of his seduction script, but now I drove to Thornhollow to see the place where the murders occurred, as if the configuration of air, grass, trees, rocks and cabin would reveal the flaw in our marriage, what was really happening. As if moving into place, the pain of not knowing had become more unbearable than knowing, would generate the unraveling. On the switchback up I saw in my mind *Tsagalalah*, the 10,000 year old giant petrograph, *She Who Watches,* on the Columbia River west of here. I saw the ancient wedding ceremony, the couple swimming north across *Che Wana* (the Columbia) he, Yakima, having swum it south to marry her, Wasco-Sahaptin. I saw Madame Dorian, an Iowa Indian (only her English name is given on the history marker), the second-known woman— the first being Sacajawea—to come west overland. I saw her hiding in the Blue Mountains with her two Alima sons all the winter of 1811-12, after their father and two other white men of the Wilson Price Hunt Party of the Pacific Fur Company were killed on the Snake by the Bannock. I heard her keening to them deep inside the cave *they will never find us.*

I found the cabin in Thornhollow. It was set back in weeds from the road, broken against a broken fence.

The twenty-year-old was found first, on the bed. Her mother found her. A resident on the reservation all her life, she was covered by a blanket with an eagle feather placed on top. A search of the cabin indicated "violent activity," bloodstains and something that tipped them off to the grave outside, a thirty year old Yurok from California, and to possibly another, as yet unfound, the third, still missing girlfriend of the rapist-killer.

Now it was morning. I apologized to Tye, told him of my ex's mother's room coming out of me, the two murdered women.

"Yes. I could feel you open up."

He demonstrated with his fingers, a man who says he wants to love me, the round of my vagina.

"It was incredible." He pulled away. "But then, nothing happened."

A year later, my marriage over, I returned to the Gorge on a reading tour of *The Book of Seeing with One's Own Eyes,* drove up the places I'd traveled with Hunter. I felt like a salmon finding my way through the ocean to the river of my birth. I had planned for the giant petroglyph *Tsagalalah, She Who Watches,* to be the cover of the book but my publisher insisted on the European *Delusions of Grandeur,* a Magritte painting of a sculpture, a naked, headless and armless Venus, her torso sliced up. I was to give my last reading in Elgin in the northeast corner of Oregon, where the Grande Ronde and the Wallowa meet, not far from the Umatilla Reservation. That night I slept in Psyche, my van, on a back street of the small town.

In the morning I found the Elgin Pioneer Café. An old guy in a pickup pulled up beside me, some exchange from his window, me as always friendly, smiling right into the old coot's leering face saying he'd love to betray his wife for me.

Packed with ranchers and cowboys, a couple was arguing in the booth in front of me, their chronic hate exploding in spits and whispers over their white ceramic plates of eggs and steak.

And a girl about twelve or nine on the stool at the end of the counter, her steamy, pouty, run-away face mirrored in the big window onto Main, sipping coffee. I felt myself as every man in the room, I heard my mother crying, I knew again the family dictate that he be the one to turn his daughter out.

The back of that girl sitting on the stool still occasionally rises in me in the act of love. My husband. Molten lava. Tsagalalah. She Who Watches.

Psyche and the Vidyahara

Through the entire two-and-a-half year affair with Tye I was recovering from Hunter, the hurting, obsessive, black reliving of us, but I came to love Tye and love him more as time went on. (Men have always told me that their problem with relationship is just the opposite of what almost always happens to me: time, familiarity and the mundane kills the love rather than deepens it.) I enjoyed being with him immensely. He was a Taurus too, my first, and the easy fusing of our Venusian sensuousness was something. In the beginning he couldn't enter me. "Sharon, please understand. I can't come inside a woman." That was easy—love is meeting the other, however they are— and he certainly made up for his handicap in other ways. And actually it wasn't long before he was joyfully maintaining an erection inside me to climax.

Maybe all Taurus' are kinesthetics. I so loved him physically. (I'm a visual too. I come to adore my love with my eyes.) He was tall, about six foot three. From the broad shoulders of his slightly humped back above his narrow hips he looked like a bull (like a bull Picasso would paint). I don't naturally think in such ways or easily value such—love is meeting the other, whoever they are, however—but probably he was the best lover I ever had—well, up there with Ĉelo. Tye was porous. He melted into me as I melted into him and we both thrilled to this. We did things I'd never done before. He'd quote Alice, his first great love, "Anything's allowable as long as both consent to it." He liked for me to stand over his face, my feet straddling the sides of his head, and masturbate. It felt a little lonely up there, exhibitionism not my thing, though I appreciated being seen as no one ever had and I did it for him, it so thrilled him, and that felt great, and then the great throbbing waves would come and he always exclaimed that it was the most stunningly beautiful thing he'd ever seen. Curious to finally check it out, especially after Hunter and the S&M accounts of his past, with a lover I trusted, I allowed him to handcuff me once, but just as I suspected it was a total, ice-cold, panicky turn-off. I love playful rough sex but no doubt thanks to my father I don't have an ounce of sexual masochism in me. Freedom is my everything. (And I don't believe the passivity and lack of revengeful anger in my other behavioral patterns is masochism either, though I understand that's the easy assumption of my S&M culture.)

Tye was a Marxist and a poet; it was a relief to be with someone both politically and poetically hip. In between lovemaking we had great conversations, sharing our stories of childhood, sweethearts, heartbreaks, hometowns and places. He told of the painful early loss of his father, his unhappy mother whose death he was still grieving, his juvenile delinquency, his evolution from Northern California redneck to San Francisco and Northwest poet, politico and art collector.

The most important event of his life was his participation in the Civil Rights voter registration movement in the South in 1963. He'd mustered his courage to do that (and it was of that mustering that he seemed most proud). He told many stories of that summer, of being in Mississippi when the three white Civil Rights workers were murdered. And then he fell in love with a black woman. Alice came to him one night when her husband was gone wearing only a silk negligee. He was preparing to sleep on the couch. She sat down next to him. She guided his hands to her body. Eventually they married. They were married for many years. He fit easily into black society, both politically (Black Panthers) and as her husband. He came to believe that he was black too, and passed as such. That must have been who his disappeared father was, and why the pull to the South was so strong that dangerous summer. When he told me this I saw it too. Then I always saw it, though in his life now he was never taken as black and wondered if it hadn't been wish fulfillment back then.

One night they were sleeping in the backyard of a friend's San Francisco apartment when suddenly he knew he had to get out of town. Maybe he was getting hooked on heroin again. Maybe he ran to save himself from that fate again. Maybe he ran from the law, the Black Panthers, the dope deals. Whatever, he ran from Alice and the marriage too. But he never denigrated her in any of the slight ways he did other former loves.

One of Tye's core stories, to which he often returned, was that he lived in the same apartment as Janis Joplin and Big Brother and the Holding Company in the Haight in 1967 or 8. "The Dead were in and out. What can I say?" he'd shrug. "Janis got hooked."

"What women don't understand," he told me more than once, "is that they are nothing to the power of drugs. Nothing. A woman can't hold a candle to that lure, to addiction."

He'd read me his poetry there on his floor mattress, Chris Isaak's whining, self-pitying bluesy bitterness against women playing from the room below, a slight snag in the sensuous mood. A Marxist but he was a poet of what I've always called right-wing poetics. His poems were University of Iowa Writing School Straight, the fetishistic first person small *I* poem of the 50s-80s era, with nothing of his political vision or hint of an aesthetic from that vision. University writing programs are taught by poets, sometimes fine and successful poets, who to maintain the job must teach a conservative poetic.

"How can your poetics be contrary to your political beliefs?"

"Art transcends politics," he'd laugh, dismissively.

"Ethics is the mother of aesthetics," I'd quote. "Marx said that when the Revolution happens the King's art will fall off the walls. Not by capitalist decree but by collective consciousness. That stuff will just no longer please as art, but be blatant testimony to imperialism, greed, class." Then I'd add, "Of course

I'm not a Marxist, I could never be a card-carrying anything, not even a poet of any particular school."

There was a young woman after Alice whose heart he broke. He didn't understand why he betrayed her, but he did.

But in the exquisite poems about her she betrays him.

"But you said you betrayed her?"

"Yes, I did, but that doesn't matter for the poem."

In my poetics of truth it does matter. If I responded with this it would have been playful. Creativity is a fragile thing, and maybe especially so in him. "Writing poetry," he said more than once, "saved my mind."

My new book of stories was being read by our friends. He praised it in literary terms and contexts, citing passages and telling me why it's great and important. But then after lovemaking he started pleading "Please please don't ever write of me. Promise me you won't." I promised. That was easy.

Some amazing things happened between us. My sister, Donna, ever on the warpath against me, fumed about my entire personality changing with him, shrinking into a little adolescent, cuddling and cooing. She didn't know the half of it! Our first Christmas Eve morning, at my urging, and Tye, inspired by my new chapbook, *Oedipus Drowned,* about my fifteen year old son witnessing the drowning of a fifteen year old girl named Joy, Tye found his long-lost son, Chehalis.

Chehalis' mother, Dana, drowned. She drowned in July 1975 in the Clackamas River on a picnic with Tye, Denny and the guys, and baby Chehalis. She was drunk. He had taught her to drink as a way to break her heroin habit. He raised Chehalis for the next two years, another accomplishment he was proud of, but then Dana's mother sued for custody for him. In court she claimed her daughter was an addict and a prostitute and so who's to say if Tye was really the father. Well, how did he know? With that he just fled, losing Chehalis altogether and himself for a long time. And yes, no doubt, Grandmother would be best for the boy.

I went down to Ashland for Christmas at my mother's new house, she having recently lost my father. Tye followed a few hours later. He was ecstatic. The grandmother had allowed the sixteen year old Chehalis to find his father. Chehalis not only looked like him but had been told everything; the grandmother had even found some of Tye's published poems for him. Then, just hours after his arrival in Ashland, a phone call informed me of the drowning death of Salmon off the coast of Baja. Salmon, my son's age, was River's son, a Mendocino woman friend and poet. This news was shattering and loaded with all sorts of coincidences, including the fact that Salmon's bride was from Ashland (which I learned from the newspaper obituary), and that I shared my first book publication with him when he was a fourteen year old fisherman and short story writer. That night, sleeping with Tye in my mother's new house, in grief and shock, I made milk. He was sucking my breasts when he gasped, "Milk! You have milk in your breasts!" It was true, it was dribbling from his mouth at my nipple. It was my pain for Salmon, pain for River, pain for his Ashland bride alone on the boat waiting for her groom to surface; pain for Chehalis and his drowned mother and the fifteen year old Joy, pain for the Child, all children that night celebrates. I was writing *Son*, I was reading my journals for the first time; it was memory. We called my milk our Christmas miracle gift.

Tye took me to Europe my first time, mainly to visit my daughter Shawn. She'd been there for over six years, had established her adult life there, but I'd been unable to garner the money for even a visit. Returning in February, on the bus from Portland International Airport to downtown I suddenly got a glimpse of the Pioneer Cemetery in Rose Park. I had been watching for this small graveyard since moving to Portland to live with Hunter—well, actually from before in all my traverses back and forth from Port Townsend, Washington through Portland.

"Wow! There's the cemetery ...." I started, rising from my seat.

"There's the cemetery Dana's buried in," he was saying simultaneously behind me.

Discovering that it was on the grave of his son's mother that I made the decision in July 1976, all those years earlier, to continue the journey with Charley in order to write *Hard Country*, my epic poem, with its main focus and climactic destiny of Charley's drowned mother was stunning.

Tye worked in Alaska four months every summer as a tree planter. After I put him on the plane that Mother's Day I drove straight to the Pioneer Cemetery, right there, just outside the airport entrance on the old trail down the Columbia, the original Oregon Trail to what became Portland.

I went right to Dana's grave. It was the one held in my mind. It was almost shocking, hard to believe. Charley and I spent all that afternoon at separate ends of the cemetery, me in profound misery over the loss of Max, my ulcer erupting again just as when my husband George, the father of my children, left. How would I be able to stand traveling with another man? I ached for my kids in San Diego at Donna's and grandparents.' I wrote in my journal, I copied epitaphs and drew headstones, trying to decide whether to go or not. Out of that writing came the poem "American Angel of Death" and then the decision to go with him. More important to me than the poem was the commitment to make the journey across the country, to try and write a big poem about Charley's suicided, drowned mother, about the drowned woman. I wanted to find the woman's heart drowned in America, to make something of my love that both George and Max had rejected. Now I lay down on her. *Beloved Daughter, Dana Lynn Kinkaid, 1948-1975*. It didn't say she'd drowned, I hadn't known that. I was high on my love with Tye, high on this astounding discovery and coincidence. I was in celebration of life, all of it, death too. With such amazing coincidences you could almost believe there are cosmic connections, even meaning, even life after death. This time I wrote to Tye from her grave.

He called me at my mother's from the BIA's Fairbanks office, told me I could not write him any more letters. My writing made him think and that wasn't good in the hard labor of the bush. He was especially horrified that I celebrated the funny bugs crawling out of Dana's grave and over me.

I had a lonely summer in my van Psyche, on the coast of Oregon mainly. I'd more than accepted making the promise not to write of him, but now I couldn't write to him. Which meant, I painfully discovered, that I couldn't write anything. Four months of writers block.

But when he came home we met again in extraordinary ways, physically and mentally. I spent most of the winter and spring with him in Northwest Portland. In the last minutes before we separated for the summer again, after our usual fantastic lovemaking, which turned out to be our last lovemaking, he said, "Look. I have to tell you something."

He guided me into the corner. Out the window was Portland's most beautiful bridge heart-shaped to the Willamette, and on the wall was an original Francis Bacon painting he'd bought in London. It was a painting of a very distorted baby in a crib. The baby was unbelievably ugly, demonic-seeming, yet looked a lot like Tye. Sometimes I saw it falling off the wall.

"I'm about to go crazy again, Sharon. I can feel it coming. I'm about to go crazy on you. I'm trying to warn you so that when it happens, and believe me, it will happen, you will have at least this. I am about to do to you what has always been done to you by the men you've loved, by the men who love you."

Well, I'd never been warned before, not by my love himself, anyway. (But men right then, with my publications, started telling me things about themselves so outside the male code that even my son would gasp, "I can't believe a man told you that!")

"I want you to understand I can't help it. I'm mentally ill. I want you to understand why." He was breathless, close to sobbing.

"You must promise me to never utter a word of what I am about to tell you?"

"I promise." I meant it. I keep my promises unless he betrays me.

"When I was thirteen my uncle, my mother's brother, sexually molested me. And he kept it up all my teenage years. This is why I became so crazed and hooked on drugs. What can I say? This is why Alice was so important. A male is different I think than a female. I think the sex part is more confusing. I mean I got off on it as you say you didn't with your father. I don't think a guy can help that. And I could not tell my mother; her brother was all she had.

"I'm telling you this, Sharon, because it's inevitable: I'm going to betray you. And then I'm going to blame you. I can feel it coming. But this is why. This is why everything. I'm telling you this because I can't help myself but at least you'll understand some. Telling you this is the only way I can love you now."

Later I learned that he'd been betraying me all along, that between our wonderful acts of love, when he'd disappear out the door, he was running down to his old friend's apartment directly beneath us, crying "Save me from her, Denny, she's crazy!"

All the world's a stage. I was finding myself on a lot of them and some were turning into disasters, in similar mystifying ways as the ones with my sister and father. I didn't fully register the disasters. Or rather, I tried to see my fault in the situations in order to learn how not to make the same mistakes again, I fought back when it seemed important, and then I let go, refusing to buckle under, be waylaid in my quest at the moment, which was the intent, my father's, my sister's and my critics'. Water off a duck's back, turn the other cheek, kinesthetics are unable to hold a grudge, this is what happens when you go public, love thy enemy as thyself. I've always been asked how I can be so open, so brave. "To thine own self be true," my mother lectured from the bathtub when I was in the sixth grade, telling again of Daddy turning his back on Richard Nixon, Nixon's outstretched hand to him to shake. Nothing's more dangerous than going along with the crowd. "Be the good you want in the world," Gandhi said who never met a person for whom he felt the negative. This is what we must do to better the world; the old eye for an eye is to be complicit with the enemy. We want a better world for ourselves, for our children. (It is very difficult to accept that there are those who don't.)

In July I was at the Tibetan Buddhist Naropa Institute, in Boulder, Colorado. I was to teach *Autobiography of the Soul* for the Jack Kerouac School of Disembodied Poetics. That summer session they had Ecology and Latin America weeks, both themes of mine, but, for whatever reason, I was put in Performance week.

Naropa, I discovered, was in the throes of serious crises, their leader Chogyam Trungpa having died of alcoholism, though the rumor was AIDS, the same summer my father died, and having passed the mantle of the organization to an American bisexual man definitely with AIDS, Ozel Tendzin. The deeper crisis was in the new master having sex with uninformed disciples, and the organization, including its famous poets, knowing and not stopping "the spiritual practice." Tendzin was now on his death bed, having just been flown from his retreat in Ojai to the main AIDS hospital in San Francisco.

Naropa has a history of controversies, the controversies usually involving sex. There was Peter Marin's *Spiritual Obedience* in *Harpers*, Ed Sander's *The Party,* and Tom Clark's *The Great Naropa Poetry Wars* and other writings verifying the much rumored story of a Halloween party at Naropa's lodge in Snowmass. "It was a wild party," Marin wrote, "Trungpa smashed, necking with a disciple and leaving teeth marks on her cheek, ordering his guards to strip a sixty year old woman and carrying her around the room and other scenes of merriment." Then, annoyed that the poet W.S. Merwin and his Hawaiian poet companion, Dana Naone, had retired, Trungpa ordered his guards to break through the plate glass door of their barricaded room. Merwin, a lifetime Pacifist, slashed wildly at the attackers with a broken beer bottle, inflicting serious wounds on several. At the sight of blood he stopped and the pair allowed themselves to be taken downstairs to the Halloween party. At Merwin's protests Trungpa threw sake in his face and shamed Naone, a fellow Asian, for consorting with a white man. Then he ordered his guards to strip them. As Naone screamed for help, "call the police!" the hundred disciples watched in silence. Only one, named Bill (or possibly Bob) King, tried to intervene; Trungpa punched him in the face and the guards dragged him out. Finally, the poets stood naked and huddling before him. Trungpa labeled them Adam and Eve and demanded they perform the sex act.

Trungpa's Tail of the Tiger Commune, the first Tibetan meditation center in the United States, was just a few miles north of Plainfield Vermont where Max, the kids and I lived in the early Seventies. The local word was to always pick up hitchhikers because Tail of the Tiger was a CIA front and Trungpa's disciples were on the roads with orders to pick them up and drive them to the Commune for him to rape. Then I saw Trungpa on stage at Goddard College. He was thirty-four, drunk and obscenely disdainful of all of us. He sat on a throne in a dark business suit looking like a fat combination of Hitler and Hirohito. His disciples knelt to him calling him "Your Highness." His drunkenness was a test—a Zen koan, of "crazy wisdom"—that only the spiritually superior could pass. He drank cans of Coors, one after another. The rumor was that not only was he sponsored by the CIA, but the Denver-based Coors Brewing Company whose owner was head of the John Birch Society was helping him to found a new institute in Colorado. For all this you could feel the thrall of most, the wanting to follow orders, to obey the parents like children. I liked Trungpa's book title, *Cutting Through Spiritual Materialism,* but all the rest made me want to puke. Where had these folks been since the lesson of Germany?

I arrived a week early to partake of Pan America week— thirty Latin American poets flown in! Though early, I was given an apartment immediately. My roommate, Maria, was an American poet and political activist who in a headlines trial had just been found innocent of smuggling illegal immigrants into the United States. She was found innocent on grounds of First Amendment violations—the prosecution had tried to use her poems to prove her guilt. She'd married the major reporter of the trial the Saturday before in San Francisco but now, she laughed, she was spending her honeymoon with me. And having an affair all week with a poet she'd met Monday morning. He'd let himself in our door, tiptoe up the stairs to her room on the other side of my wall, and they'd make love. She made it clear to me that her bridegroom, whose phone calls I regularly picked up, must not know. I remember sitting straight up in bed one night realizing I was experiencing shock. Maria was a leftist hero in the political struggle of Central America. That she was deceiving and betraying her new husband just as Hunter had me at the very moment of marriage, the pain from which I was still reeling—well, it's not that I'm a prude, or a dummy—but I was and am mystified and hurt by such clashes in morality, in behavior. She actually seemed to relish my being a witness to her infidelity, as if proving something. Maybe that she wasn't trapped? By husband or prison.

Maria left at the end of the week and then I had the apartment to myself and my work week began.

On the first night of Performance Week Anne Waldman gave a three hour lecture on ecstatic poetry, on the Shaman tradition of invoking the gods. She'd studied in Bali where ecstatic poetry is at the spiritual core of the culture. Along with this goes (or used to) the tradition of the scapegoat in certain villages, where every year an old woman is chosen and over a week's time chased through the alleys, roads, and market places, the villagers falling into chanting states of ecstasy as they stone her to death, purging themselves of the year's accumulated sins. Margaret Mead's famous 1930s film of a Bali scapegoating was showing every night of Performance Week.

Anne is one of the great, original performance poets (if you can take her hissing snarling ranting style). She concluded the lecture by reading, in her ecstatic orgasmic performance persona, Amiri Baraka's poem "Rape the White Girls" as an example of the tradition in American literature of calling down the gods. And then she also read the Haitian poet Rene Depestre's Sixties poem with exactly the same refrain repeated over and over: *"Rape the white girls/rape the daughters of the Southern white judges!"* When it was all done, there was stunned silence—I mean we were mostly white and half of us were "girls"—except for Victor Hernandez Cruz who clapped "Yeah, Leroi!" (Amiri Baraka was born Leroi Jones.)

The headline of the Boulder paper that night was "Rapist on the Bike Path!" It could be seen in the newsstand on the patio behind Anne as she read. Reports of the rapist, a black man, had been front page news the whole proceeding week. The dark Bike Path was the path most would take back to the apartments. On my first day I'd been encouraged to use this tree-lined shortcut. "Aren't there usually rapists on the bike path?" I laughed, not knowing there actually was one, but I always took the lit, populated, if long-way-around path. I had in my lap the results of my first day with my students and many of these, by both the males and the females, were stories of early rape and other sexual abuses—very common results when the assignment is to write an early traumatic memory. I waited for someone else to respond. Any audience I'm in someone will do the right thing, and do it well. I knew better than for it to be me. Any words of mine, outside a prepared written one, would only cause confusion and accusations. I assume this is because of my speech difficulties, my words in childhood having been so often slammed back down my throat.

But no one did. Allen Ginsberg and Jerome Rothenberg jumped to the mic and responded to various scholarly points of Anne's lecture. Then we were about to adjourn. No way then could I not speak up. No way could I betray my students, their stories that I myself had elicited, burning in my lap.

"Before we go," I said from my back row seat, "I want an invocation for us white girls." The place went completely nuts. Pandemonium! Ginsberg jumped to the mike, accused me of calling for censorship.

"No," I explained. "I am not calling for censorship. But I'm afraid now. Of being raped. I'm afraid for my white students. I want a blessing from this group, for all of us white girls, to ward off the powerful negative energy just called into this room."

A black man rose and spoke unequivocally against the invocation to rape. A student, a blonde girl, spoke in support of the need for a blessing invocation. But the scholars overruled—in the name of the national issues of freedom of speech, the importance of everyone being able to write, paint, sing *anything*; Baraka's whole poem must be heard to judge its intention. Ginsberg and now others kept repeating that I was calling for censorship. "This is exactly the issue of censorship," Allen said, "going on with the NEA and Jesse Helms." He was the president of the new International PEN committee formed to fight censorship's rise including the Iranian government's *fatwah* death sentence on the novelist Salman Rushdie. There was his own situation, he has a lot of fuck-the-boy poems. As a gay writer, there was a new threat to his *oeuvre,* his life's work.

An old European scholar on The Ecstatic jumped up and said "To be honest I prefer pornography to short stories because it's more effective."

"Hysterical identification with ideology is always risky," Anselm Hollo said into the mic, "but if we exclude the expression of any state of mind, opinion, or emotion as ideologically incorrect, we're in trouble, or end up with nothing but Susan Polis-Schutz, the female counterpart to Rod McKuen."

"There's a rapist out there on the bike path," I protested, "and his powers have just been evoked. Anne's invocation was a success. I'm thinking of my students. Let's have an invocation now for the white girls."

"Will you give yourself your own blessing?" Anne asked, sounding as tired as I must have sounded.

"No, I can't. I'm disempowered by the violence put on us by those poems. The group must do it."

"Oh, for Christ sakes!" Anselm Hollo shouted in the most patronizing tone. "A goody-goody! Somebody, pul-lease, escort the girl home."

"I am not for censorship," I said again, slowly, clearly. "Out of those guys being able to print that stuff, bring that stuff out in the open, being able to vent publicly, came the Feminist Movement."

"I'll take her home," Ginsberg said. "The truth is, for art's sake, aesthetically, I'd like to see a snuff film."

"I want to walk home by myself," I snapped back. I didn't say go see Margaret Mead's snuff film, it's showing all week.

As we were leaving Jane Fonda's and Tom Hayden's daughter, a very white girl, the one in the Zen movie, *Baraka,* ran at me shouting, "Racist! Racist! Don't you know you can't talk that way?"

As it turned out, I went home in Ginsberg's limousine. The

driver was a bald headed white woman with a big bone in her nose named Simmons; she'd just gotten out of Bellevue. In an eerie way she seemed an incarnation of my great grandfather, the Lumbee/Seminole Christopher Columbus Simmons. Allen was telling me of his former student Andrea Dworkin, and what a bad turn she's taken with feminism, mainly with her infamous book *Intercourse* asserting that sexual intercourse for women is always rape. "Have you read it?" I asked. "She says that only once, a small phrase in a long anguished poetic riff about rape, nothing like the insistent "rape the white girls" of Baraka's and Depestre's poems. Have you read the extraordinarily beautiful essays in *Intercourse* on Joan of Arc and James Baldwin's homosexuality?" Simmons, her bald head gleaming under the dome light, winked at me in the rearview.

Allen was staying in the apartment next to mine on the second floor. We kept talking over the balcony railing looking down to the patio below. I asked him if he knew Robert Kelly's poem "A Map of Annandale," a justification-for-rape poem that I'd found in my teaching bag that very morning. Coincidentally the note on it says it was reprinted from the Fall 1965 issue of *Silo*, the Bennington College literary magazine, "ably published" that year by Anne Waldman. I told him that the only play I'd ever wanted to act in since high school was Amiri Baraka's 1964 *Dutchman*, about a beautiful crazy racist older white woman named Lula (one of my names), rumored to be based on the poet Diane di Prima, who taunts, then murders, without consequence, with collective immunity, a young black man. I told him of being a part of the Peace and Freedom nominating convention in Richmond California in 1968 in which Eldridge Cleaver was selected as our Presidential candidate. Cleaver had just gotten out of San Quentin for raping white girls as a political act which he aptly explained and apologized for in his book *Soul on Ice*. I said my urges toward this subject are no doubt related to my own history, are attempts to understand

and find ways out of our rapist culture. Maybe this is true of Anne too.

"I'm an anarchist," I said. "Freedom's healthy. I don't believe in censorship, as difficult as that gets sometimes. As long as there's repression we're stuck, we don't know what's going on, we can't evolve. To print for all the world and posterity *"rape the white girls"* exposes the sick feebleness of that reaction and helps us to get on down the road to real solutions, to sanity and freedom."

But even so I could not seem to communicate to him that I wasn't calling for censorship.

Now I know that as a disciple of Trungpa, Allen Ginsberg, one of the founders of Naropa, an actual defender of Trungpa's Merwin and AIDS debacles, for all the important poetry and work he did in his life, was an advanced disciple of the Nyingmapa tradition, a believer in the spiritual lineage through reincarnation of the holy, infallible, one-living master; that is, into obedience and power, sadomasochism and hierarchies (always misogynist), not democracy, not communication.

"Trungpa is questioning the very foundation of American democracy," he said. "Naropa's Vajradhatu is an experiment in monarchy. Trungpa like the Pope is infallible. Humiliation by the teacher of the student, by the victor of the loser, is sacred Tibetan tradition.

"The Merwin incident," Allen continued leaning over the railing, "was not a mistake, but a lesson the meaning of which the disciple is not wise enough to decipher. Trungpa was about to teach Vajrayana, a form of what is called "crazy wisdom," in which the mind is freed of moral shackles, and all action becomes play."

I could hardly believe my ears.

"In the middle of that scene," he said, bringing up the Halloween party, "to yell 'call the police'—do you realize how vulgar that was? The Wisdom of the East was being unveiled, and she's going 'call the police!' I mean, shit! Fuck that shit! Break down the door! Strip 'em naked!"

In the morning I received a letter from Tye accusing me of all sorts of absurd but hurtful things, including a poem that seemed based on that funny sex act of ours. He who had once sighed to me in adoring, joking allusion to the now famous Naropa quote about Merwin and Naone, that I was "overcompensating physically" wrote
Thighs
blood cut white
where the moon
wiped its knife....
Silver blades carve
as she writes
her bleeding name
across the maniac's face.
But there was also a barely-legible scribbled note thrown in.
Please stop me before I destroy everything between us. I'm out of control now- Please just one last post card with a kiss of forgiveness on it—love, nothing more. When I heal, when you come back from Europe, we'll be friends again. I love you still too much. Tye

My reading was Tuesday night. I read with Jerome Washington and Xam Cartier, both black. (Naropa hadn't qualified last year for NEA grants due to its all-white faculty, students and poet guests; there'd been a serious revolt among students who formed The Student Union for Ethnic Inclusion which was behind much of the best energy of that summer—the Latin American and Ecology weeks. And clearly, I see only now having written this, behind some of the vehemence against me. "Rape the white girls" was Naropa demonstrating that it wasn't racist, the sexism so blatant they were blind to it.)

Xam is an Oakland novelist. She read a chapter in a jazz cadence about a blonde who rips off black guys from black women, a black society groupie, basically. This was a hate-Blondie chapter. She did start by saying that by the end of the book the narrator and Goldilocks realize they're sisters, but sitting in the front row the reading was hard to take. The description of Goldilocks' hair was a description of mine.

Jerome read from the *Iron House* stories, of his years in Attica. Coincidentally his book had just been published by a press run by close Mendocino friends. Then I read. In my selection I was responding to the charges that I'm a "goody-goody," that I'm for censorship, that I'm a racist. I selected pieces that are of sex and political consciousness.

I started with "Forests Forever Is a Feminist Issue," which I had just written for Redwood Summer, for Judi Bari and Darryl Cheney, bombed that spring in Oakland by, we all were convinced, the FBI. Darryl had asked me to write it in the effort to make ecofeminism more broadly understood by the sexist, redneck element in the Earth First! movement. Several male professors walked out immediately, protesting the word "feminist."

It was hot. Half way through the reading I took off my leather jacket (which I was wearing in the first place as a security blanket) and kicked off my sandals. Jack Collum rose from a back aisle and walked out, shouting that I was strip-teasing. Strip-teasing! Rather the opposite of goody-goody. I was in Performance, but I didn't remove my jacket as performance. My mother had bought me the sandals to go to Naropa, I was wearing them for the first time, they were preventing me from reading well.

I read "Photograph of the Virgins on the Sun" from my South America manuscript of my daughter and me at Macchu Picchu as an example of my own ecstatic poetry. I read from "Beauty and the Beast" in my newest collection of stories, when the fourteen year old narrator refuses to kiss the beast but dancing with him recognizes her own bestialness that he's aroused.

And I read the story from "The Warriors," the pending rape scene that pivots on the moment when the Oakland black gang leader spits in the narrator's face, "Are you prejudiced?" "No!' I answered, smiling truthfully at him." They let me go.

And then, to show further that I'm hardly for censorship, I read the part from "El Niño del Salvador: A Love Story" when the narrator swallows a few drops of her Salvadoran lover's urine. In this early 1980s story the narrator encounters a black Salvadoran on the run from his country. He's walked to the mid coast of Oregon from San Salvador. He tells her the story of his brother next to him in the lineup who dies when the soldiers gun them down. They make love and she discovers his body is riddled with the scars of bullet holes and surgical scars. Just that afternoon in the bookstore she'd opened the latest *Mother Jones* to a photo essay, a full page color photo of three decapitated heads of young people, very beautiful people, two men and a woman, all three of them with castrated male genitals in their mouths. Just their heads in the corner of a hut in El Salvador. She had the magazine in her backpack. It was an image she'd seen more than once as a girl, from World War II, from Korea, from Algiers, from Vietnam. There was a film she saw in college of a battleground of heads, just rows of men's heads with their genitals in their mouths. And photos of the American practice of castrating black men and then hanging them with their genitals in their mouths. And photos of the U. S. Cavalry wearing the scalped vulvas of Indian women on their hats. We don't just kill each other, we sexually mutilate each other. This is not aberrant behavior. This is not individual with the killer, or nationality or race or time or place. This is human. (At least, the male human.)

My story is a conscious working with the contemporary controversies about pornography. What is obscene? The narrator drinks a few drops of his urine as play, as sex, as love. She shouts *"Take this, you decapitators and castrators!"* It's done in the spirit of countering that image she's just seen in *Mother Jones*. She takes the most despised aspect of the human body, its waste, and honors it, loves it, celebrates it. What is obscene? War is. War is male hatred of the body that women make. Her relationship to urine is different than, say, a pornographer's, and maybe most men's. The first time she held her son he peed in her face. Sheer joy of life! Annabella Plurabella! She changed diapers for years as a mother. Her gesture is a healthy, life-affirming act. Going to the limits, yes, but done in love, done in the spirit of humanity. (Needless to say, this was before the AIDS disaster.)

Afterwards, as I came through the volatile crowd, Ginsberg hooked his arm in mine and said, "That's the best poetry reading I have ever heard in my life!"

And then he whispered, "I have never tasted urine but I hope to before I die."

In the audience that night and at the party afterwards were several of my University of Denver students from the previous fall. They were there to deliver the news of a betrayal that was far more devastating than Naropa's stake I was being tied to.

We were in a crowded Mexican bar. I felt good about my reading but Ide Hintze whispered, "You should know there are many who are not happy with what you did tonight." Ide was at Naropa that summer to learn how to set up a similar writing school in Vienna, Austria. "There hasn't been a writing school in Europe," he kept saying, "since Sappho, twenty-seven hundred years ago." I was talking with Ed Dorn, an early poet hero, who'd been teaching my epic poem *Hard Country* at the University of Colorado for years and had recently written a favorable review of my latest poetry collection, and then to Stan Brakhage, the film maker of *The Act of Seeing With One's Own Eyes,* the autopsy film that inspired my story of the same name that C.D. Wright, one of my publishers, named as one of the top ten stories of the Eighties. I was a bit ecstatic, you might say.

I'm an ecstatic poet, I'm so happy to have finally gotten here. It was hard to register just how bad things were going against me.

"How dare you read about a black phallus!" A young woman (white) stormed through the crowd at me, screaming and gushing big tears.

"Rikki has been spreading it everywhere that you tried to seduce her husband and are out to get her job," Marc from Denver said beside me.

The stab was almost debilitating. Rikki, a close friend of C.D.'s, was the one who got the job for me (to temporarily replace the Denver's tenured poet on leave for impregnating one of his students and causing his wife to have a breakdown). She and her husband Guy were my only non-student friends in Denver and I'd loved them, especially her. In my last week we'd gone out on the town together and she'd confided to me her affair with the head of the English Department.

After the shock I got what Rikki was doing. Adulterous of her husband with the head of the English Department, she was afraid I'd go to bed with him too—maybe with both of them. Well, if *she* did (goddess, that she *could!*), why wouldn't I? The head and I did have one dinner date later that same last week, which I considered strictly professional. He was definitely not my type, but much more to the point, even if he had been, I'm unable to use sex as a bargaining tool. That's an act I've never been able to do. That's the power-wielding Hollywood talent scout of the second grade to whom I couldn't recite "Mary had a little lamb." "I shouldn't have told you that!" she gasped just after she did. Maybe she was afraid too that I'd write it. Guy might find out. As far as he went, he was even less my type than the head, but even if he was, husband has never been my type. That's my father, my mother's husband whose rape of me made me the other woman. Maybe she felt insulted, for her guys. Or maybe, the hardest for me to get, it's just me. If I go to bed with the head, the way she got the job, she might be replaced. Maybe telling me was deliberate too, a part of a mischief-making, COINTEL-PRO, spin-control, "crazy-wisdom," Vajrayana, doubletalk conspiracy. Once she told me of deliberately betraying the writer Angela Carter even though she was dying of breast cancer. "Of course I had to," she said, "for the sake of my own career." And of sleeping with publishers to get published, something Guy himself seemed to approve of. Wow, that people really live that way, continue to wake up and continue to breathe that way. Well, her novels reveal that they do, her writing is about life lived that way. Maybe I don't get it enough that my truth and honesty aesthetic is threatening. No one seems to get that my fidelity to my loves is higher than to my writing aesthetic. Though as I've had to learn, as I first learned with David, my sister's second husband, if you betray my sister, David, I will know it, I will be released from the promise not to write of you. My life has been altered, taken wrong turns because of the lies told to me and of me. (My friendship with C.D. was destroyed in part by Rikki's lies.) And maybe I am dumb after all. In the years ahead there will be other women friends who will excitedly share their secrets with me, the sexually free woman they assume I am, and then immediately end the friendship and spread similar lies as Rikki's about me. I haven't seemed able to prevent or counter this.

"You betrayed me and my people!" Emelia from my workshop and Peru, to whom I'd dedicated my reading of the Macchu Picchu virgin poem, was now storming through the crowd, screaming. "How dare you write of Peru!"

The next morning a man named Paul Shippee showed up in my classroom. "Of course I can see that you've been crying," he said. "But your reading was extraordinary." He was there to show his solidarity with me against Naropa.

We went to a Chinese restaurant for lunch on the mall. He was the leader of the group that had broken off from Naropa, in shock and protest to the AIDS/Disciple scandal, and editor of the group's newsletter. I was relieved to learn of this group. The big issue, he explained, after the disciples diagnosed with HIV, was that having dedicated their lives, not to mention inheritances, to this path, they were now spiritually stranded. The only way in the Vajradhatu path is to be personally anointed by the current Master in the lineage from the great Milarepa, 1040-1123; it's a system of succession by reincarnation. Chogyam Trungpa Rimpoche was discovered reborn in 1940 as the eleventh incarnation of Trungpa Tulkas. From age two he was raised to be the Supreme Vidyahara of the Sumang monasteries of eastern Tibet. Now the Supreme Vidyahara was the American dying of AIDS but still fucking his uninformed disciples. But to overthrow him would be to abandon the thousand year old spiritual path.

Something about this man kept reminding me of Tye. Maybe just that they were both about the same age and size. Then, stunningly, half way through our meal, I saw Tye stand up out of Paul still seated across from me, turn, and walk out the door. It was so real, so graphic, so Tye, I was speechless for awhile.

Afterwards we walked to his nearby house. He showed me copies of his newsletter, and letters from all parts of the world from the still faithful condemning the breakaways—spiritual obedience is fundamental. It was hard to believe in this day and age that anyone could defend such a position, especially someone like Allen Ginsberg! On the way back to my apartment he told of living in the same apartment as Janis Joplin and Big Brother and the Holding Company on Ashbury Street in the Haight in 1967 and 8. "The Dead were in and out. Janis got hooked." One day he looked out the window and saw a little troop of orange robed disciples parading down Haight and knew in the instant. "The feeling I had was I've been looking for you a long time, and, oh, there you are. It was like coming home, or something." And he told of helping to build the stupa in which Chogyam Trungpa was cremated in Vermont, of the high honor of being one of the chosen to light the pyre under the Venerable Vajra's body, and of now planning the permanent stupa here in Colorado, specifically to commemorate the Buddha's descent from heaven to teach his mother, which will be known as the Great Stupa of Dharmakaya Which Liberates Upon Seeing, and which will hold his ashes and skull.

But what about your protest movement? I didn't ask this. Could you have been one of the one hundred disciples at Snowmass that night?

I called Tye. He started in, hissing and ranting that he hates me. He wants to kill me. I'm evil. That word again, that accusation my sister keeps throwing at me, that charge again. Whatever have I done to evoke *"evil?"*

"Oh, Tye don't," I pleaded. "If you knew what is happening to me this moment, how devastated I am, you wouldn't. Surely you wouldn't. I know you said you would, but ….well, at least not now at this moment."

Then I blurted, "I just met an old friend of yours. Do you remember Paul Shippee…?"

"Satan! Get thee behind me!"

I hung up.

Then sank deeper in the hole, spinning in the hurt and bleakness of it all, unable to even pray for tears or insight.

Paul was blown away by my connection with his old roommate, Tye, who he hadn't heard of in twenty-two years. "Part black, right?" Later in the week he said he'd been trying to call him but getting weird responses. "Does he still carry a gun?" I think Paul wanted to be my lover but, mainly because of Tye, that wasn't a possibility with me.

I was urged to come to the big tent Thursday afternoon for a talk by a visiting Zen Meditation Master from Asia somewhere. Anne and Joanne Kyger and Bobbie Louise Hawkins all individually urged me to attend.

The tent was packed. A young man in a dark business suit entered fifteen minutes late, sat down, and farted. Then, lifting his butt to the mic, he farted again. "I don't know anything about poetry," he said to us poets. "But well, it's like being horny when you're fourteen and fantasizing fucking a woman's body." Did I walk out then, or wait through the crap? Whatever, I made clear my contempt. Anne and Joanne glared at me.

There was a meeting Thursday night of the whole community to discuss what to do about me. I was at the party next door with everyone in and out from the meeting, not a single person informing me what was going on. Four official statements against me were drafted.

On Friday Tye's last communication with me arrived, another scribbled note on a two-by-three inch notebook page.

"I know now for certain that you are an evil person because you risked my committing suicide by hanging up on me yesterday."

On Friday night Jerome Rothenberg, Ginsberg and Bobbie Louise Hawkins read. Jerome read poems from his Ethno-Poetics book. Unlike Anne he performs these like an objective scholar at the lectern.

Allen read a funny but silly poem about a young Naropa boy student trying to suck him off and failing. And a poem he'd found by George Yesenin about Isadora Duncan's disgustingly flabby thighs. Ha ha.

Bobby Louise introduced her reading by addressing the difficulty of writing her memoir being Robert Creeley's ex and mother of his four children. The room of Naropeans lunged forward in their seats, *don't write it Bobby*. "But what am I going to do?" she sighed, "that was my life." She spoke about truth and history and literature and the woman's movement that empowered her and her fidelity to Naropa that saved her too from the Bolinas shed without plumbing that Creeley left her in. She read a story about a woman and her four children being deserted in Mexico when the famous poet-husband disappeared with a young girl. Then she read a story about a blonde girl working in a drive-in. It seemed directed at me who as a blonde teenager worked at her parent's drive-in and has written of it. It seemed directed at the controversy about me.

During that reading someone entered my apartment and stole my leather jacket, the one that had become an issue because I took it off during my reading.

This theft was terrifying: the thief entered my apartment with a key. I'd been made to feel a fool for being concerned about the rapist on the Bike Path. The thief poured him or herself a glass of wine, making sure I couldn't miss this. That night, getting back there and finding this became one of the more terrifying long nights of my recent life.

On Saturday mornings, at the end of each week, Naropa had a Colloquium in the tent with the faculty of the week. This Saturday there were several hundred people in attendance.

Ide told me right off that Allen's apartment was robbed last night while he was reading, of about two hundred dollars, and other personal keepsakes. Mine too, I said.

We were seated at a long table in front. There had been that meeting about me, still unbeknownst to me. Bobby Louise Hawkins on my right leaned into me and seemingly with compassion whispered, "Don't respond to this. Don't ever respond. Just keep your mouth shut."

Four prepared statements were read condemning me as racist and sexist—as grandstanding, as exhibitionist, as disruptive, as ego-driven, as being guilty of the Buddhist sin of not having dissolved the self. Two came from students suddenly sitting with us on the faculty panel. Xam named the number of times I referred to the black male penis (a redundancy she seemed to miss) in my reading, labeling this as black studism. (How many times could it have been? Surely she wasn't counting the castrated penises in the mouths of the beheaded. How many times did Xam refer to me as Goldilocks in racist scorn, not as in my writing of the penis, in love?) Next she ridiculed "Photograph of the Virgins of the Sun." "How *dare* she call herself a Virgin!" (Did she not know the definition of virgin, *"she who is unto herself"* as I was most profoundly in that moment? Did she not hear the line, the narrator's to her daughter, *"Oh honey, all women are virgins because we have not yet been loved."*)

Then Jerome Washington, sitting on my left, close friend of poet friends in New York and Mendocino, put his hand on my thigh and whispered: "I have to do this, you understand. For career reasons." He read his statement condemning me too of black studism, of racism and sexism, his hand still on my thigh until I swept it off.

The dream I had at my daughter's the first night Tye and I got to her 18th Arrondissement apartment in Paris played again in slow motion across their heads. It was my first night on mainland Europe where ten million women were burned, and six million Jews, and gypsies and homosexuals and soldiers and untold zillions of all the other categories. I nightmared my daughter being burned at the stake set up under her three hundred year old building.

I still have the drawing of the nautilus shell earring I doodled as all this was going on. It turns up at the oddest times in my teaching files. The earring my mother had given me had begun to hurt in one of the three pierced holes of my left ear and I'd taken it out, placing it on the table before me.

Jerome Rothenberg's wife in the back of the tent stood up, sobbing.

"You are making her the scapegoat!" she screamed, "that we saw in Margaret Mead's film!"

I've been grateful for that.

In the concluding discussion I was asked to make a statement. I was in my far-away, pixelating place, I don't remember what I said but it seemed I did alright. According to Ide's interview, later published in Germany, Allen defended me, defended writing of "the perverse, the abysmal, the threatening, all contradictory emotional revelations." And he said to all of them, "It was the best poetry reading I've ever heard."

Sunday morning, in Joanne Kyger's apartment, waiting for the ride to the airport, we were all jolly and civilized, happy to have gotten through the week. I was still upset about the theft of my jacket and let them know this again. And about the wine.

"Allen said you were sexually molested by your father," Joanne laughed. "Being diminished in public, that's classic. That's what happens to someone who was sexually molested as a child. You have a need to be shamed in public, to take on the scapegoat role again, right?"

On August 25, Ozel Tendzin, born Thomas F. Rich in Passaic, New Jersey, in 1943, died in San Francisco after extensive retreats in La Jolla and Ojai. In his apology he said "as the Supreme Master I somehow believed that I and the people in contact with me were protected from AIDS."

I spent the next two months in Psyche, my van parked on the Mendocino Headlands over the ocean, alone, mute, missing Tye, and still in the soul struggle with Hunter. "Don't respond. Don't ever respond. Just keep your mouth shut." Okay, I just made things worse by trying to defend myself (and the white girls). Just let it go. Don't honor that crap.

Did the Cheyenne at Sand Creek have a need to be shamed in public, to have their vulvas scalped and worn on the hats of their killers, the soldiers?

Obedience begins in adulation of and helplessness to the parents. This is why the early Soviets and the Israeli kibbutz' took the children away from their parents.

What is trying to birth?

The genitals in the mouths of the beheaded. The one being stoned through the grainy streets. The father confessing. The lover going crazy giving you the gift of warning. The drowned mother in the cemetery the son being stripped of Psyche's love of Eros their son drowning in the grief of his insanity don't write of me don't write of the boy.

He called me in Ashland, introduced himself as a Portland filmmaker making a film *In Search of the Poet*. I laughed and said I'm searching for her too. He'd read my newest book of stories urged on him by a woman writer friend who said he and I were made for each other. "She's the only artist I know besides you who's still working on our generation's vision." At the end of the day's work I walked down to the Log Cabin. When I walked through the door his camera was on me. He smoked a pipe, wore a tweed, leather-patches-at-the-elbows jacket, a beret, and had all the arrogant mannerisms of a Hollywood director. No way were we made to be lovers, but friends, oh yes. I loved the first story he shared, of being on a bus in Greece on the way to a film job with Jean Houston's Goddess group and slowly realizing that the two women sitting in front of him were Jean Houston and Peggy Rubin. Realizing in overhearing them that he did not want to work for them, and so did not get off with them when the stop came. Obviously he'd seen their posters around Ashland put up by my sister.

And I loved his funky station wagon, Truth, and his big hairy black girl dog Morticia.

I was beginning to realize that with my publications I'd gained the reputation of being a woman who's had many lovers and remains undaunted by this shocking fact, a woman who epitomizes the sexual freedom of our female generation. But the fact is the man with whom I can be intimate is rare, appears few and far between. The emotional appeal has to be equal to the sexual appeal, and vice versa—there's no way around this. I've tried to get around it, there are stories in my books about trying, but finally it has to be love and it has to be sexual, equally, for me to be physically intimate. I can't tolerate sex for sex sake or sex for heart sake—no doubt this is from my father's messing with me. Only within the all-encompassing house of love do I love sex. Then I can really get into it, then it's "making" love.

For all his humble situation and artist's lifestyle there was an arrogance about Tom that was a total sexual turn-off.

He rented a storage room in a warehouse in the railroad district of Ashland, continued to make his documentary of me, but also to show interest in being my lover. After a couple of weeks I knew it was time to set him straight. Dear Tom, I love you but you must understand I can't make love with you, that will never happen. I gave him the letter at the end of a Saturday night of dancing.

He drove down to Safeway, read it in the parking lot under the big lights. He pulled out, was stopped within a block by a cop car. The cop was a young woman.

"I stopped you because you were weaving. Have you been drinking, sir?"

"No," he said. "Well, a wine awhile back. I've been crying."

She ran a make on him, came back and said, "I'm sorry but you're under arrest."

"What for?" he gasped.

"I'm sorry, sir, but they didn't say. Just that there are two long outstanding warrants for your arrest."

She allowed him to drive ahead to the warehouse, to lock Morticia and his camera inside. Then she handcuffed him, hauled him to Medford.

He called me the next morning, Sunday, from the Jackson County Jail. I was horrified. He still had no idea what he was in there for.

"Honest," he laughed. "I haven't the foggiest."

"I'll bail you out."

I'd been saving every penny for my trip to France, to be there for my daughter giving birth. That was some of the film he'd shot, me selling my books to the local book stores to scrap up the money. But jail is evil, there was no question, I'd bail him out.

"No, no," he said. "I'm a documentary filmmaker, it's kind of interesting in here."

Well, I could understand that, but still....

He wanted me to go down and let Morticia out for awhile, to feed her and get his camera, take it to my house where it'd be safer.

I got Morticia, I got the camera, I got the $200.00 bail out of the machine, and drove the fifteen miles north to Medford for three o'clock visiting hour.

"He'll be transferred by bus to Portland," the guy at the desk reluctantly told me, "probably Tuesday or Wednesday. No, today's Sunday, we've no idea what the charge is."

Visiting jails and prisons always devastates me. Filled mostly with young men, visited by their mothers and sweethearts and wives and babies and sons and daughters sobbing and/or freaking out in some way.

The man who finally came through the door at 3:30 P.M. in jail pajamas, and set behind the bars across from me was not the arrogant man I'd been dealing with. Through the bars (or whatever the barrier was, probably bullet proof glass), there was none covering him. All his posturing was gone. He was without masks. I couldn't take my eyes off him. He was beautiful— deeply, miraculously moving to me, as naked and genuine as the man I've always longed for, have always maintained an impossible faith exists.

"I'm bailing you out, Tom."

Even then, especially then, my words were a question. I'd waited with the bail to visit him, to make sure just in case he was serious about staying for the research and experience.

"Okay," he said in the tone of whatever.

"It's un-American," I snapped. "And illegal," I slapped down the twenties. "To jail a person without telling him the charges."

When he came out I had the camera going. I filmed him coming through the door to the free world as beautiful, as naked, as pure as a newborn. Then a stunning thing happened. I witnessed it through the camera's eye. When he saw me with it his mask came back on, and all the armor. Goddess, I'd captured it on film!

"Go back to jail, Tom!" I teased. "I want my money back."

Instantly, the mask came off.

We went to his fifty dollar a month pitch black windowless warehouse room along the railroad tracks and made love among the stacks, on the plywood slab that was his bed. I had an experience unlike any I'd ever had—well, there was that last time with Hunter—or have had since with any other man. Just before his penis entered me I came, vaginally.

This would happen every time we made love. His cock was like a magic wand. Maybe the shape, or the hang of it, or our particular chemistry together, I don't know, I tried to figure it, I'm still trying to figure it, it was almost bizarre, it was almost not even sexual, it wasn't a matter of foreplay, of building up, of the gradual stimulation. The orgasm was instant and deep in the G place.

Back in Portland for his court appearance he finally learned his crime—failure to pay child support. "When I couldn't be with my daughter, not even for visits, my visitations being too disruptive for the new family, the rich and famous husband who had been my old film partner, I stopped paying."

All the month before leaving for Paris, I lay in my narrow Guthrie Street bed between my high files and the book-lined wall and night after night tried to be in my body, vessel of all memory, of all experience. The courage to heal. What happened to my body? It must have hurt. The key is to remember physically. I must have felt it in my vagina. There must have been tearing.

I was seventeen. I was a virgin. I was getting married in two months. A vaginal examination was required by the state of California to detect syphilis, and, if desired, to obtain a form of birth control. I chose the diaphragm.

"Only a brute could penetrate you," the doctor said, looking up from between my sheet draped knees. I had to have surgery to cut my hymen, the thickest he'd ever seen. He told me there are women who can never have sexual intercourse, and some who can't for two years of trying. And then it's very painful.

The look on Daddy's face when I told him I had to have surgery. Our insurance will pay for it, I assured him.

It was scar tissue. I came out of the sodium pentothal truth serum sobbing.

I worked at remembering. It must have hurt. But nothing.

Then one night I was awakened from deep sleep by a piercing stab up my vagina. Excruciating, searing pain, like a butcher knife. It was shockingly painful.

In the morning I looked. A white butterfly shape spread across my vulva, the white wings flaring into the inner sides of the labia.

I picked up Tom in Portland and we made our way to Seattle from where I would fly to Paris. I was leaving my van Psyche with him for however long I'd be gone. But first I had to lead a writing workshop for sex offenders in Monroe Penitentiary. I was grateful for the last minute job and tickled about the name Monroe for such a place. We continued to make sweet love, with always the same stunning inexplicable experience, so distracting it was hard to know what was happening with him. I was beginning to feel a little guilty about this.

Judith, who arranged the job, was leading us out of Seattle for Monroe when Psyche broke down in a dangerous, steep curve in the road. We had to get to the prison by noon, then my plane by early evening.

"Don't worry," he said, "I'll take good care of her."

From Judith's car window I waved goodbye to Tom and Psyche broken in the middle of the dangerous canyon turn. The Monroe guards took the photo of Patrick's new baby boy that I used as a bookmark in my book with poems about him. "No nude photos allowed in this place!" they triumphed for finding the contraband. The sex offenders were wildly emotional. Captured brutes but like Tom seemingly without bars and masks. Some of them sobbed unashamedly when reading aloud their boy memories written in our circle. On the plane to Paris I meditated on the weird butterfly in my labia, saw out my window a white winged creature flying through the night alongside us. It was a universal joint that went out, a chronic condition with Psyche. But in all the hard miles and years afterwards, the universal joint that Tom installed in her never went out.

When I returned to Ashland six months later I was diagnosed with *lichen sclerosis*, with the strong possibility of cancer of the vulva. I had never heard of cancer of the vulva. She said I might need a vulvectomy. She scheduled a biopsy. She asked me if I'd been raped as a girl. She said I had to confront my past. She said it was killing me.

I did the research. *Lichen sclerosis* is a rare condition seen in very old women. The blood vessels atrophy in a butterfly pattern around the vagina; *lichen sclerosis* is often the first stage of cancer of the vulva.

I didn't look like an old lady anywhere else. I was still often taken as a girl. I was always carded at the dance place doors.

A packet with the history and photographs of vulvectomies came in the mail. The entire genitalia is removed, and skin is grafted, actually pulled from the inner thighs and down from the stomach and buttocks to cover the big wound.

I didn't make the biopsy appointment. Later when the

butterfly disappeared (Tom too when I couldn't make love with him anymore, his mask back on), and I began to tell friends, I'd laugh, "Thank you, Doctor but I'm going to my grave with my vulva intact." I took the chance that it was just Psyche again, her wings trying to hatch out of the worm cocoon. I knew better than to let her fall into the AMA's hands. Instead I would continue to open to my past before it killed me.

Our War

Ferida Durakovic was a poet from Sarajevo. My assignment for Ink Fish was to have a conversation with her rather than a regular interview. Vicki, my editor, thought this would be appropriate given my themes of women and war, poetry and politics, democracy, racism and genocide, my vehement anti-fascism.

1995: I didn't understand much of what was happening in Bosnia, but I knew well the near-successful genocides of Native Americans and Jews, and the US atrocities in Vietnam. The despair that washed in and out with the tides those mornings reading the single paragraphs on the back pages of the A section of The Oregonian was, for me, of hopelessness. Muslim males as young as ages twelve were being rounded up and marched off from their villages at Serbian gun point, never to be seen again. The waves roared, pounded, and hissed—how can this be happening again? When Vicki called I drove the almost two hundred mile round trip from Waldport on the coast to the library in Eugene, did as much research as I could cram in before our scheduled conversation. It'd been just five years since I'd planned a trip to Yugoslavia with Tye. Then his love ended, then there was no Yugoslavia.

Was it possible to write this story? Could I write myself as causing anger, insult, pain when I felt unconditional respect and concern, and even (impossible) hope. The reigning poetic ruled that genocide was impossible to write; write of one death, not six million. (The reigning poetic taught that there was no such thing as genocide.)

As I entered the reception for Ferida Durakovic at Sitka's Art and Ecology Center north of Lincoln on the Oregon coast, its magnificent architecture of polished wood and shimmering glass, the cedars outside dwarfing the tall room of rich patrons, I felt a wave of collective disapproval coming at me.

She was tall, thin, with white skin and dark hair, and she wasn't dressed to kill—a funky black turtleneck and jeans, huge, out-of-fashion, black horn-rimmed glasses. But right off she too seemed to regard me, dressed similarly, with cold suspicion, as if she'd been warned about me. This vanished into warmth midway through our encounter, but at the end returned with a vengeance.

Her sponsor, who had helped get her out of Bosnia to this residency, was handsome, aristocratic—well, snobbish is the right word. We talked a little over salmon and cheeses. I'd read his essay, *Beauty and the Beast,* about her and Sarajevo; I told him I much appreciated it. His pregnant wife glowered at me from across the room. He was teaching the year at Portland State. When his eyelids lowered simultaneous with his nostrils flaring, I swore I smelled the lamb that was now his vest. There was something shining on each blond strand of his hair. He spoke of the baby coming, that Portland was a stopgap—he actually said that—toward his goal of being a professor in a prestigious Eastern university and of becoming a successful writer. When I asked him about his poetry the sneer that lifted from his thick lip to his small nose disappeared, but every time the topic turned back to Ferida or Bosnia the contempt was unmistakable. Bosnia was his territory, she was his ticket out of Oregon. Their huge hairy dog, Latte, the color of coffee and milk, watched us from the sunny deck, thumping his tail.

A young woman whose skin glistened in a sheer sundress weaved in and out of the clusters of mostly older people. It was to her house we were to have dinner and the conversation.

She drove us north to Pacific City. It was a relief that the sponsor didn't accompany us.

As we drove Ferida told of watching Clinton's inauguration on TV, "those of us who still had electricity. How much hope we had, that he would help us."

Then, exhaling smoke through her nose, gesturing to the spectacular coast, she said sarcastically, "Oregon is peaceful."

"How much good it would do *this* country if he'd stand up for *your* people!" I harrumphed behind her. Maybe that was the offense, that I spoke of the benefits for us. "It would do us so much good if just one president just one time did something for the good."

"I think American democracy," she said, "is not a grown-up girl yet."

I had never been to Pacific City, a hidden fishing village tucked west off Highway One behind a tall, cedar-covered islet. The young woman's mother, a painter and long-time resident of the coast, had died in the house of breast cancer three weeks before; her mother's death was no doubt what she had been addressing as she weaved through the little groups of older people, her mother's friends. The house was done entirely in Native American décor. There were portraits, Ed Curtis photos, landscape paintings on the walls, baskets, weavings, and the classic books on the tribes shelved on the walls. I spied a rare Jaimie de Angula novel. The woman whose house this was originally had deeded it to her mother, they were longtime lovers. This generous woman had also gotten the daughter into an elite school in the East. "Brown," she said, when I asked. "I know a poet who teaches at Brown," I responded. "C.D. Wright, she's one of my publishers." Yes, she knew her, she'd taken a class from her.

"I was born April 18, 1957," the tape begins, the guitar of John Williams playing Segovia in the background. I could still smell the cigarette she was lighting. "The youngest of four children." I was taken again by her accent.

"In '59 we moved to Sarajevo, so basically I've spent all my life in Sarajevo. I'm not a real born Sarajevan, but I consider myself a Sarajevan."

"In order to help us better grasp this terrible situation"—from the beginning I tried to be careful —"I want to focus on your personal story as it unfolds within the larger one. If any of my questions are too personal or offensive in ways I am ignorant of you must let me know. OK?"

"Ok!"

"Is the fact that you weren't born in Sarajevo considered important? Does the town you were born in classify you in a certain way, does your native town mean something?"

"Yes, of course. It means a lot to people whose families have been settled down in Sarajevo for hundreds of years. So in that sense I'm a very new Sarajavan, but in a sense of being a citizen of Sarajevo, in a sense of *loving* Sarajevo, I am profoundly Sarajevan. And the man I love is of an old Sarajevo family."

"And who were your parents?"

"My father was a Partisan during World War II. He was a peasant. After World War II, he worked at different jobs like salesman, and finally he finished evening school for salesman. All his life he has been salesman and or a clerk. My background is lower middle class."

"Mine too."

"I'd rather say working class, but it's something in between. My mother never worked, she was dedicated to our education and to raising us. She has only six grades of primary school because she was a child when World War II started, and she never started again, because she married my father at the end of the war at eighteen.

"That's it, that's my background. I used to live partly with my parents, I couldn't afford, in that time before the war, an apartment of my own, it was very expensive and my salary and income from poetry books wasn't enough to pay rent, so I lived partly with my parents in our house and partly with my sister, Keka. She used to live in the now occupied part of the city, she is divorced and she has two kids. Now they live as refugees in Denmark. She got divorced, she didn't love her ex-husband, but when war started she fell in love with him again." She laughed. "It's a time-of-war story! You know, wonderful! They got divorced because he was pretty wild, and he didn't want to live with young kids—he was irresponsible. He got killed at the beginning of the war."

"She had fallen back in love with him before he was killed?" I was stalling here, wanting the story of his death, but not sure how to ask, a story I regretted that I never got.

"Yes! It was wonderful because they finally discovered that they loved each other. War is to blame for that. War—war can make wonders. War itself is awful, but what you experience during this war can be miraculous."

"Yes, because you're right there...."

"You are on the edge, all the time on the edge. Nowadays I don't want to spend my time with some people because I know what's basic, I discovered who was my friend at the beginning of the war and who wasn't. It's like black and white, you can believe?"

"I can believe...."

"Someone is very cocky, for instance. In the middle of the war, shelling is all around, everything is horrible, you are afraid, I was afraid first for the people I love, and then for myself because we were spread all over the town and it was very dangerous to go around the town to discover that some of your dear people is dead. It was horrible. I have a pretty strong feeling of responsibility and I felt responsible for them. Those moments were the moments when I discovered who I really love and who I don't love. And my sister and my brother-in-law, they finally discovered they were so foolish about this getting divorced, having fought all the time, and it was very good, but it didn't turn out very well. It's a common war story.

"He was killed mid-November of '92 and she left Sarajevo with her two kids at the end of November. It was very hard to leave Sarajevo, it was a relief operation, they finally took her on the bus."

"I remember that time. They were trying to get people out...."

"Yes. These long convoys for women and children."

"And what were you doing then?"

"I was trying to get my sister and her children on the bus!"

"You didn't want to go yourself?"

"No, no. I have my parents, I am responsible for them, they are old and they are sick. They are not alone, my two brothers are there, but I feel I am the one responsible for them because I don't have family, my brothers have enough trouble with their kids. I *never* gave a thought to leaving Sarajevo until now. There is a cease fire until May One, it is relatively safe right now. I earned some money working with foreign journalists and I could leave them some money, so it was an appropriate time to get out. I just hope I can make it back before anything worse starts.

"The relief food is from all over the world, so it is often old, out-of-date, food that didn't pass inspection, bad food. Many Bosnians are sick now, getting cancer as we didn't so much before. So many are malnourished. Some have starved to death. When the war began many young people fled. A lot of older people have been left behind. Sarajevo is full of old and sick and lonely people in cold houses."

"I hope you will forgive me for my inadequate understanding of what's gone on there...."

"Even I do not understand very well. In my youth we never even dreamed about this war which has come to our door. That is my message: nobody knows the ways of war. Something, anything can happen. We do not learn our history. At the beginning, this evil became so profound. We were so easily stepped on, life was so easily expended."

"I loved it when you said at dinner that Susan Sontag had to go there to find out for herself because it is so confusing from here. Actually, though, I'm very suspect of why we can't understand it. Why is it so difficult? I've read the papers, watched and listened to the news, I've asked people about it, and still, it's confusing to me."

"David Rieff, Susan Sontag's son, wrote *Slaughter House*, it's like *Farewell To Bosnia*. He was very well informed, he was there first. 'You should come,' he told his mother.

"Sontag, who is a member of the American PEN, brought a large sum of money into the country by strapping it to her belly. She made it by car, through all the check points. It was an extremely brave thing to do. Then she put on a play there, *Waiting for Godot*, and when she came back she did a full story on Sarajevo in the Fall '93 New York Review. So many writers have visited our country through the years. Now they don't help us. But Susan Sontag is one of our heroes!"

"She was *my* first contemporary woman writer hero, way back," I responded. "And I appreciate that someone in Congress said it's very clear who the victim is and who the victimizer is in this war."

I couldn't remember who it was no doubt because he was a right wing Republican whose stances were often appalling. But I was impressed by his informed efforts for Bosnia.

"Robert Dole, yes! He was the one who proclaimed Bosnians are the victims and Serbians are the aggressors. It was the first time in this war anyone declared this publicly. Nothing happened, but we were very happy. He claimed the right for Bosnians to defend themselves. It was a very noble step to take. Currently the Bosnian government has asked for the lifting of the United Nations-imposed arms embargo. I was once a pacifist, but I think the embargo should be lifted so that both sides can be armed equally. I don't believe it will finish this war, but it will give us a fair chance to defend ourselves. I was never a person for arms but now I want equal strength to fight back. We've lost our faith in Europe, and to a great part, in America.

Now we have no hopes, only to survive somehow.

"We had so much hope when Clinton was elected, he said he would help us, he was young, Democratic, but very soon we were disappointed. I published an open letter to Clinton in a Sarajevo newspaper last year. I said you fooled us all so skillfully. I realize now all your lies were just part of the election process. I called him 'just a propaganda hologram!'

"If I was the American president or government I wouldn't let these Serbians fool me. This lack of action is *not* about Bosnia, it's for the sake of America. But to let this monster kid around with American democracy is a dangerous thing."

Segovia soared. I felt again the Navajo blanket I was sitting on, the Pomo baskets full of arrowheads, the Hopi pottery. I will fight no more forever, Chief Joseph said.

It was Jaime de Angula's compassionate and kind priest that the California Indians hated, and eventually killed—not their cruel enslavers. When I read his novel years ago I was thunderstruck, but I understood. He was despised for the same reason liberals are despised.

"When did the war begin?"

"The official start of the war was on 6 April, '92."

"That's the day you fly back, the sixth."

"Yes, it's a kind of terrible anniversary. I came here for rest, to recharge my batteries. On April 6 I fly to Atlanta, then probably Zurich. Then I will have to just wait till I can get on a UN plane to Zagreb. It was very difficult to get out. Things are very tense again, with more and more snipers. If they start to shoot again, all UN roads and flights will be cut off. I'll have to crawl back in through the mile-long, dark, muddy tunnel under the airport. I have, how do you say it—claustrophobia?—I did not want to go through that to get out, but now I will have to crawl back through it again to get in."

"Go back for me to...Yugoslavia. I want to talk about poetry, since we are both poets, and the politics within this situation, your personal history, your education, how you became a poet, at what point the political situation becomes.... I mean such profound changes happen through there, the 80s, there's Yugoslavia, that's what I used to know."

"I used to know Yugoslavia! It was a time when I had another kind of homeland, Yugoslavia. It was my only homeland. Bosnia, my present homeland and I hope future homeland, was a part of Yugoslavia. Yugoslavia was a federal country, it consisted of six republics. Our language is Serb. Different dialects, but it is all the same. I was a pretty happy child there, in Yugoslavia. I belonged to a generation which didn't feel oppressed by any political ideology."

"Is that right?"

"You know, the generation born in '47, '48, up to '50, they were directly influenced by the new Communistic regime. We lived a kind of socialist, communist regime, but *I* never felt it as a pressure, because I had the opportunity to be very well educated. I am highly educated, I studied literature, I think I have the kind of education which the normal intellectual, the normal writer in Europe probably doesn't. Because the education system was that good. And I was a very curious child, I had the opportunity to gain as much knowledge as I could pick up.

"So my childhood was very good. I attended Sarajevan high school, I have three-four languages. It had its name, Fifth Grammar School, Sarajevo Grammar School. There used to be five of these high schools. And in '76 I started to study literature at Sarajevo University."

"Why literature?"

"Because I am fool! When I finished my university I realized I didn't want to study literature, because it's foolish, it's not practical." She laughs heartily. "It was very nice for my education, but I should have done something else, like horticulture. I love everything about flowers and herbs. Like please tell me, what is that huge white blooming plant outside the front window there?"

"Rhododendron!" I exclaimed. "The Northwest Pacific coast is famous for them. In another month they will be blooming everywhere, in the woods, on the rivers and beaches, in all colors, and there will be festivals...."

"We have rhododendron in Sarajevo, but not like this! And Sarajevo was once filled with trees like Oregon, but almost all have been cut or destroyed during the course of the war. There are just two parts where the trees are preserved, by a miracle. When I see the remains of all the cut trees, it's like seeing the dead people.

"It's so beautiful here, in Oregon, I think people must be very peaceful. Do you know what Oregon's motto is? 'She flies with her own wings.'"

I laughed. "But there are many chauvinists here, too, to use your word. Racists and bigots. I used to ponder this mystery, why rural people in beautiful places are not more peaceloving, more liberal, more generous."

"So I was young. I wanted to be *writer.*" More laughter. "I had my first book of poetry published at twenty. And so that was reason I studied literature."

"What kind of literature did you love, or focus on?"

"In high school, I finally became a young and angry intellectual, as we all do at that age. I pretended to understand Sartre and Camus and all those existential philosophies. We all pretended to understand it. The generation before me was a time of this absolutely wonderful craziness about *Catcher In The Rye,* that generation, my brothers', they loved *Catcher in the Rye,* but *my* generation was very much influenced by *Siddhartha* by Herman Hesse.

"Before the war I was a poet, in general. I was a very intellectual girl. I was young and innocent. I gave readings in all parts of Yugoslavia, in Croatia, in Macedonia. Now I am neither innocent nor a girl. My poetry is much more simple now. I think my poetry has improved a lot. To talk simple is God's gift. I think I have always been an idealist, an ordinary intellectual woman dealing with the world's troubles."

"What about women, were there women you studied? What about Simone De Beauvoir, did you...."

"Yeah, yeah, it's okay...."

"Okay...?" I laughed again.

"Everything is ok, but, ah, I was too young to understand everything they wrote. And we all knew we didn't understand it. And finally you discover something else is alive!"

"What do you mean you didn't understand it?"

"It's too hard for a young girl of eighteen... you know, it's philosophy. I'm sure you read this wonderful discourse about suicide, by Camus, *The Myth of Sisyphus*. I was so sure that I understood this text but really it was too hard. I was so young, I should have read something else, I think. So when I was almost twenty, I realized what was my kind of literature—fairy tales."

"Fairy tales! That's wonderful!" I laughed. "I received a similar education in existentialism, so I know what you mean."

I can't detect anything in my enthusiasm that could have revealed to her that I'd always disliked fairy tales and that at eighteen it was precisely Sartre, de Beauvoir, Camus and Sontag who saved me. I was dying of the boredom and fairy tale oppressions of my childhood.

"It's a little amazing to realize we got the same thing in such different worlds. In that period, myth, and fairy tales, and make-believe and the folk traditions, and certainly gender studies, all of that was taboo."

"That's it, that's it."

"It was scorned, and...."

"It was a mistake by our teachers, I think, not to pay any attention to myth, to fairy tale, to anthropology, at least. Fairy tale is a form of anthropology."

"Absolutely."

"And we all loved Antonioni as a director, because he was so macho and *blah blah blah*, and American film was *second rate* film. At the same moment I realized I loved fairy tales, I confessed to my boyfriend that secretly, all my life, from fourteen to almost thirty, I wanted to see again *The Sound of Music*."

"I've still never seen *The Sound of Music*." Actually, I think I saw it in high school and hated it.

"And *The Wizard of Oz*."

"I've never...."

"You've never seen that picture...? You never...."

"No, I never...." I was never drawn to it. Musicals have always seemed absurd to me. Unnatural. Recently I learned that the author of *The Wizard of Oz* was the governor of South Dakota who urged the genocide of all Native Americans just the week before Wounded Knee. I thought of course. That's why I've avoided seeing that thing. Somehow I knew.

"Oh, gee, I'm a better American girl than you used to be."

"No doubt," I laughed, not ironically, "in a number of ways."

Chief Joseph laughed too. And the Mojave girl.

"You know there is a stage in your life when you discover that you are something else than what you are pretending to be." She lit another cigarette.

"You asked me to describe myself at twenty. I was a very intellectual girl. No make-up. Overalls, nothing to show I am woman. My mother saying all the time to get married, you'll be too old to have a baby. I wasn't interested. I was *never* going to have a child. When I was thirty in 1988 I wasn't at all interested. And then you find out something else is alive.

"I never wanted a child. Then right in the midst of the shelling this huge desire came over me." She clutched her stomach.

"I have known this man for fifteen years. I like him, but to him we were just friends. During the shelling I decided I would go see him if I could. It was very dangerous. When I finally got there, when he opened the door, I fell on him!"

We both squealed in delight.

"Now we are very close. He loves me very much. He is an architect. I'm going back to be with him and my parents.

"And during the shelling also I wrote *Miki's Alphabet,* a book for children. I just started writing it, during the heaviest shelling I've ever seen, in so much terror, suddenly feeling so much joy—for life. It saved my mind. Then I knew art is absolutely necessary. Not a luxury.

"The Center says I can stay here, my mother said please stay there. It is for my loved ones' sake I'm here now, to get some rest. It is for their sake I must return. I couldn't bear it if something happened to anyone I love while I am gone, I couldn't. I came here to get some rest, to talk. I've enjoyed every moment of daily life, the quiet, the unbelievable beauty here. Now I am over my war weariness. I am ready to return next week."

"You are so beautiful," I said, "in your time-of-war stories. It's an important thing to know, that life is a continuous passing through stages. If this could be understood sooner we would be empowered, collectively and individually—to know that we don't know. For instance, I always knew about being a woman! My education in being a woman began in the crib! I was a teenage mother and wife. Now I'm discovering the joys of being a very intellectual girl." I laughed again.

"Partly," I continued, "for me, for you, it is that we are from people who didn't have an education, so what we're getting is something so profoundly different than what we've known, it's freedom."

"You want to grab it all," she jumped in.

"But you have no tradition on which to hang it, really, at least at first, when you're young. Later, when you've digested the education with your traditions it's very powerful. Certainly it makes you a poet!"

"Exactly."

"And a politico. Communism is similar. It had to reject and deny so much, or at least it thought it had to reject much in order to advance a certain idea."

This is when she began to warm up to me.

"Yes, exactly, and that was the main mistake."

"Oh boy, what's happening in Eastern Europe, it's so clear an example of the inevitable collapse of denial systems."

"The mistakes are so obvious." She laughed.

"All of it counts, everything that's in the pot, that has to be the lesson of the past decade. You can't repress or suppress or oppress anything because it's going to come back at you as the killer. You have to allow all of it into your political theory and plan."

"The mistakes are obvious as stitches!" She weaved her fingers together, "you know what is wrong. You are an American, you can tell what is wrong with American democracy, because the stitches are obvious. I wonder all the time how people can't see them. Obviously they don't want to see them."

"It's denial, they are refusing to see. So much of the intensity, the hatred and insanity of the Right, is plain and simple psychological denial." But alas I knew too, it's much more than that.

"And why I know that is because I discovered I knew what was coming in Bosnia, a war. But I rejected it. I denied it."

"How did you know this?"

"All you have to do to know what will happen is to read some smart and good books. You can foretell anything—please try to do this—after reading ten good books. Not only horrible things, but wonderful things. History is so simple. History is the history of power.

"And the Balkan Peninsula is a kind of mixing of the power of the East and the West. Sarajevo represented an ideal. It's not dead yet. An old old city. Multi professional, multi ethnic, *multi multi multi*. We have a very old Catholic Church, Muslim

Ulema, and Jewish Synagogue, all of which existed six hundred years before Sarajevo. The intermarriage rate is very great. Anyway I'm lucky enough, you know, there is an old saying, I think from the Far East, which says, may you live in interesting times."

"Yes," I laughed. "I know that saying."

"It is very hard for my life, but it's very interesting at the same time." She laughed ironically now. "So we felt something in the air, something started...."

"When did you start feeling this?"

"Two or three years after Tito's death. 1980. Fifteen years ago. Something started to fall apart."

"In 1980 you were still in college...?"

"I graduated that year, I graduated a couple of months before Tito's death. I was twenty-two, twenty-three, I was young, and I was *so* prepared to change the world. I was a pacifist, a member of this pacifist movement. Tito died, I didn't want to think too seriously what would happen with my homeland, because there were people whose job that was. My job was to write poetry, to be smart, to be young, and to have a boyfriend, to improve my knowledge, to travel more. I'm not to blame for all this, there are some other people to blame, some very seriously to blame people."

"What did you feel about Tito?"

"I had a great respect for Tito, even though the mistakes he made are obvious, they hopelessly pierce your eye, they always did, but I have a great respect for...a certain period of his life. It was magnificent in '48, when he refused to collaborate with Stalin, this was very good. I'm not the only one who has some great respect for him. Finally, when you have somebody important like Tito you are trying to carve his good side from his bad side. He obviously had a very bad side, much more than good, but you know I lived as Tito's pioneer, and I didn't feel his bad side. If I weren't there in Tito's time, my parents probably wouldn't have had a chance to give me an education and to move to Sarajevo and to improve our family intellectually. So I do not intend to speak negatively of Tito, it's not decent, *at least*, or at last, it is not decent.

"Americans have their right to hate Communism. They have their right to hate Socialism, they have their right to hate whatever he built, but I lived there, and I didn't hate it. And partly, you know, Yugoslavia fell apart, it's ok, but you know I have my loyalties.

"It began to fall apart...step by step. The big changes started, I think, with Romania. With the murder of Ceausescu."

She pronounced it as mostly h's and s's. I could hardly believe she meant Ceausescu, he was portrayed here as a total monster, his downfall a great victory of the people.

"I can't remember the exact year because I thought what was happening in Romania was the worst, the most horrible thing that can happen in the world. We saw it on TV, moment to moment, and we saw Ceausescu and his wife executed."

"Christmas Day, 1989," I interjected.

"...and I saw the demonstrations, I saw how some people got wild, monstrously wild, and I said this is the stuff of human ego, but I realized that there is more horror to happen, to ex-Yugoslavia. And that horror happened in Bosnia. I hope that it won't be so severe in the future, but I don't have much reason to believe this."

"Can you say what it is?"

"Can you imagine that there are people who make their political platform on *chauvinism*. Even racism. On hating your neighbor. Just because he belongs to another nation, or religion. That is what's happening there. And, can you believe, in other things, like raping women, as a political system, as a means of political struggle, as a systematic weapon of ethnic cleansing. The only thing that I used to always say, as a pacifist, is that a man who rapes just one woman deserves the death sentence. How high this evil can go, when as a policy of war, of aggressing the war with raping women of another nation— and it is happening there, I think about forty to sixty thousand Bosnian women were raped, deliberately raped during this three years."

"Yes, I've been very aware of that, the rape policy," I said, but inside I was gasping. Capital punishment is always wrong. I've struggled to grasp the depth of the horror, to not be in denial, but she was talking about my father. She must not have ever been a real pacifist. "One of the things that I've pondered, is how many children have been born from those rapes, and who are those children?"

"I know some of the stories. I know some young girls who rejected their babies after delivering them.

"They kept them in concentration camps until in high stages of pregnancy, so very few succeeded in having abortions. The simplest thing is to have an abortion if it's done in time, but the greatest number of them had to deliver a baby. Each and everyone of these women has her horror story, you know, it's tragedy one by one."

"And that is the purpose," I cried, "of the rapes. To divide and conquer, to totally devastate the women, to craze the men, to decimate a race. You have this new population growing up that belongs to no land, that is utterly alienated from everything from the beginning. And in fact this has always happened, it's always been military policy everywhere in history. There's the classic book on this, *Against Our Wills, Men, Women and Rape*, by Susan Brownmiller. The Gulf War bombers were shown S&M films before taking off, but of course this kind of thing is hush-hush, for the sake of the niceties, morale and patriotism. You wouldn't want to think of your heroes, your sons and lovers, your grandpas as rapists, your husband having sex with the enemy. You might not want them going off to war."

"And of course the opposite happened too, of women loving

their babies, however they got them, *this is mine.* I was lucky enough never to experience this, I live in Sarajevo, almost all these cases happened over Bosnia, Herzegovina, in remote villages where they could get wild."

"What happened to your parents' village?"

"I think it's destroyed. Because on that mountain we were born, these monsters have their headquarters."

"Oh, god. I am so sorry. What's the name of the mountain?"

"Romanjia. And Saseveci, little place on Romanjia mountain, they have their headquarters."

"And your parents were born there, and their parents, all the way back?"

"Yes. We have a little cottage there with a garden. My parents grew their vegetables there, during the summer, they would come home with wonderful vegetables and fruits from their garden and they were very proud of all that and it was destroyed. I think our relatives are alive but they live as refuges all over Bosnia, they don't live in their villages anymore. And of course that kind of war is called ethnic cleansing.

"Oh, gee." She started to cry a little. "It is very hard to talk about this."

"It's okay that you're crying. We can stop if you want."

"No, it's okay. It's okay."

"What do you think will happen?"

"I'm not very optimistic about it. We will have to have a mediator, the hate is too deep now. But, you know, I have some hope without any basis." She's laughs now through her sobs. "I'm just that kind of person, so all the time I have some foolish hope something good will happen. I still believe the good part of this world will realize what is at stake. The reality doesn't show me it will happen, but being fairy tales lover, I expect somebody to just jump in and make the end of my homeless story."

"Would you tell a fairy tale that's native to your land?"

"Because of the language differences it is very hard to retell some of them, but there is one folk fairy tale, about a guy who is a *fate*, actually who is a *destine,* we call it *oosod,* the word *oosod* means *destiny*, it means creature-who-decides-your-destiny. It's a very long tale, but basically if you have a problem, a very hard problem and you can't solve it, you have to put on your iron shoes, and you have to go on foot over nine mountains and over nine rivers and over nine seas over nine lakes to find this man called Destiny. Of course during your voyage you experience all kinds of things, wars, horrors, the most terrors, Orks. You meet even fairies and fairy ladies. At the end of your journey if you are good enough you will meet Mr. Destiny and you can ask him about what you can do about your problem.

"There's a story about two brothers, they both had plans. One brother worked so hard, so very very hard, but he never had a good harvest. And the other brother, each and every day he would lie down in the meadows, under the sun, and he had absolutely wonderful harvests. The first brother decided to go and ask Mr. Destiny, to tell him it's not just if he works all day and his brother doesn't do anything and gains this wonderful harvest. He managed to get over the nine *nine nine* lakes and mountains, and find Mr. Destiny. Mr. Destiny told him 'Each and every morning you wake up with bad thoughts. You begin your day not with good thoughts, you are worried all the time, you envy your brother for being so happy and having a good harvest. This is the first thing you must change. And the second thing, your brother has a wonderful daughter, she is beautiful, she is smart, and she is a child born under the lucky star. And that's why her father doesn't have to do much.'" She laughed. "Because he has a child born under the lucky star. So the brother went home and asked his brother, can I borrow your daughter to live with me for awhile? And so his niece came to live with him, and of course he didn't wake up with bad thoughts, but with good thoughts and finally he was rich. Each and every year he had good harvests."

We laughed together. Again, the Indians on the walls whooped!

"Can I ask you something that may be disturbing?" Perhaps it did disturb her. "I don't mean to attack your fairy tale, but in the spirit of trying to find the Good in the world, and where the Bad comes from, I want to ask you one thing. Is that fairy tale not unlike the way the chauvinists think? *We* have this line to the magic, *we're* lucky, *we* are not poor, we were born under a lucky star, somehow we are superior, our luck is proof of it, we have these rights, we deserve our riches."

"Yes, perhaps, but there is something very important about them, the chauvinists: *they are not happy.* They are not happy because other kinds of people, other races, religions live here and they must destroy them in order to be happy."

"It is not the same thing as feeling born under a lucky star and feeling superior to the bad luck brother...?"

"No. Even after the horrors I've gone through I can be a child who was born under the lucky star. Because I am alive!"

"So lucky star is spirit, is love, is the life spirit."

"Yes, yes, of course. To be good. To be good to other people. Chauvinist—he is evil itself. He can't be happy until he sees his neighbor of another nation dead. And I don't think he will be happy even then. Because he wants more evil."

"I understand what you are saying, but people who are classified as evil under your explanation—which is mine also—don't believe they are evil...."

"Yeah, they believe they have their course."

"I think they believe they were born under a lucky star. Somehow we have to start defining clearer what we mean by magic, and love, and good, to investigate these things. For instance in my country, middle class people, I mean some of the people I've loved all my life, would be shocked to realize they are evil to many in what they're not understanding, in what they're denying and refusing to get. In their need and their belief that they are doing right by living a certain way so that their children can have the best, can enjoy life and if their children go to college and become professional people, they were born under a lucky star, while out on the street, in foreign countries in trouble, well, those terrible people somehow deserve their bad luck. You know what I mean?"

"I know exactly what you mean, but I disagree in just one thing."

"Please disagree in all ways you know!" I laughed. "And as you said part of the problem here may be language. Even your word chauvinist—for me chauvinist is not that serious a word, it's been cheapened, I think, by its association with our somewhat jokey 'male chauvinist pig.' Perhaps I'm not really getting what you mean. I'm remembering too your sponsor's essay of you walking through Sarajevo after the War Conference of the Writers' Association in plain sight of snipers, talking and joking loudly. What you are telling me is making me understand that kind of reaction better."

"I had a very hard time to—I was not poor, but I was not rich either—to gain my education, to gain everything I achieved, but I did it alone, and my lucky star is that I don't have to be grateful to anyone except my parents who delivered me. And pushed me into the world, to become a good human being, I believe I belong to *good* human beings, so whenever I see what you are talking about, I can't understand it anymore. Because this materialistic thing, I don't have anything, I used to have my house, I don't have my house anymore, I used to have a wonderful library, I don't have my library anymore, I don't even have my letters, they are all gone with the fire, so I can't understand those people, I would like very much to live a normal life, not wealthy, but to live a normal life, and not have problems with money, but my values are something different now. I don't expect you or other people to understand me because I don't want you to have this experience. In some sense I'm richer than you, but of course in some sense I'm more tragic than you are. You don't have to die in order to have an experience of death, and write about it. So you don't have to experience war in order to become a better person. I'm the same person from before the war, but I know some people who changed, became monsters during the war, and that's the most striking."

"Why do you think that happened? What happened to them?"

"If I can explain it I will find the solution for this war!"

We laughed.

"I know my questions are sometimes ridiculous, I just keep trying to look at the most basic, perhaps unexamined, overlooked things, looking for clues. What religious tradition are you from?"

"Islam. I'm a Muslim. I am not a believer. I'm not a mosque goer. I know how to say three prayers my Mama taught me, my parents are very strong believers, but my Mama never wanted to influence any of my religious beliefs. She told me when I was leaving Sarajevo, please say this little prayer out loud I taught you, long time ago when you were little girl. And she said I would like you to be a real Muslim but I know that you are not that kind.

"So I say the little prayer for my Mama. Bosnia Muslims are victims of this war. I never declared, before the war, I never declared myself anything. Basically I am a poet, my nationality is a poet, but when I see how many of these people, these Muslims, are killed and raped, wounded, how many children are handicapped for all their lives, being Muslim is kind of a political attitude, not nationality. We have gypsies in my town. If they were so victimized as Bosnia Muslims I would declare myself a gypsy."

"Yes, of course."

"I'm not better person or worse person for being Muslim, I'm just normal person, and the only important thing is whether I'm good man or bad man, nothing else. And that is the thing I like about America, I can say without terror I am Muslim, nobody will be surprised by that, *whoof!* nobody will be scared about that.

"And there are Serbs that I love, who love us, who want to live in our city with us, and they see this war as evil too. And they are normal people. No! Nothing will change me even though I am killed for this kind of thinking."

"To be good, to be good to other people, to become a good human being, the only important thing is whether I'm good or bad —this is basic vision in me too. Could it be our lower middle class, peasant roots? First generation up, it's as if we carry this code like the Arc of Covenant? Fundamental, but Ferida you make me realize I rarely hear this expressed in the world I live in now. To be good? They brand us "emotional," "romantic," "sentimental," when we make moral arguments in this reigning value system of economic interests. I have a letter Richard Nixon wrote to members of his administration in 1972 which was photocopied by Norman Mailer and mailed to librarians around the country, saying the problem is clear: the working class have gotten educated. We must stop this!"

We laughed.

"They've been stopping that revolution ever since by stopping free education."

I took a deep breath. "Is it a religious war?"

"No, no. But, you know, if nothing happens, and it keeps on like this, at last it will be a religious and civil war. But now I can assure you it is not."

"It's not Christians against....?"

"No. That's a mistake. It hasn't anything to do with this, anything. If it was a war, Islam against Christianity, why...?"

"Christianity against Islam."

"Which ever, yes, but *they* claim it is Islam against Christianity. Serbian forces attack Sarajevo, attack Croats who are also Christians, of another kind, they fought Croats in Croatia, it cannot be a crusade, they both belong to Christianity, and they didn't join together against Muslims in order to make some kind of crusade, that's not true, it's stupid to look at this war like that, it would be very stupid. Simplified and very untrue. What is happening is this: the war is Neo-Nazism, it is like Hitler's Reign of Terror, the Nazis claimed to be better than Jews, so they tried to exterminate them."

"And you don't think that's a Christian....."

"I'm positive of that."

"Because Neo-Nazism is on the rise here too and it's coming from the fundamentalist rightwing Christians. I keep thinking: the Nazis were Christians. What is it about Christianity that evolves this hideous evil attitude of superiority. I mean I know it can be true of all religions but...."

"The Serbian side is eager to convince the rest of the world that this war is Islam against Christianity. If America especially, abandons the Muslim people, we will be exterminated. I know. I'm a Muslim, but I am political Muslim. I have visited Libya and other Muslim countries, I am not that kind of Muslim. My roots are South Slavs, I mean I belong to the European tradition, which now we try to start to despise because Europe doesn't want us. You know Europe claims to be democratic—I don't believe it, it's bullshit. No body helps us. The easiest thing in this war would be to annihilate Bosnia Muslims, and after that to negotiate about dividing whatever can be divided between Croats and Serbs. The only thing, the little annoying thing is the fact that there are four, five million Bosnia Muslims there. We are a kind of annoying fact. If we were not there everything could be wonderfully divided. And being a part of that tiny small unknown nation I feel, from day to day I feel, whenever I think about my nation it's necessary to be a part of it. I am an intellectual, I'm sorry to say, but I am!"

She laughed. "I belong to this intelligentsia."

I laughed with her. "I'm not sorry! I'm not sorry for you or for me, I'm glad we got that. Nor am I sorry for the world that's got us!"

"Me too. This is my task, to belong to the victimized side. It is the task of smart people, the intelligentsia all over the world. I know that Americans hate the intelligentsia, because it is a product of Europe, I would hate it also, but I have to admit that I'm a part of that, though really of the self-made intelligentsia, but...."

"Pacifists are often anti-intellectual, too—some of my Buddhist poet friends tell me I think too much. Ha! My father always said that too! The free-thinking mind is dangerous to any system of thought or enforced order. Well, there's a new intellectual that has to come, a holistic intellectual, if you will. It's as you said that America as a democracy is a young girl, and earlier you said that democracy hasn't happened yet, but it has to happen, someday. But the idea of democracy is where it happens, the possibility of democracy happens every moment as you go through each day, and you have these choices that can be made, each person has their little choices, and then collectively it happens and...."

"We can do it together."

"And this kind of thinking is a product of *mind with heart*." I laughed. "You can have all the education in the world, or you can be, as most people have always been, isolated in your own little world without books, and still be an intellectual. The brain is an organ whose function is to think!"

"You have to share your good thoughts with others."

"And your good action. And when the time comes to stand and say *this is my place*...."

"In order to improve whatever place you live in."

"And then when you can do that, you want to have children! And then...."

"Because then you miss something, you miss something. Something else is alive. And then you are complete."

"Alright...!"

This tape ends in laughter.

I returned for the second half of our conversation three days later in her studio at the Center. On the door was the plaque: The Louise Morley House. She poured us large glasses of organic Oregon Chardonnay.

Over those three days I'd become increasingly moved by her, increasingly devastated by the situation in Bosnia. I'd continued to read the library material. The United Nations persuaded the Bosnian Army to give up its weapons in exchange for its peacekeeping forces, then these peacekeepers did nothing to stop the Serbian sieges. In the three years since 1992 some 250,000 Bosnians had been systematically killed by the Serbian Army, and more than two million had been displaced. Allowing the destruction of the Bosnian Muslims, it was actually explained by some US, UN and European leaders, was the price that had to be paid for the continued peace of the rest of Europe. By now the genocide had been largely completed and a multiethnic state had been destroyed. The photos of the concentration camps, of emaciated, tortured inmates, were hauntingly similar to those of fifty years ago in Germany and Poland. I was particularly devastated by the individual accounts, the fathers and sons, in order to save the rest of their families, forced to orally castrate each other, parents made to witness the mass rapes of their daughters, the throat slittings of their sons, the burnings of their villages, the many accounts of the male roundups, the hundreds put in warehouses with polite, encouraging words, then shot from all sides by the Serb gunmen, then burned. A woman with her nursing baby and nine year old daughter on a floor of one of the concentration camps. They had witnessed their father and brothers killed, the woman's milk had dried up, the baby lay starving on her chest. She begged the soldiers to get milk for it. The one yanked up her baby and blew its head off with his gun. Then they killed her, then they raped the little girl, who survived to tell this.

And the Serb killers, who were they? And how did they become mass killers? How could anyone let that happen to themselves?

I talked with my mother about Ferida. My mother was upset that she was going back. But I was profoundly moved to meet such a person. I knew in the marrow of my bones that if I were in her situation I'd go back. She seemed a soul mate. I wanted her to know this.

"I met Louise Morley once," I told her now. "In her big house on Cannon Beach. She was a patron of my second husband, she commissioned him to make sculptures. He took me there to meet her."

She and her billionaire husband were sitting on their big foggy deck at sundown over the Pacific Ocean, Hunter's bronze "animistic" creatures mounted around the railing overlooking the roaring ocean below. She was dying, they both were, but she was imperious to us.

"I think she's dead now." I sort of laughed the old joke. "It doesn't matter how much money you have your death's going to be pretty much the same as the rest of us."

I'd been trying, through the lingering sorrow of this exchange with Ferida Durakovic, to see myself in the conversation, to see my contribution to the hellish confusion, that I not be blind to myself as I see most others being, that I grow and change for the world's sake. That I meet her.

"I would like you to tell us about your bookstore, about the fire, the story of what happened to you and it."

"I worked from '86 till the war in a culture and sports complex, very huge, in the center of Sarajevo, downtown, this center was built for the Olympic Games in 1984."

I remember the 1984 Olympics. That teenage girl from Portland who had two guys injure her main competitor.

"It was dedicated for sports, exhibition events, for youth cultural programs. That was my job, to work as editor, as manager, and at last as a head of this bookstore, in this youth culture center of Sarajevo. I was an organizer for literary programs, it was very good. Two years before the war, I fulfilled my dream of having a wonderful small bookstore, with the books *I* wanted to have and to sell to people. I did it, I was very satisfied with it, we called it alternative bookstore, because it was not just a bookstore, it was a place to stay, a place to talk to people who know books, a place to have a coffee or wine during your stay there, to read half a book if you want and nobody will blame you if at last you don't buy it, and the most wonderful part of this bookstore was a small space to have literary readings, to have jazz sessions, whatever, it was absolutely wonderful for people who want to entertain and to be entertained, that was the main purpose of this bookstore. It was not *my* bookstore, but I intended to buy it, in time, I wanted to be an owner of this bookstore. But alas, it was not to be.

"It was a relaxing place to be, that was my main goal, to kind of educate people who are not just buyers, who come just to buy things, but it was for those who enjoy the fact that they can look around for something, exchange their readers' experiences."

"That's wonderful. There are so few such places in the world." This was the Communist still in her, I thought.

"Yeah, I tried to make freedom with my bookstore. I dream of that time and place in the world now."

"Well, you make it now with your person."

"Thank you. I try hard."

"What was the name of your bookstore?"

"Valter...Walter.

"In the Second World War there was a Partisan guy who is half myth and half history who defended Sarajevo from fascistic attack in '45. It was wonderful. Fifteen or more years ago a Partisan film was made entitled "Walter Defends Sarajevo." We all learned about Walter Peric, he was a national hero who organized the defense of Sarajevo when fascists wanted to enter Sarajevo, so we thought it would be appropriate. Our bookstore was not the first place titled *Valter*. A youth generation newspaper was titled *Walter* in '87. And after that there was a chain of these wonderful youth things and we all gave the name to bookstores, newspapers, youth enterprises, *Walter*. Because it was a kind of political attitude to name it *Walter*, a kind of resistance. When war started I was so proud that my little bookstore was named *Walter!* He had this Partisan guerilla movement.

"I never saw the fire. It was at the very beginning of the war, I think in July and August, '92. The shelling of Sarajevo was so heavy that we couldn't go out from our shelters, so I never saw my bookstore burning, I just heard it on the radio that Olympic Complex, especially the Youth Center, and my little bookstore, *they* were burning. Nobody could possibly go out. From the very start of the day till... I can't tell you the last day, the story.... it was shelling all over."

"You will someday, you will write a book."

"I hope so! I remember the day this youth culture center was shelled, on the 27th day of May 1992. I know this because I was hiding with my sister and her two kids in a shelter and with some of our friends, and it was the most horrible time of this war because you couldn't possibly go out, whatever you needed you couldn't have it, because it was from the daylight to midnight, it was shelling all around, we were hiding and the only thing we had was radio, that is one of the reasons I love radio, it was the only connection with the rest of the world. Somewhere around midnight on the 27th of May I heard that Youth Culture Center of Sarajevo was heavily shelled, and it was on fire, and some of my friends, my colleagues were there trying to put out the fire, I was in a position just to hear, not to go there to fight the fire and even today I feel bad about this, but I could not go, there was no way."

"It's the thing I identify with you, the core understanding and need and intent to be where the fire is, to stay when they are trying to burn you out. To be witness."

"Yes. I want to be there. If I can do anything, in order to help anyone."

"And you can, just by your presence. Just by witnessing."

"Thank you! When I think about this bookstore, it so hurts. Part of my life was burning, gone. It was just a part of another burning-out of parts of my life, the series of burnings which proceeded after that. The National Library, for instance, was shelled in August, the fire burned for more than three days, more than a million books, including 155,000 rare texts and manuscripts. The Serbs shot at the firefighters. One librarian attempting to save part of the collection was killed by a sniper. When we heard the library was burning, my friends and I went there to cry. It was impossible to imagine someone shelling the National Library. That was the place to exchange opinions, that was where everything began for me as a poet even if it turned out that I spent more time in the café with boys! I knew the man who ordered the bombing. Nikola Koljevic, a Shakespeare scholar is now Vice President of the self-styled Serbian Republic. For awhile I met him daily for coffee or a drink, we played table tennis together in the loft of the Literature Institute, I cannot explain to you why Nikola Koljevic plotted the destruction of his own city.

"Before the war Nikola made a video which began with him reading his translation of Rebecca West's *Black Lamb and Grey Falcon* from the balcony of this library. Then he destroyed it. Can you imagine?"

"You said even your letters were burned. What do you mean by letters?"

"My parents used to have a house and I was a part of that

house, and all the letters I used to treasure, all of them were burned together with my parents' wonderful house."

"Your correspondence?"

"Yes, my personal letters. The first time when we fled from the house I was carrying *Little Prince,* and Tolkien's *The Lord of The Rings.* I thought these were the most important things to carry out from your house. Of course, along with a little bag of your underwear, and nothing else, I didn't bring anything else with me. And my mother, when we decided to flee from the house, was carrying two huge bags and I asked her "what are you carrying along?" And she said "I'm carrying the things everybody needs." And it was food. *It was food!* I never thought that I needed to bring food. I was so embarrassed by her reply because she never thought of bringing her necessary things, no.

"So we fled from our house, my personal letters were left there. We were there again for three or four times but each time we had to get out. I didn't have enough time to think of my personal letters. I dragged out this old album of photographs from my past, so I'm not lost, I'm not without *any* past, but it is a small thing to have. My room was filled with books with dedications—like you gave me your books with dedications— book as book is wonderful, but if you have it signed by the author who wrote it, it is something so personal, that makes you richer."

"On the other hand when you read it it's inside you and no one can take that from you."

"Yes. You probably know what Bulgakov said about manuscripts and books. 'Books can't burn. Books can never be burned.' You have it here. It hurts anyway."

"It's a true record, when you're trying to be clear, to see, to know, this is not fantasy, this happened. This person said this. You're a writer, you write it down. That's the difference finally between writing...and just thinking and knowing and dreaming and meditating and praying."

"Yes, yes. This is real. You have some need to write it down, not because...."

"You're writing for someone else, you're writing it to be read. You are making product, material, in a very odd way, even though you are not a materialist. I'm here now and this is what's happening."

"When I was young I didn't have need to write down things, because I was sure I would remember everything. We have a wonderful saying 'whatever is remembered it fades away, whatever is written down, it can stay.' If you feel something it is important to write it down. If it is burnt down it is hell because it is burning your history down.

"My sister Keka, she used to have apartment in the now most horrible occupied part, we had to flee from it, to a friend's house, then we had to flee from there, so then we had to just walk around the town. She never brought anything with her except her kids and her sister, that's me, we fled out from her apartment in her car, you know, meaning, we will be back soon in two, three days. Nothing, nothing she ever had was with us, but never mind she lost her apartment, everything, the only thing she regrets is the children's photographs."

"I've heard this before."

"She is so unhappy about this. I say never mind about the photos, you have your kids, and she told me, yes, I have my kids, but my kids don't have their past, because photographs— all these boring photographs, birthdays, and candles with grandma and grandpa—I remember my birthdays, they were so boring, posing, you know smiling, but that was so important, Keka is so unhappy that she doesn't have photographs of her children to show them one day. It's your past, but you have to prove to someone that you have your past. Even though these kids, now almost thirteen and ten, remember their past, nobody will believe them, very soon."

She poured more Chardonnay, the smoke from her cigarettes

a constant around her. The cedars out the window wavered in their infinite love.

"I want to ask this, because you are a poet and prayers are poems, but if it's offensive please forgive me. Can you share the prayer your mother asked you to say?"

"No. No, it is too personal."

"Good! Okay. Why was *Catcher in The Rye* so appealing to your brother's generation and *Siddhartha* to yours?"

"When I was in high school I read *Catcher in the Rye*, it was wonderful, but I didn't consider it as a cult book. I was born in '57 and something else appeared on our horizon, something very funny—Herman Hesse!" She laughs. "The generation of my brother, born in 1951, absolutely adored *Catcher in the Rye*, probably because of this feeling of liberty, feeling free, whatever. I loved it, too—it was all around the world. Can you imagine, we lived behind the Iron Curtain, but somehow, information leaked to our part of the world about *Siddhartha*."

"Books the fire can't destroy...."

"Yes! We lived the same lives as North Americans, everybody suffered for *Catcher in the Rye* and everybody wanted to be a part of that world, and that's wonderful, absolutely wonderful.

"Four of my friends gave me a present, *Siddhartha*. It was so different from the experience we knew about, it was this Far East philosophy and there was Herman Hesse to make us acquainted with this kind of philosophy, that's wonderful too. And I loved *Damian,* as a wonderful poem of friendship. *Siddhartha* was a very serious book at that time to accept as an icon. You can't explain, you are young, someone gives you some information about this wonderful book, and suddenly it is the book for your generation. For some generations it is *The Little Prince*."

"You were a pacifist before the war. Perhaps *Siddhartha* was an appeal to pacifism?"

"Yes, that's it."

"And the history of your publishing, please tell me what your books are."

"Basically they are lyrics. I published my first book when I was twenty. *In the beginning was the word*," she laughed. "I had a friend who said whatever you write down I want you to bring to me. Many were not even typed, and he made a selection. He lives in Germany now. He took it to a publisher, he made a radio program of my poems, he made everything for me. Suddenly I discovered at the age of twenty I have a book of poems. I was so young, and so amazed that my first book is there without any of my effort. I was just a gifted girl who gave all of her poems to someone who made a book out of them. I didn't know anything."

"It almost sounds like Mr. Destiny. As if you were born under a lucky star. They recognized and honored you, imagine! So now you recognize and honor them—Sarajevo."

"I write from inspiration, not all the time. In fragments."

"That's the poet. That's one of the reasons it's hard being a poet. When you're not writing your identity is threatened.

"What do you do as Secretary-General of PEN Center of Bosnia-Herzegovina?"

"Mostly," she inhales. "I write letters to people begging for help, for money."

"Your father was a salesman. What did he sell?"

"When I was a little girl, he was clothes salesman."

"What I'm wondering about, in a Communist country, in my understanding, you don't have salesmen. Salesman is sort of the archetypal capitalist."

"No, no. He worked for a sales factory, in this long production, he wasn't an individual salesman. No, he was just a part of this working chain. Oh, I would like to have my father as salesman! Not an important person."

"You made a distinction between working class and lower middle class? Lower middle class was the term my mother always used to designate us. She lectured that we were never to use the term working class, that working class was insulting."

"I think it is the difference between parents who want to give their children education. That makes the difference between working class and lower middle class. When you are working class, wherever in the world, you are not much interested—no! It is very rude and stupid what I am thinking—in having books in your house. My father eagerly wanted to give us education. He wasn't very well educated, from time to time he read a book, but world literature was not important to him, but he wanted to give his kids an education that he didn't have, so he raised us to a little higher educational level than what he had. This is the slight difference between working class families, and my family. My father claimed all his life that he was just a worker who wanted to give something better for his kids and he worked absolutely hard for that. He made me feel very proud of that. He gave me the first push to try to exceed in the outside world, that was enough. I felt very lost and I felt very bad but at last I feel very glad to be in the world my father pushed me into. That's the main meaning of lower middle class. He didn't want me to stay as he was. He wanted me to be equal, something he considered as better. Of course this is true of all parents."

"I told my mother, a beautiful and wise woman, about our meeting. When I told her you were thinking of going back and having a child, you were having those stirrings, she said why doesn't she just stay here? Why doesn't she get pregnant, come back here and create a life for her child? She has a voice. She can write of Bosnia. Why does she want to go back to that place at war?"

She was laughing harder than ever.

"This is from my mother—her mother died when she'd just tuned four, most of her family died before she was ten—so it's not that she doesn't know what she's talking about, she was offended that you want to go back, she wants you to stay right here, she wants you to get pregnant, somehow—of course *only* by the man you love back in Bosnia and birth the child here on the Oregon coast and—and forget about your country—no! she didn't say that, my mother would never say that, but something—that life, creating new life and then protecting it is the most important, the responsible thing."

"That is beautiful, that is wonderful. Please, please, give my love to your mother. I feel that also. But you know I told you, I have my promises to keep."

"Yes, and I love you for remembering your promises."

"No matter what I want now, there are some people I am responsible for. And those people want me to be here. My responsibility is to be with them. Nothing else. I feel very good about this. If I stayed here now as I have the opportunity, I would be very unhappy."

"The United States is made up of people who took that opportunity, who got out, escaped, our whole history is this, it's one of the great things about this country but there is also the dark side, we are the people who fled. And certainly we are not a very happy people.

"I want to address now the fact of your being a woman," I go on, exuberantly—in part, no doubt from the wine, but mostly from what seemed genuine bonding. "I think I understand what you told me, that you denied the fact of being a woman, there's that in your history, your growing up and education, Camus, Sartre—I keep seeing Simone de Beauvoir wandering in shock through Nazi-occupied Paris in rags, no make-up, rashes and boils on her face from malnutrition, hair turning grey, falling out, and in this unattractive state thinking about being a woman…."

"Not denying, just not liking being a woman."

Oh. Surely she meant—I heard her as objecting to the categorization 'woman,' not objecting to being a woman.

"I'm a feminist," I said, "but perhaps not the kind of feminist that is commonly assumed by that label, but in my situation of privilege and comfort, so different from yours, to use it to investigate and explore. I'm tracking something, many people are, which has to do with denial. The history of what's denied is often of what is the most natural. So I'm wondering—you told of wanting to have a baby during the shelling, of walking across Sarajevo to find this man you always loved. This is wonderful, I...."

I wasn't sure where I was going because we were interrupted then by the sponsor, followed by his wife and the girl from Brown and the dog, Latte. The squeak and pop of the cork can be heard on the tape from more Chardonnay he was opening. It must have had something to do with ecofeminism.

"The only thing is: I am not a feminist." The sarcasm I had first heard from her was back.

"Which is only a word, a label...."

"That's right, only a label. It was very unusual for me to think about all these female things, I consider myself as a normal person. So if you are a normal person you don't have to think thoroughly, I didn't think of myself as so-and-so. I just told you a story which can explain *me*."

She gulped her wine. We all raised ours to each other in greeting.

"I used to be in a period of Communism. That is the only *ism* I can accept. That was the only *ism* I lived through and nothing else with *ism* can I accept, I would never be a part of any *ism* any more. Except perhaps *romanticism!*"

We all laughed.

"There is Ferida-ism," the sponsor said, in a tone implying that I was a groupie for her.

"No, no." She did dismiss that.

"What does your name mean?"

"Unique, one in a million. My last name means fool, it comes from Russian language." She scoffed, "it has some Turkish root, it means *durable*."

"My name is Russian too, maybe the same root. You said with some passion that there are some people to blame."

"Yes of course. Do you want the specific list? The aggressor is Serbian with Milosevic as President, he wants to make Greater Serbia, at whatever cost. It means Neo-Nazism is at work. He is like Hitler of course, but he is not as smart as Hitler, and…" Her voice turned witheringly sarcastic here. *"How lucky the German people not to have another Hitler.* Milosevic. He is the Balkan Peninsula tyrant." Then gathering herself she says, "If you want to give names you can say…."

"Those four names," the sponsor interrupted nastily, "are available everywhere."

"Yes, thank you!" she puffed and sipped. "I am trying to talk seriously."

"It's so easy," he snarled, "to name those people who are to blame for this war in Bosnia."

"Yes!" she said, "I want to talk anthropologically about the war because it isn't just another war. It's part of spreading this Neo-Nazism worldwide. Be forewarned: it is a right wing, e-mail conspiracy between generals around the world. They are after control of the Mediterranean and the oil to be piped from the Caspian Sea, this is the reason. The fall of Communism is to blame. Communism was the check and balance to this."

"I would like to give a suggested reading list with this interview. Is *Balkan Ghosts* a good book?"

"No!" he snapped. "That book is part of the problem. There is a book by Noel Malcom, *Bosnia: A Short History* which you can read, the last few chapters have all the names. And Tom Shelton's *Sarajevo Daily,* is a good book. Michael Glenny's is okay, you'll get all the names. And David Rieff's *Slaughter House.* But the best book is Noel Malcom's *Bosnia: A Short History* because one of the arguments used repeatedly by politicians around the world is to suggest that Bosnia is not a country, it is a hodgepodge, artificial thing. But the fact of the matter is, as Malcom is very clear, from very early, Bosnia has been an independent country, it has its own history, its own culture and he lays that out so that when you hear somebody like Clinton, and Warren Christopher, the dithering idiot, suggest that these are ancient enemies, ancient hatreds, there's no resolving it, a rap they got from *Balkan Ghosts*, you know that's pure bullshit. And you'll understand *why* it's been obfuscated, first by the Bush Administration, now the Clinton Administration, as a way of allowing them to justify inaction."

I was thinking that's the same stand Israel takes with Palestine, but suddenly she was practically screaming.

"Yes, that's it! *You* have the luxury to be a pacifist. *Lucky you!* I used to be the same as you."

This time there was no doubt. That *you* was directed at me.

"Yes." Her bitterness was withering. "That's it. I'm so much a pacifist now, that I know that this kind of pacifism, that all the people in the United States who call themselves a pacifist, is bullshit!"

"When it's really American inaction," I tried.

"Pacifism is a wonderful idea. But a wonderful idea too is to have a good time all the time. The other day I read a generalist asking Gandhi what do you think of Western Civilization? And he replied, it would be a very good idea."

"What about Gandhi? What would he do in this situation?"

"Gandhi was *not* a pacifist!"

"Gandhi was a sexist for one thing," I laughed, trying to ignore her increasing anger, trying to get us back to where we were before they walked in. "He did not carry his philosophy over to women, into his personal life, and maybe he didn't in terms of class, so in this sense you are right, he wasn't a true pacifist. And pacifism is not, of course, the same as passivity, as Rebecca West maintained, along with her pervasive racism against Bosnian Muslims. Pacifism requires constant vigilance, consciousness against war. True pacifism would have stopped this war before it started."

"When Susan Sontag first came to Sarajevo, she had her platform." The word "platform" spit like cigarette ash from her mouth. "And the second time also, but the third time—she had a press conference and she told us a wonderful thing. She said I used to be a part of all pacifist movements in the world. I traveled all around the world because I wanted to be a part of this peaceful peace movement. When I came to Sarajevo I realized I'm not a pacifist anymore. You can ask her, I just quote what she said, and she didn't say this just for the sake of Sarajevoans, she—it is a part of her way of thinking now."

"So it makes her the only figure on the left in America right now with a brain," he said, matching her sarcasm, pouring us all more wine. "Because she's the only one who has tried to rethink the legacy of Vietnam and to think about what it means, in the Clinton era, that the sole super power on the planet, with a $300 billion dollar military budget, cannot *act*."

The next thing I knew the four of them were snickering together with their newly filled glasses in the window corner. They were definitely snickering at me like children on the playground. They were making big warding-off gestures at me.

I quoted to them, as my goodbye, from the poem she wrote on her first day in Oregon.

"Those who know what
I am writing about
will not need to keep on
reading these lines.
And those who do not know
what I am writing about
will start another war
far far away....

"May you endure, girl poet, woman intellectual. And Sarajevo and Bosnia."

I drove the sixty miles south, the sun descending on the Pacific, to my mother's in Waldport that late Sunday afternoon, not drunk, but having had too much wine to pass a breathalyzer test and therefore focused on getting past the sixty miles of seven police, sheriff and Highway Patrol stations without calling attention to myself. Statistically that year there had been more DUI arrests on that stretch of Highway One than on any other highway in the country. Neo-Nazism on the rise! Cold sober, I was hurt and sick at heart. The picture of the four of them on the other side of Louise Morley's white pristine studio, huddled together, snickering, warding me off, intensified with each new ray of the sunset. He was fairly easy to shine on, a familiar, opportunist, self-serving asshole—a kind of Koljevic. But for her, I kept aching. I kept seeing myself from her eyes, big, blonde, exuberant, arrogant, blithely carrying on about feminism and pacifism while her people are being genocided. Not a grown up girl yet. A Clinton hologram. The ugly American.

Waldport was the home of one of the major work camps for World War II Conscientious Objectors. No war in recent history has elicited the degree of contempt for men who refused to fight on the grounds of their consciences. Waldport's camp subjected these men to logging work so brutal that several died in the woods. Many COs were artists and Waldport is credited with being the root of the San Francisco and Northwest art renaissance of the Fifties. The poet William Everson printed and published first books of now significant poets at the Waldport Conscientious Camp.

There's a poem Everson wrote to Churchill on hearing his 1939 speech calling America into the war to help save Europe. It is not an issue of saving Europe, or anyone, he says. Some of us will not kill no matter what, or who. Some of us know the self as holy and all the other selves as holy.

"Love your enemies," Jesus said in the Sermon on the Mount.

"Bless them that curse you, do good to them that hate you, and pray for them which despitefully use you, and persecute you. For the sun rises on the evil and on the good, and sendeth rain on the just and on the unjust."

And Albert Camus, the Algerian-French World War II Nazi Resistance fighter, wrote *Neither Victims or Executioners* petitioning the world not to hang the Nazi war criminals. In dismay he wrote "...of a world where murder is legitimate and where human life is considered trifling.... All I ask is that, in the midst of a murderous world, we agree to reflect on murder and to make a choice... to accept the consequences of being murderers ... and the accomplices of murderers, ...or to refuse to do so with all our force and being."

All my life, most consciously with the birth of my children, I've held myself at the center of this vision, that life, all life, even the lives of killers of millions, of genociders, is sacred. *Thou shalt not kill.* The cycle of violence will end only when the cycle is broken. My resistance to armed intervention in Bosnia was great. There's almost always a way around arms if found in time. The legacy of Vietnam does not so much demand rethinking, as it needs continued pursuance. But as a mother, as a woman whose life has sometimes been threatened, I knew too that there are times when it's too late to be passive. The clarity of my sense of protection of my children, then second, of myself, has always been fierce. But even then, in the dangerous moments, my deepest instinct has been to *stop* the would-be killer—shoot, stab him in the arm, leg—to protect him, helplessly crazed, but one of the Universe's ("God's") children too.

There was a widely published photo of a Muslim woman from Srebrenica, Bosnia, who had hanged herself that summer. To see your children raped and murdered before your eyes, the throats of your parents slit, your husband and brothers beheaded—there are experiences too terrible to bear. There are experiences that must not be borne. In the photograph she hangs from the tree, her face to the trunk, dressed neatly in a Western short skirt and dark blouse. She doesn't seem dead, she seems serene, almost elegant.

It was luminous twilight when I got through the Seal Rock Highway Patrol trap, came down the twisted stretch just before it opens on the sand dunes and beautiful mouth of the Alsea River. The forested and ocean bluffs here seem undisturbed by civilization. My mother's house was in the dunes, which had been the burial grounds of the coast Indians. "Burial" is the wrong word, "resting place" would be closer since the dead were laid out in full regalia to return to earth, sky, river and ocean. Because of this, the area was the last place on the Oregon coast to be settled by the whites, beginning only in the 1890s. The skeletons lay for miles up the coast from the north side of the Alsea, a native word meaning peace. Yaquina John, chief of the coast further north, resettled on the south side of the river to watch over his dead son at rest on the north side. The first thing the German settlers did to settle Waldport was to strip the corpses of their regalia and finery and throw the bones in the river and ocean. The exchange with the traders, schools and museums became their first American money. There were still occasional accounts of kids playing in the dunes and finding the magnificently dressed corpses in the tall dune grass. And stories of their good industrious parents explaining away one of the greatest, if most common, evils.

A tidal wave from Alaska in 1962 washed directly into the mouth of the Alsea River and destroyed the town of Waldport, Oregon.

My Beard

On his seventy-first birthday, his seventy-second Valentine's Day, he told us it was terminal. I don't know how he told Donna but he took me for a walk through Shamrock, the RV Park they were staying in near Sacred Heart Hospital in Eugene, Oregon. A narrow asphalt path circling down through thick waving trees that followed the river. His rawhide moccasins, his tears. His arm up around my neck awkward, heavy. Surprising, I was almost as tall as him. "I should have named you Valentino," his mother wrote him on his thirty-seventh, deep in her own dying. I know this from her diary.

First he scolded me to never visit them again unannounced as with my last visit, which brought tears to my own eyes and a deep hurting stab to the heart. I didn't know then that he'd had a secret orchiectomy three months before and was waylaying me from showing up unannounced at any further castrations.

There are photographs of that late afternoon taken by my sister. My hair is up in a rare ponytail, I'm at my thinnest. A long bamboo snake from Tijuana that she brought back for him is around my neck. Our father looks, well—terminal. In one photo it's not possible to tell whether he's laughing or crying, the painted bamboo and wire circles of the snake slithering around his thick neck. He's dancing me up and down the RV aisle, Donna snapping away. When did I grow as tall as him? When did the cancer metastasize from his prostate "to every bone in his body, to even a spot in his left cheek bone?" I'm still in such denial about the Edens I don't know that my sister is jealous of our dancing, that she's photographing us as in documentation, a kind of proof. Never mind that his relationship with me had always been abusive, that I am still his Lady Godiva, my younger sister is forever the child who'd choose incest, physical violence and psychological abuse over neglect. (Or thinks she would.) When he dies she will demand the snake back. I, the non-materialist of the family, will bring it to her lovingly, apologizing profusely, how did it end up with me? Our mother, our saintly host as always, is not in any of these photos. I did not know then by even the dark clutch of my nightmares that she too was jealous, but my sister did.

Mama told us he came out of the doctor's office, asked to be taken to the mall. He sat there all day. Terminal: he just wanted to watch human beings. At some point on that birthday/ Valentine's Day, a Friday, sitting in the front seat of the Buick while she ran into the store, Donna and I in the back, he reached over the seat back and grabbed the book in her lap, a biography of Bob Marley and began reading with an intensity that was like fire.

My sister and I, opposites that we've always been, or as we've always been told we are, both noted his sudden interest, as he was dying, in Bob Marley. Weirdly, Rastafarian, reggae and Jamaican things kept popping up—his last real estate deal, for instance, later in the summer, will be with an Oregon man named Bob Marley. I was careful to just stay open to the ongoing fact, not to interpret or jump to conclusions about what these coincidences might mean, but Donna read them as clear signs of his next life. Rebirth in Jamaica, for sure, perhaps political and spiritual leadership, like Marcus Garvey.

What we were witnessing in his grabbing her book was shock, fear, overwhelming self-grief—he was reaching for anything to distract himself. What do we do with our emotional selves when told our emotional self is terminal? My sister believes it's precisely the emotional self that survives. When he dies, seven months hence, she will claim him. She will negotiate with Heaven for his soul. She will go to the Sierras and set herself up for a week, to make the first contact. It will take three days. He will be hers in death, she will be his savior, she will devote the rest of her life to saving him from me, from what I no doubt will write of him, proving she's the worthy one, his true love all along, meant to be hers from the beginning. Between his death and our mother's eleven years hence, their second daughter will be in psychic control of the family, while I will remain faithful, ever principled, ever blinded.

We went to a Chinese restaurant, just like we did as a young family in South Central Los Angeles. We'd meet the Bill Hogans there. Every February 14 Mama baked a heart-shaped chocolate cake which we kids decorated with red hot candy hearts bought from our pooled allowances. I told this in my first book, published the week before his cancer diagnosis. My book so hurt them, our mother will tell for the rest of her life, that she cried for days. She told this, the first time, in the same letter she told the news of his prostate cancer and scheduled surgery, but that wasn't why she cried for days, it was my book, feeling exposed and seeing, so shocked, that I was an unhappy child. Still, I must not—"your dad's worried about this too"—feel guilty about his cancer. So now at his last Valentine birthday celebration I couldn't even bring up this wonderful heart-cake memory. There's very little of my childhood in that first book. Though come to think of it, there is "Father," a poem about fishing with him

> *until our story (You, the ruthless boy*
> *so young*
> *you outlive me)*
> *is turning into*
> *foam*
> *and the great birth*
> *from your severed and flung*
> *genital.*

This is not a castration wish, I always maintained before reading it to an audience, but an allusion to the Uranus-Gaea-

Chronos-Venus myth. Uranus the father is so brutal to his children they're unable to stand up from the crawling position; in some versions he eats them. Castrating his father at his mother's request, Chronos throws the severed genital into the sea and from the foamy splash arises Venus, the Goddess of love. In one sense, I go on, the myth is a metaphor for evolution. Uranus the father to Chronos the son as in chronology; the four-legged animal to the upright human; ejaculation to conception to Love.

Believe it or not, the fortune in his cookie was *"Soon all your troubles will be over."* Believe it or not—my habit of denial, my positive-thinking, my sunny side (though in the family I'm the Dark One)—my first reaction was—I actually said this to him, "See, Daddy, you *will* get well."

He gave me that look, one he'd given me all my life, the questioning of my integrity. Quit pulling my leg, Lu. You and I both know the truth.

My integrity did need questioning (had always, but hardly in the way he'd controlled it from infancy, or in any way, for a lifetime of trying, that I could fathom). He was acknowledging in that look that as always I was being disingenuous, I was not acknowledging the truth about him. I was a liar. Therefore I didn't love him as I was pretending, I hated him, I'd be glad when he was dead. It won't be until Mother's Day that he'll confess—that's not quite the right word, though it may have been the right one for him—his sexual molestation of me as a girl.

I'm often told that I'm perceived as a mystery. "I have a reserve," my mother used to say of herself, "I'm not like other people." This was true of her, maybe of me too. Maximilian, my old love, asked more than once, "Is it the Indian in you?" "Yes," I'd say, "my mother," though uncomfortable with both the classification and stereotype. By temperament I am naturally reserved most of the time, ninety-nine percent of the time, but at odd, surprising times, outrageous characters come out of me. My wacky side. My reserved side is my mother, my wacky side is my father. His announcement that there was no hope had something to do with what I did later that night.

I'm trying to get out of Eugene. I can't find an on-ramp to I-5 North. My heart is pounding too hard, like the pounding cold rain. My husband, a sculptor, is a judge tonight in Portland's Annual Erotic Art Show. I have to get there. It's his birthday too—his forty-eighth. And Oregon is a Valentine, too. February 14, 1859, the reason the Erotic Art Show is on this date every year. The woman who married us the previous October, the daughter of Portland's police chief, a well-kept secret in her social life, had asked him, between her instructions and our vows, to be one of the three judges. The two other judges would be herself and her assistant, Julie. They'd been meeting, reviewing the entries ever since, Hunter obsessed with my revelatory feminism (but deeper, with his new feminist knowledge as authority over the two women), with the issue of what's erotic, what's pornographic, what's the difference? So I want to come up with something outrageously erotic to wear, out-there-outrageous being high-artist aesthetic for him. I won't know for another year, ten months to be precise, that he and Julie, our wedding photographer, fucked at our wedding, also between our instructions and vows, in the backyard woods of that beautiful Portland West Hills manor.

After driving Psyche, my Dodge van, in dark, pouring-down circles around Eugene, trying not to think of my father (trying to think deeply enough to save him), I finally find the on-ramp to 5-North. At about Cottage Grove, alongside land that belongs to Ken Kesey—I-5, god, no wonder Kesey's insane—I'm able to get KBOO. The Valentine Erotic Art Show has already been busted! For the Garden of Vulvas and Penises growing in rows between high green grass in the display window. A man with a grade school daughter who passes by the window every day called the police. Lee, the Garden's creator, sobs to the reporter. "I meant to honor our sexual organs, I didn't mean it to be obscene." The station assures us the show goes on.

My father was Coyote, the great Trickster in the bone game of my life. (He was a swan, a seagull, a fish, a snake. A pedophile. A rapist. An incestor. A homosexual?) I loved him and from earliest memory prayed to Jesus to stop him, that he be forgiven, that he not die. Mama would say in her ongoing, sideways explanation of him, that always, since a little boy, he'd been fascinated with snakes. "Why do you think he's so fascinated with snakes?" she ruminated through the years. I still don't know, I never thought of answering that question, but I see him emerging from the garage under the Ramona house when we were teens, a long fat green and gold garden snake in his hands, curling around his waist. "Let me introduce you to Gertrude," he laughs—oh my father's laugh, of such intelligence and irony and pure joy. Gertrude was good for his garden. I had only a sense then, from my grandmother who pressed the etymology and genealogy on me in the admonition to never forget, the meaning of our name, Edens. When I was little, trying to learn to read and write, I'd hear my mother on the phone spelling our name, "like the Garden, but many." The snake in the Garden of Eden was Lucifer, an entity, or concept at least, my father wrestled with from early boyhood. From my birth he called me Lu, "for your middle name, Lura," my mother explained. (At two he called me Lady Godiva and loved for me to traipse nude in front of company while he recited Tennyson's poem, *"Then she rode forth, clothed only with chastity. And rippled ringlets to her knees."*)

I don't know for certain that he led a homosexual life but the circumstantial evidence since our mother's death, especially regarding Shane, Odie, Dee Rupp, Bill Hogan, and Sam Gardner suggests it. They called him Red. But in his lifetime, and for the eleven years until her death, for all my questions, and the sexual, volatile, violent, terrifying, and sometimes positive experiences with him—and aching, thinking, praying (*"Forgive him Father, he knows not what he's doing"*), wrestling with and meditating on him—and what seems now our mother's lifelong, self-and societal-censored attempts to tell me, such a notion never crossed my mind.

Maybe he explained to her his sexual attraction to me in the same way he explained, that is, apologized his reaching for her breasts the first day they met. "I've been living with a man, I'm trying to be excited by a woman." (That was the first thing she told me, and repeated several times, in her efforts to explain him.) Maybe on some level she even approved of his attraction to me, to encourage his heterosexuality. Our mother carried the burden of our father's sexuality like a mother carrying her helpless infant, a handicapped child. (After all, they both explained, a man is quicker to the trigger than a woman.) That he tricked her into marriage three months after they met by taking her virginity, she eighteen, he twenty-two, meant that he could never trust her love. "The School emphasized that a woman who wasn't a virgin would never have a family. Men married only virgins." My mother raised in an orphanage coveted a family. She succumbed to his pressure, her tarnished state, and married him.

He was pan-sexual even if that didn't include sex with men. Sex was the heart and core of his being. "Your father is the most sexual man I've ever known," she said many times. Only in writing my childhood memoir, *My Father's Love*, did it occur to me to respond to my dead mother, "But Mama, how many men did you know?" (Not many, I know, no matter what I don't know.) He was also a user, an emotional blackmailer as my sister grew up to be, though Donna always insisted that she didn't know about sex until college, she who witnessed all her childhood our father being sexual with me, she who was in our Hollydale bedroom the night he raped me—I was seven, she was five, our brother was four; she and I both had heart attacks as the echo-cardiograms reveal, I'm not sure what happened to Clarke except, for sure, the boogie man was real—and later in Ramona when my thirteen year old lover, Ramon, climbed the pepper tree and came through the bedroom window, her bed just feet from mine. (She was eleven, our ten year old brother in a room of his own.) That's how denial works—or was that lying? And well, whatever, she'll take his hugs, thank you, the chest and groin grinding embraces. Gladly.

That he was a trickster meant we all were.

Aries Wrecking Yard, where Hunter and I lived, was seventeen miles southwest of Portland. A bronze sculptor, he'd lived there for years before I met him, for his work— his sculptures, his women. Our living space was a 1957 U.S. Forest Service bus that he'd fixed up in fantastic ways—the kitchen behind the driver's seat, under the ceiling window, a desk and crimson velvet sofa down the length of the bus, two vintage Cadillac bumpers welded into an antique wood stove, and twin jet canopies for skylights over the loft bed. The acre of wrecked cars, the wrecking yard workers, the dynamiting and excavation of the gravel pits, the ongoing shooting at the Washington County Gun Club that bordered the north side of the property, the train tracks which bordered the east side, the train coming through late at night, the pack of howling coyotes that ran the tracks most nights, the frogs breaking out in song at the oddest times were all part of the surreal environment which mostly I loved. Aries had been a pig farm before becoming a wrecking yard. The smell of pig urine was almost too much when it rained. "Pigs are holy to the Goddess," I'd sigh.

I dress in the cold bathroom of the cavernous barn that is his studio. Naked under the glaring 100 watt bulb, I shave. *"Your electric hair,"* the poet e.e. cummings names it. Then I glue it around my mouth, a perfect dark blond goatee. The pound of the rain on the tin roof, the pound of my heart for my father, the pound for what I'm doing. I slip on my floor-length flesh-colored silk gown that originally belonged to the actress Susan Strasberg, Marilyn Monroe's closet female friend. Maximilian and I found it at a 20th Century Fox studio lot sale. I choose a pair of red antique high heels from Hunter's collection on the wall. I find my reddest lipstick.

My father was always sexual with me. He was sexual with me in the crib, it's my earliest memory. He was sexual with me every day of my remembered childhood until I told my mother at twelve, and then all hell broke loose. He'd attack, accuse, twist my words, all within the frame of being the one attacked. How could you, Lu? Do this to your own father? The scorn, the disgust, the hate in his voice, the hitting and slinging was devastating. Trying to tell him, tongue-tied to the double cross—he'd molested me but I'd betrayed him, I had told— Daddy, I love you, I am not out to get you.

I see only now that the fights were almost always in the presence of my mother, and usually, in the presence of my sister and brother. For the most part he didn't attack me when it was just the two of us (though one time when no one was around he hit me in the head so hard I flew all the way across his garden.) He was in the process of demonizing me to them so that they wouldn't believe what I had told Mama, or might tell.

At least I always stood up to him. I'd stand back up, refuting his accusation and scream "Go ahead, hit me again," Mama, Donna and Clarke watching silently. But I was helpless against his size, his strength, most of all his conscious intent; he knew exactly what he was doing to me, to them. I refused to know he was capable of such ruthlessness. I believed it was all a mistake. Dear Jesus, forgive him. Help him to stop. Help me to see my own faults in this, help me to stop the fights. But Jesus was helpless to prevent them, as I was, because I refused to know that my faults were because I had told and that my mother was deep in her own crisis about it, thus not protecting me. I was in denial. I believed in Jesus, I loved my father, I loved our family, there was nothing worse than a snitch, I would not know, I would not think.

In a drive with a carload of poets from Mendocino California to Port Townsend Washington, which turned out to be a permanent move for me, I stopped at my parents new place in Florence Oregon and the six of us spent the night—I can still see the sleeping bags across the living room, the deck, one down on the beach. Recently one of those poets, Caitlin, told me that she saw very clearly that my father was trying to steal my chi.

Our mother always described him as a kind, sensitive, principled man; he was brought to tears easily, he had so much compassion for the underdog, he could be friends with anyone, "high or low." Now I have to ponder that it wasn't just her submissive role as wife that she cultivated, or psychological denial, but that she was, at least in part, or subconsciously, glad of his cruelty and brutality to me, it proved he loved her more than me. It proved that I was the fault, I seduced him, I vexed him, I deserved what he dished out. I never saw my mother brought to tears (though she said she cried for days when my book was published), not even that most common, sudden watery veil across the eyes. This was understandable. (No, woman. No cry.) Most members of her immediate family—parents, grandparents, aunts, uncles, and cousins— were dead by the time she was fifteen, all of social diseases, grinding poverty, abusive working conditions, abusive laws and "unchristian Christians" (not to mention the genocide of her ancestral North Carolina tribes). Her maternal grandfather breathed his last in her arms. She survived by "controlling" her thoughts, by "the power of positive thinking", by forgetting, or rather, by remembering it all in a positive, triumphant way. She loved life, life is worth it she always said.

She started hinting, or so it seems to me now, of his possible homosexuality very late, never using that word, to explain him, to explain the inexplicable. To explain his sexual, violent, possessive and psychological abuse of me, and her (the orphan's) allowance of it —because she knew that I might write of it, of him, after they were gone of course, destroying her carefully constructed story of the perfect marriage and their successful lives, that he loved her, he was faithful to her, even in her months in the TB sanitarium (when it happened). Only the rape that hammered my seven year old body into pieces and caused my heart to explode and her second daughter's heart too in the bed next to mine hurt more than being made the other woman to my mother. We kids lived in unspeakable fear of the boogie man returning. Then the fear of my telling, the fear then of my writing that they worked to silence—where is the bottom of hell here? I catch glimpses of why my sister as a grown woman would risk everything to silence me, including her reputation as a New Age healer (years of helping other incest victims so that she obtained the authority to say I was making it up), but I still can't quite articulate it, or understand it. Something about jealousy, something about power, something about hate for the Chosen (the raped) one.

I study his photographs as a young man and I think I see it—a gay man. But then worry that I'm reading into them. I think back on his buddies I knew as a girl, study the photographs and have to consider now, could they have been his lovers? Handsome (beautiful) Dee Rupp especially seems to shine in this late light. And Odie, and Bill Holden and Sam Gardner. And Shane. Shane was Aunt Alice's first husband, the father of her girls, Billie and Shirlee, the one who mysteriously disappeared. Why does the image of Shane making love to my father over me in my buggy on Cade Street in Long Beach seem so real? And their giggling ring so true though I couldn't have possibly grasped what I was witnessing?

I don't know. Someday I hope to. Maybe as the result of my publications. One of his lovers conceivably still living, or the child of one of his lovers, will come to me and say, yes, for sure, your father was my father's lover. Or at least, yes, my father, your father's best friend, was gay. Most recently I've searched, unsuccessfully, for the sons of Dee Rupp (last in Newport, Oregon) who might, but of course might not, know.

But if he was homosexual, from everything I understand about him—homosexuality not a negative judgment on my part—he suffered for it; he suffered for his male identity. When he confessed to me he said he always suffered for raping me. He sobbed he'd never forgotten for a day of his life. "I hated what I did to you. I tried to forget it but I couldn't." His suffering is in all the twisted and twisting images of him in my memory and nightmares. I've always suffered for my father's suffering, I suffer for it now. Hate the sin, not the sinner. I hated what my father did to me. I hated what it did to him. I didn't hate him.

Four months before he was diagnosed with prostate cancer, a week after my first book was published, I dreamed him wearing a yellow dress in the Pasadena Rose Bowl Parade. Yellow was my mother's favorite color, watching the Rose Bowl Parade, an annual, beloved ritual of our family of very few rituals. This started New Year's Day, 1946, when the Los Angeles Times ran a front page photograph of him and other wheel-chaired vets lining Colorado Boulevard for the early morning parade. **War**

Heroes! For over a year he was a patient in the Pasadena Army Regional Hospital, but not for war wounds, he always chuckled. For prostatitis caused by the immunizations. 1945, Europe or Asia, that was the problem, they didn't know yet which theatre he'd be sent to so they shot him up for both. *"Dreamed of my father turning into a woman in a dress like a float in the Pasadena Rose Parade,"* is the way I put it in my second book, *"a dress of all yellow and real flowers. World War II planes flying over his head."* Eventually the treatment was a vasectomy, the reason they didn't have any more children, and perhaps a twisted root in my buried consciousness of dreaming him as a woman. Vasectomy, statistically, can be a factor in prostate cancer. Prostate cancer can be a result of earlier venereal disease which is the disease listed on his Army discharge papers. Our mother always emphasized it as "non-sexual" venereal disease. His discharge papers say this too.

I've long suspected my father witnessed his father molest his older sister, Lucille. She was called Lu, left home as a teenager, never to return, even to visit her mother and brothers. And maybe his older brothers molested him—two were twins, Kermit and Kenneth, which brings up another interesting statistic: same-sex twins are more likely to be homosexual than single birth humans. Certainly my father was bullied by them. He witnessed his father's raging jealousy of his second son, Kermit, who was his mother's favorite. "He'd hit Kermit but never Kenneth and never your father," Mama would say, blithely. There are entries in Grandma's diary—granddaughter of the infamous Tennessee Confederate traitor and Union supporter, John Chitwood, and devout (submissive, obedient, dutiful) Baptist wife and loyal Confederate, Francis Martin Chitwood—addressed to her dead father, George Washington Chitwood, "a kind and compassionate man" in clear shock of what was happening in her home.

My husband is coming down 9th NW to the Pearl District gallery with Julie, sees me pull into the parking lot, pretends he doesn't. It's still raining but now it's the misty, sensuous rain of Portland, hardly noticeable; nothing like the tropical downpours of my home, LA.

When I walk through the door Lee hands me a big pink rubber dildo from the dismantled Garden, apologizing that the hairy rubber vulvas really did look obscene. "I didn't mean it that way, honest, I honor the female."

The place is jammed with Portland's artist society. Hunter is interviewing people with a mic and cassette recorder strapped to his meaty shoulder asking their feelings about the exhibit, asking the erotic/pornographic question about what they're viewing, Julie following behind him, photographing. He barely acknowledges me, but this isn't unusual. I come behind them doing my own interviewing, holding the dildo to people's mouths in mime of him and his mic. "But more erotic is the shave!" I chime to those who are hearing the fast-spreading rumor of the source of my beard. "Would you like to see?" I keep applying my True Red lipstick.

Second place is a framed photo of a dozen shots of male groins, lower hip to upper thigh. How different individual penises and testicles are! The twelve penises, the twenty-four testicles seem to carry the stories, personalities, ethnic heritages, and most amazingly, the faces of their possessors.

First Place is a large acrylic of a rabid black dog. He plunges head first out of the frame straight into the viewer's face. His murderous rage is shocking. Bared fangs, raging mongrel: *what the fuck does this painting have to do with the erotic?* And I know, without knowing yet the true nature of my husband, this is *his* First Place, his pressure over the two female judges, the woman who married us, the daughter of Portland's police chief, and Julie.

That night after it's all over, having gotten my dismay under control, I show him, my One and Only Valentine (well, no, there's Daddy). I give him my birthday present. We married October 18 but he didn't consummate the marriage until January One. Since then we've had six weeks of fairly normal marital sex (though in a story I wrote a year later I say we had sex that New Year only, and since factual truth is a deep aesthetic but denial a psychological weakness I can't be sure). To show him in that funny, exquisitely tight bus, jet-canopied, starry space wasn't exactly easy but it was erotic, at least for me. After showing him on my knees, I swung down the pole and paraded up and down the aisle.

"Sorry, but I couldn't possibly have sex with you now until it grows back."

And he didn't.

The photos of me that night at Portland's Annual Erotic Art Show were taken by Julie, as are half the wedding ones. (My sister took the other half.) I couldn't have nightmared then that they'd fucked at our wedding. I didn't know my sister was jealous, nor our mother, though all their behavior was trying to blast me open to the fact. But the Erotic Art Show, I'll be told, was too weird, the feminist erotic/pornography question a growling howl from deep sickness. And I hear myself being blamed. And I see Julie looking at me. The rabid dog is in the background of every photograph she took of me in my beard. When your husband is cheating and you know the woman without knowing, later you will remember how she looked at you. It is an unforgettable look, even though you didn't know.

A month later, still two months before my father confessed, I dreamed a fish following me down a mountain side snapping (lovingly) at my ankles, to the mouth of the Siuslaw River and the Pacific Ocean where he lay dying. I dreamed the Pacific Ocean as God's Eye eyeing us.

I was on a long trek up the Sierras, or maybe Mt. Hood, with a man, some version of Hunter, when suddenly I remembered I'd forgotten something, I had to go back. The man, though annoyed, said he'd wait for me.

As I turned to return, my feet in the whirl stirring up the dirt like ocean waves, this fish was lying there right on the path, a foot long, on his side, scales shimmering silver in the sun, his eye taking in all of me.

I started down. He flopped along as fish flop when out of water, on his side just behind my running feet, his ocean eye ever on me. This fish loves me, I thought, he follows me just to be near me, though dangerously out of water. I kept descending down in my flip-flops, in prayer, for worry of him. How will he make it through the dust, the dirt clogging his scales?

We came through a large gate. "Whose property is this?" someone asked. Some version of my father, the real estate broker. My feet flew over another fish, half-buried, the scales of his middle disintegrating like crumbling rock. My flopalong fish flopped down on this dead fish so happy to feel him! Rubbed back and forth on him. He rubbed and rubbed his brother, his paradise, down to Topanga Beach in Southern California where I raised my children.

A man was waiting in the cabin for me (some version of my former love, Maximilian), then stood at the window with me. We watched my fish, gills gasping for joy, enter the ocean. Instantly he became a frolicking red Irish Setter. You could see his happiness for this. Then the high wave drew back, and my father floating on his red back in the inner curl just before it crashes, stretched his left leg across the water, the beach and sky, "there's no getting away, Lu," and became a giant woman's leg that stretched to mine standing at the window.

I woke crying—actually sobbing. (Like my mother I never cry.) Daddy, you dog. Topanga Beach is where I first remembered and wrote of the "lesser" molestations. Your fish in the bath,

Daddy, your fish in the rooms and garage and cars and city plunges and Sierra and Cascade rivers where we fished, and backroads and beaches ever after me, your little girl, your big fish in your hand, your paws on me, when you were called Red.

When I got down to him that day on the Siuslaw's mouth, amazingly (there's that word again), he'd had a fish-dog dream too.

"I was throwing bones and meat to the dogs on the beach when a huge fish leaped out of the wave and grabbed everything."

His old dog-eat-dog looking up at me from the bed, his ocean eye on me still not remembering. Just that I'd forgotten something, which for all my journeying I still had to return for.

There is pain so utter it swallows substance up, then covers the Abyss with trance. Such a contemporary understanding, but that's Emily Dickinson. *So Memory can step around, across, upon it. As one within a swoon goes safely, where an open eye would drop him bone by bone.* Freud says the fish is the phallus and Oedipus means swollen feet from the sea and Christians say the fish is Jesus and my oldest reference book says Raphael is the angel who was sent by God to warn Adam of his danger. And he traveled with Tobias into Medea and back again, instructing him along the way how to marry Sara and to drive away the wicked spirit. In art Raphael always carries a pilgrim's staff, signifying the journey, and a fish, alluding to his helping Tobias catch the fish who performed the miraculous cure of his father's eyesight.

I don't understand these leaps, the penis into the fish into the dog, Oedipus from the sea who blinds himself on realizing his incest with his mother (the eyes? Why not whack the thing off?), Raphael to Jesus the Pisces (ruled by fish). I'm moved by the many photographs of my father fishing through the years, mainly from Pacific shores. Though he was endlessly discussed by the family, mythologized, referred to, excused, explained, made a hero, he was never, not ever, by any of us in any way, psychoanalyzed. From earliest memory he called Freud Frood, sometimes, Fruit. And his first name was Cecil. Cecil means blind musician and one of his few songs, maybe his only song, was "Amazing Grace." *First I was blind, but now I see. Amazing grace for a wretch like me.* We played all the recorded versions we could find of *Amazing Grace* the final week of his life.

The instant they crossed the California border back into Oregon after the fabulous caravan trip through Mexico he got sick again. He'd been feeling great since the orchiectomy in November which enabled him to continue taking the female hormone DES, a form of estrogen. The DES worked, he felt great, the tumors vanished, but the drug is dangerous—he had the orchiectomy because the DES caused a small stroke which permanently destroyed the peripheral vision in one eye and caused his testicles to swell like balloons—a man can only use it for a year.

Sometimes I wonder if they were elsewhere the several months they were supposedly stranded in a Texas garage, the garage unable to find a part for their motor home. Maybe at one of the Mexican cancer clinics of natural, alternative healing. We always joked about Oregon being the cause of his illness.

Less than a week after the fish came the swan.

Daddy and I are flying on the back of a white swan across the Pacific Ocean. He's in front riding it like a horse, with stirrups and reins. I hang onto his back, my arms around his middle. The swan is beautiful, big, powerful, muscular, its feathers rowing the wind in a song. We are in happiness and delight.

When I came out of this, a writing workshop trance in Seattle, I was almost crying again. Then came the memory. My father made me a fantastic white swan rocker when I was very little. I named the journal entry "Leda and the Swan. Or

Swansong."

Ever since I've been astounded. Did he know the myth of Leda and the Swan as he knew of Lady Godiva? Where do these myths come from? Why a swan? Is it simply because the swan's neck is phallic—and beautiful? In the Greek cosmology the swan's rape of Leda is the origin of war. The rape produces Helen, whose beauty is so great nations war for her, bringing about their own destruction.

"Whatever happened to my swan, Mama and Daddy?" My question over his death bed was met with stares and silence, as if something happened I'm not to remember.

"Didn't you make two swans, Daddy, one for Donna?"

I swear, they clammed up.

But the truth will set you free. The words are on my tongue, I'm in danger of actually saying them, the words of my mother and grandmother, the words of Jesus my first words, my first literature, the Bible, though I'm not a Christian now, except genetically, temperamentally, psychologically, philosophically. Instead of an eye for an eye, turn the other cheek. Love thy enemy as thyself. Forgive them, Father, for they know not what they do. How is it that we, a so-called Christian nation, have forgotten Christiantity's most basic principle, the Golden Rule, do unto others as you would have them do unto you? How is it that these very words of Jesus are now labeled psychotic, heretical, even illegal, could lead to the same old State crucifixions? You're either with us or against us. Most forbidden of all—politically incorrect, anti-Semitic, radical, revolutionary —Jesus, the Bible says, came with a new testament in protest of the old.

I left Aries Wrecking Yard early that morning, Mother's Day. We'd been married seven months.

When I walked in, an afternoon of pure Oregon light

shining off the ocean and silver dunes, they were sitting on the couch together. Donna and Clarke were there too, and Donna's boyfriend, Jeff. My parents' eyes met mine. It was like running into a wall at high speed.

He had to arrange to get us away from Mama and Donna who were being disingenuous, that is panicked, to prevent this. All four of us were being disingenuous.

I drove us to town. "One night I came and got in your bed. I was naked."

My mouth broke out in cold sores, my face in pimples. As he told it I saw it, a bad movie seen too many times, running and rerunning across the windshield. He was running in front of us naked down Rhododendron screaming *no! no! no!* He was running naked back down the Hollydale hall screaming *"no! no! no!"* He was running from me on the bed in a pool of blood and feces, trying to get my heart to start again.

"I was out of my mind," he sobbed, "but I don't want to make excuses for myself. That was the only time, right?"

I couldn't speak.

"I didn't hurt you, did I, Baby?"

"I was a little girl, Daddy," I finally managed.

"Yes, that's right. You were a little girl."

"I always wanted to talk to you about it," I gasped in not much more than a whisper, "but I was never sure you remembered. I was always afraid it'd give you another heart attack."

"I wanted to forget it. Always I've wanted to forget it, but I never could. I've never forgotten a day of my life what I did to you." Then he said again, "That was the only time, right?"

I stuttered something about the lesser, ongoing molestations. (I didn't say that I've never forgotten the demands to see my growing breasts, to touch them, repeatedly showing me his penis in his hand sticking up through the bath bubbles, how I had to watch him, and of finally telling Mama at the end of the sixth grade.) He said he didn't remember that, he was uncomfortable with the word molestation, "hard to know where the boundaries are, if that was molestation." And then he said what I wish he hadn't. He said none of that had anything to do with our fights. The fights which started after I told Mama and she probably threatened him legally and the sex ended, were even harder for him to admit. Perhaps because, after all, he was a man, but not, not ever, a bully.

I pitied him. I was terrified of him. I loved my sinner as myself. I was mute in terror of his sin against me. I'd do the same thing again. I'd forget if that's what it'd take to protect him. I did forget. Sort of.

The truth shall set you free. And now what I must never forget, what I learned only with my coming out: he molested, with the identical sex, his son's daughter, my brother's girl. My protecting him led to his abuse of my beloved niece.

I told Donna that night. She was my sister, a healer, we'd long talked of his verbal, sometimes physically violent abuse of me, and her guilt in not taking my side, but that she too was suffering from the family and now his approaching demise. I never dreamed then she'd been jealous all her life of our father's attention to me and his obliviousness to her. If I'd realized it what could I have done?

Our orphan mother mythologized our father. She made him flawless, like a god, attributing unquestioned virtue to his behavior. Then my sister and I did too. We made him a hero precisely because he wasn't. It's why he felt unseen, unloved. For my sister his confession to me as he lay dying was the final act that proved our father to be a truly great man.

But it was also salt to her oldest wound, Daddy choosing me. Very soon she declared to all that I made it up, Daddy never raped me, how could I say such a thing about him?

There's a photo she found in 1968. Daddy is sixteen, a very handsome, actually, a beautiful young man. But the five-by-seven face is pin pricked by stabs of a needle from my eight year old son. I can barely remember that he bullied and humiliated my son, I was so used to seeing my father that way, I thought it was the way of all fathers and grandfathers. There is one sentence in an apologetic letter from my mother speaking very directly of this, saying he loves Danny even if he treats him the way he used to treat Clarke. That's how denial is passed from mother to daughter in complicity with the man. Could he have molested my son, too?

I don't know for certain that he attended the Scopes trial in Dayton, Tennessee. But I do know the Monkey Trial had a major impact on his psyche, on his life. His mother, the ex-schoolteacher and Mine City Baptist Church Sunday School teacher, was the area reporter for the three major Tennessee newspapers. It was a major crisis. It was all anyone talked about, God and Darwin, the Survival of the Fittest, evolution, the Seven Days of Creation, Life Everlasting, Genesis, belief and lost faith. Salvation. The church and the state. Heaven and Hell. The soul. Dayton was sixty miles northwest of Ducktown. I see them catching the bus. He's nine.

My grandmother was not confused about the Theory of Evolution and her faith. She was a Mary Sharp College graduate. Her aunt, Mary Corn Sharp, after liberating and financially supporting her deceased husband's slaves, including passage for the many who chose Liberia (as in liberty) Africa to start anew, gave the rest of her fortune to help establish the first US female college with a curriculum equivalent to the top male universities. All through my childhood my father's mother cited Genesis, saying that everyone knows the Seven Days of Creation is a poem. She explained metaphor. Despite the current fundamentalism, the Baptists, some of whom are my family's direct ancestors, were the ones who got the First Amendment through, the guarantee of free speech. She was a Chitwood—John Chitwood who fought for the North was her grandfather—and a Reagan, a Martin, a Winn, a Corn, a Hancock—from a long line of people who left England for religious freedom. She was a poet, she wasn't confused, but maybe this is what happened to Daddy as a boy. (What did his father believe? Son of a Confederate soldier, raised a Primitive Baptist, he would have been a Creationist. Still another split.) I know now from Aunt Lucille's oldest daughter that my father did to me what he saw his father do to his older sister. After all, we're descended from monkeys. Maybe what someone— his father, his brothers, his minister?—did to him, was because we're descended from monkeys. He watched, at his mother's side, his father beat his older brother, Kermit, his mother's favorite, the one he was closest to, while he and Kenneth, Kermit's twin, were never touched, and from which came, at least in part, his sense of entitlement. He watched his father train pit bulls to attack others. He played Clarence Darrow in the high school play. Darrow lost the trial but that was nothing to his humiliation of William Jennings Bryan, ridiculing his belief that God made the Universe in six days. Maybe when he touched me he was being the fittest, he was being a monkey, a snake. His eyes and hands would devour my bare chest and he'd say you should grow up to be Clarence Darrow for the defense, Lu, you're such a fighter for the underdog. "It affected him deeply," Mama always said.

In her diary my grandmother writes of seeing my father in a Downey church "all by himself, praying" a few months after his rape of me. Daddy alone in church—not a social obligation or ritual—backs up my sense that he was spiritually anguished, that he suffered.

Your father doesn't go to church, Mama always said, because of what happened to him in church as a boy. I never asked what happened. These days, given all the molester priest and preacher stories in the news, given how often she repeated this, I have to wonder.

"She's writing it all down for when we croak," he said that night after our "talk" when Donna's friend, Jeff asked what I was writing. Just before sleep he moaned to Mama that God is an angry, vengeful God. "Where did that come from?" she moaned herself. Believe the worst will happen, he believed when they first met, and then you won't be surprised. She believed the opposite: believe the best because whatever you believe will come true. See the beauty and love and the goodness in the world. Her belief in God being a loving God and that her husband had finally come to believe her was of fundamental importance to her.

And there was the time from that bed over the Siuslaw he looked at me in great severity. "Someone said you don't believe in God, Lu. Tell me that isn't true."

He was envious of our generation, of our sexual freedom. Mama often quoted his bemoaning that he wasn't born in our time, how he would have fit right in. Men now get to wear colorful clothing and long hair. All his life he had to wear the same uniform: drab pants and shirts. As in my dream I can believe my very masculine father fantasized wearing women's clothes, maybe even a bra, he so loved unhooking mine.

In the Bible the youngest son is often the favorite son, like Joseph. I see his funny, giggly side when being sexual with me, as if he's entering childhood play again, not the meanness and sadism of some men. Except for the rape, and the attempts to silence me. Again, and again, I have to force myself to remember his rape of me. And his demonstrations to the family, the psychodramas, his sadistic emotional abuse of me and the many times he hit me. And again, her abuse through total silence and submission. My very presence provoked in him these attacks, anger and cruelty. Mama always called this love. Love vexes. Besides, I was just like him. We were just alike. He was so jealous of me when I was born, he put his fist through the hospital nursery window. I took her from him.

Sometimes—this temperament of mine—I've tended to think my father just made a bad mistake. He should have confessed back then, pleaded for forgiveness—well, could he have? What could he have done once he'd raped me? I imagine self-hatred, I imagine his panic, I remember our neighbors, a lynch mob if ever there was one. I see his mother dead on the spot of her bad heart, I see my mother dead of her TB.

It wasn't a mistake. That's you, still a Christian, forgiving him. And it's not just jealousy, as Mama maintained, not just natural possessiveness due to love, as your father has for you, he loves you more than daughter love, he loves you so much, she warned long before I had a boyfriend or any thought of one, that his jealousy of any future boyfriend made him sick.

It wasn't just jealousy. Fathers who have messed with their daughters are afraid of the future boyfriends, lovers and husbands who know, or soon will know. He must oppose her man. In the very least he could be in serious legal trouble. At the most, maybe, he worried about his soul. Which may have been the motive behind his confession, rather than the freeing of mine.

In the end I changed my father's diapers, washed his groin, washed down that tight humid place in between the cheeks, the genderless place of his castrated gonads, his orchiectomy. Even then I saw only his beauty, the baby boy, the suffering man like Jesus. I saw what once was the origin of me.

When he died I stopped bleeding.

Because my estrogen level remained high it was diagnosed as traumatic menopause. The uterus and the prostate are analogues, the identical organ at conception before the differentiation into gender. Like a father's sympathetic labor pains, I thought, I've suffered sympathetic prostate death with my father.

Actually, eleven weeks after his death, many rivers still to cross, and the raging hot flash firestorms, my marriage came to an end, just before midnight, December 12. That afternoon I had finally started again.

Hunter kicked me out. That was it. The end. My last menstrual blood. No, woman, no cry. I had married him because he convinced me that he wanted our child. Hunter's parting words were "you're no longer erotic to me, Sharon." He also said as I fled the bus into a raging ice storm, something that will haunt me more. "Well, it's about time you took the hint, Sharon."

A few weeks later, into the new year, Hunter found me at my mother's in Florence. He drove me out to the ocean. His manner was almost contrite and remorseful. "You were the most erotic thing I've ever seen," he said of that Valentine night. He was acting contrite as a way of relieving himself of guilt. He told me that after completing the installation in the afternoon, Julie invited him to her apartment for a shower. He stepped out and.... He maintained typical male sexual helplessness. In fact this was four months after they'd been meeting, discussing, debating, judging erotic art. Four months of fucking. One night, sleeping beside me under the canopy, he woke from a dream and told me of fucking Julie plastered naked to his molding table. All those nights he didn't consummate our marriage, he implied now in his high shamanic seriousness, he was being faithful to her. He was such a principled man. He fucked her at our wedding. And ever since. I will be informed of this by the woman who married us.

I lost respect for sculpture. The art of capturing women in stone. Carving them from stone. Pygmalion perfecting God's work of the flawed female. He threatened to call my father about his sexual abuse of me to pay off his karmic debt, so I'd be forever in his debt.

He found then, soon after my midnight ice storm flight, my pubic hair beard, my merkin. He made an altar of it. I never saw it, I was never in Aries again, but when I learned I went crazy. There were altars in the barn and wrecking yard of his former women, altars I'd lived with, accepted and honored as art. I'd been happy to know his stories of these women, now shrines, happy for his sharing. Most men are sealed shut about their former women.

In those consciousness-crashing months that followed, I demanded my pubic hair back. "Send me my merkin NOW!" I screamed on a postcard of the Florence bridge. I didn't care that it meant dismantling his precious art. It wasn't precious, it wasn't spiritual, it wasn't art. It was me.

He demanded then, in exchange for my merkin, the bronze sculpture he'd given me at our wedding.

I didn't know what he was talking about. I didn't remember. It took a week. I was in Sausalito, I wrote on a napkin: *the slab of bronze I held in my hand*. He had me hold it while we made our vows.

A pig fetus! A caste, lost-wax bronze pig fetus.

Aries, a pig farm! Pigs: sacred to the Goddess. A pig fetus preserved in the barn's freezer. He had me carry the fetus sculpture through the wedding.

I had to search for it, through all the upheavals of moving. Still another week later in Ashland, I found it. It was buried in the secret money drawer of the box my father made for me to fit between the driver and passenger seats in Psyche. "For your money," Daddy grinned in presenting it to me. Me, the moneyless! My father the box maker! All those nightmares of him punching a hole in the toy box he made for me. Where I hid my bloody pajamas.

I held it in my hand. It had thin lines of blue-green mold growing in the bronze crevasses. Good, he'll know it's been buried in Psyche, not in my palm.

Yes, he said. The pig fetus looks just like the human fetus.
He had me carry it during the wedding.
Suddenly, I knew. What he wanted me to know.
Pygmalion.

The bronze was not of a pig fetus, but a caste, lost wax sculpture of his own aborted fetus from one of his former girlfriends. His fetus kept in the freezer until he cast it in bronze.

I mailed it back, letting him know that I knew. He was so proud of his ingenuity as a sculptor. He mailed back my merkin.

On the early September morning before Hunter kicked me out the phone call came from my mother. I was dreaming one of those dreams deeper, more real than day life. Over the weekend I'd had as bad a time as it gets for a poet. I'd spent months—all those months my father was dying—preparing a twenty minute presentation on the designated theme, "Family and Gender," for Bumbershoot, Seattle's annual literary and music festival. Five poets, three local, myself, and the bestselling novelist and super star poet, James Dickey, were on stage in a large auditorium. Much to my surprise Hunter was sitting in the middle of the audience. He hadn't told me he was coming. Why didn't he come with me. He came because of Dickey, that as husband of one of the panelists he'd have the opportunity to meet him.

I was the last to read. I read from my prepared paper on the subject that had been Bumbershoot's choice of theme, but did not get much into it when Dickey rose from the other end of the panel, lunged toward me with his fist clenched, snarling, "Do you know what we do to women like her where I come from?" The audience explosion in favor of Dickey was something, but the female voice screaming "Hey Blondie, why don't you just shut up!" brought the audience to its feet in jubilant approval. Hunter rose from his seat and took off.

At the party afterwards, going over it with poet friends who I expected to applaud my effort, more attacks. I drove the three hours home to Portland in the wee hours of the morning.

I climbed up to the loft and lay down under the cockpit canopy skylight beside my husband. In the half hour sleep, I dreamed my mother and father on the south end of a cold, isolated beach. My father lay dying across my mother's lap, she lovingly bent to him, a high rocky bluff behind them, the Pacific lapping ever closer to them. Everything was a color between purple, blue, and silver. The color of sand, tears, eternity. They were the classic Pieta, mother and son.

The phone rang. I got down the pole.

'Come," my mother said. "It's time. Now. I need you now." My mother had never asked for help before.

I packed knowing it could be weeks, was back in Psyche and on my way south within the hour. At some point, haunted all the way, stopping for coffee, I drew the Pieta dream image in my journal.

All those many five hour journeys from Aries Wrecking Yard down to Florence on the mid-Oregon Coast the winter, spring and summer my father was dying, I wrote as I drove, lines for a long poem, *My Soul Is a Seagull*. This writing at the wheel kept coming, on my way to my parents, on the return to my husband. "Lu," he said sometime in the last weeks, "when you see a seagull know it is me." My father is the seagull of my soul, that prehistoric scavenger, that survivor. I'm descending the exquisite but dangerous, creek-mouth hairpin curve where the imprisoned Takilma of the Rogue River Wars starved to death the winter they surrendered—well, many drowned trying to grab fish from the crashing waves—the seagulls swooping into my windshield so near it seemed I could touch them, a landscape, a seascape, earth so beautiful it's no wonder we universally believe in a Creator.

Two years after his death Donna encountered our father on the Goddess site at Apis, Egypt. He was coming up as she was going down. Together they reinforced the Cosmos' Script that I am Lucifer, the Snake, the Most Beautiful, Most Powerful, Most Evil Archangel sent here to destroy the Edens.

Eight years earlier, in June 1979 forty-one sperm whales beached on the Oregon Coast and, after many agonizing days, the TV world in witness, died. The mystery of why they came ashore in front of my parents' home remains troubling to this day. My father's photos were around for years.

My father spoke of them on the day he died.
Of walking dwarfed amongst them, dead and dying, their giant
greyblack hulks snorting, letting go
on the beach in front of his house.

Sharon Doubiago is the author of eleven collections of award-winning poetry, including the recent *Naked to the Earth*. *Psyche Drives the Coast* won the Oregon Book Award for Poetry. She's a recipient of three Pushcart Prizes, two Oregon Literary Arts Fellowships, and is a National Book Award nominee. She's written four book-length poems, *Hard Country*, *South America Mi Hija*, *The Husband Arcane The Arcane of O* and *The Visit*. Her four award-winning memoirs are *The Book of Seeing With One's Own Eyes*, *El Niño*, *My Father's Love, Vols 1 &2*. *My Beard* is memoir in the form of individual stories rather than the on-going narrative of traditional memoir. She lives in North Beach, San Francisco.